Voodoo Gold

By

James H Jenks

Visit WWW.Voodoogold.com for exclusive material.

I dedicate this book to my loving wife Sue and our two boys, Tyler and Tanner. I appreciate the courage Sue had to face managing the family while living with the unknown of the whereabouts or condition of me while serving in Iraq.

I would like to give special consideration to my other two boys who served with me in Iraq, Kevin and Josh of Tactical PSYOP Team 1282. I'm proud to state that we served together and without the two of them on my team, my experience in Iraq may not have been as rewarding.

I would also like to recognize all military service members who are currently or have previously been in uniform. Without them volunteering for service, none of this would be possible.

CONTENTS

Voodoo Gold

CHAPTER ONE

LIGHTNING, LIGHTNING, LIGHTNING

EVERETT, WASHINGTON

I was in the lobby of Lang Manufacturing waiting to meet the President of the company and their Information Technology director to convince them that they needed to replace their existing T1 line with an OC-3 line. The current T1 line was working just fine and cost roughly $500 a month. The proposed OC-3 line cost $20,000 a month and had way more horsepower than they needed, but I needed them to need it. This was Christmas bonus time! I was just shy of my number and this deal would put me over the top. I needed to earn this bonus so I could take my boys Tanner and Tyler to Disneyland in the spring as I had promised.

I had arrived early and had rehearsed my sales pitch in the car a few times. I was confident that this deal was mine. The secretary told me that the President was already in the boardroom. I spit out my gum into my shirt pocket and made sure it was safe for use at a later date. As I stood up, I patted down my thick black hair that has a habit of sticking up when I don't want it to. "Pretend that you don't need this deal, don't look desperate." I took a step towards the boardroom, then looked down at my feet and watched my toes wiggle. Oh shit! I wasn't wearing shoes! I was in bare feet. I froze. The receptionist stared at me with disbelief as she shook her head. Surely her next move was going to be to call security. How could this be? How had I got so caught up in the details that I forgot about my shoes? Suddenly a loud booming voice broke through...

"LIGHTNING! LIGHTNING! LIGHTNING!"

KUWAIT: March 2003

My sales nightmare transformed into a far darker life threatening nightmare of a United States Army soldier in Iraq. This was no dream, this was a full meal of horror.

"LIGHTNING! LIGHTNING! LIGHTNING!"

The words popped and hissed out of the loudspeaker like a chorus from hell. Between each repetition echoing around the base camp, a siren blared giving me the eerie sensation of both having my guts sink while simultaneously wanting to spew up. The siren started slow and low, gradually gaining intensity in a terrible long scream and then faded away. One deep breath and it started over again.

The second siren scream drove me out of my cot. I sprang to my feet, grabbed my chemical protective mask and pulled it on, wrestled into my Kevlar vest, and threw on the helmet. This exercise was all pure instinct. I felt detached from my body as I executed these reflective tasks. A few minutes passed before my semi-conscious brain processed the screaming message from the loudspeaker. The message was short and simple and it only had one point to make. That point was Saddam has launched his SCUD's[1] and they are on their way to blow you into eternity.

When we first arrived at this military installation, we were warned that such an attack might be launched against us, but I didn't believe it would really happen to me. Watching the news and having some journalist hide under a table during a SCUD attack and describe the event made you believe this only happens to other people. This was no fire drill like we practiced in elementary school, this was the real shit and I was looking for my table.

Luckily I had taken the precaution of sleeping in my uniform. If there was going to be any kind of trouble, I wanted to be dressed for the situation.

When we first arrived at this camp and went through our orientation, they told us the story of some poor asshole that had run out of his bunker naked at night during an attack. Apparently he decided that this war wasn't going to change his sleeping habits, and more importantly his comfort. He always slept in his skibbies at home and being in Kuwait wasn't going to change a thing, until the first SCUD attack happen. His comrades were real uncomfortable staring at his naked ass while they were all huddled around in their bunker.

---

[1] SCUDS — A series of tactical ballistic missiles developed by the Soviet Union during the Cold War, and exported widely to other countries.

My boots were strategically placed beside my cot so I could jump right into them. My M203[2] was already in my arms because I had been cradling it in my sleep like it was an old girlfriend.

The lights went brilliant and SFC Hunter who was in charge of us for this deployment appeared with his protective chemical mask on yelling: "GIT JOR APPS UT DER BUNKER, FGHT, FGHT."

The mask made him impossible to understand but we knew what he was shouting, "get your asses to the bunker, right now."

No one asked him to repeat the order. No one needed him to repeat the order. I brushed passed him and was out the door like Speedy Gonzales.

I sprinted towards the bunker, it was easy to find because we had placed a big sign in front of it that read "361st PSYOP Cigar Lounge" the day before in honor of the few of us who liked to smoke cigars. We were forbidden to smoke them in the tent because the camp Marshals assumed we were irresponsible and would burn down the tents with our carelessness. We took this as an opportunity to design a sign in order to designate our bunker. Our creative minds decided that these bunkers are not only for people to take cover from missiles, they are also the only place that was fire proof for

---

[2] M203 - A single shot 40 mm grenade launcher designed to attach to a rifle.

smoking cigars and as a bonus, they provided protection against the hot afternoon sun.

Before making a beeline to the bunker, I made sure my Team Assistant Sgt Brown was also on his way to the bunker. Running next to him was my Specialist and the youngest member on the team, Spc Carson. We ducked inside for cover and assumed our seats in the bunker.

I peered outside over the top of the sandbags that were stacked up in front out of the bunker. Three tracers were racing towards the stars in the sky. We knew these were SCUD's on their way to destroy our asses. Seconds later, I watched our Patriot Missiles race through the skies and intercepted them.

"Oh hell ya, blow the shit out of those bastards," someone yelled out with excitement.

Outside and on his way to the bunker, one of my colleagues was doing the forty-yard dash towards us. This individual was SSG Dumas, a Team leader for TPT 1283. Dumas was a little scrappy guy about 5'2" tall. The bunker's entrance was just a little shorter than he was. He was running at full speed, eyeing his spot inside the bunker where he would sit. He jumped for his seat as he made his approach, but he forgot to duck and so his head slammed into the concrete. His feet flew out from underneath him, making him land flat on his back. His chemical protective suit went flying into the bunker everywhere and he landed on the weapon that was slung on his shoulder. His Kevlar helmet shot off his head because it had not been strapped on properly.

"Ugh," he groaned. Once we realized that he survived the blow, everyone started to burst out laughing because his misfortune provided us a much needed comic relief from the SCUD attack. After I had a good laugh, I grabbed him by his upper fatigues shirt and dragged him into the bunker and threw him onto the bench. Sgt Brown who was behind me grabbed the rest of his gear and tossed it at his feet. SSG Dumas looked as if he had been slapped stupid.

"Hey SSG Dumbass! You gotta duck when you enter a bunker," Sgt Brown yelled through his chemical protective mask.

We all laughed at his expense. He was always the butt of short jokes, like, "hey SSG Dumas, you can stand up now when you talk."

We were all now sitting on the bench looking at each other, antsy with adrenaline-fueled anticipation, our fingers were playing with buttons, hooks, and straps, our toes were tapping like a jack hammer.

"Do you think these ones will have the chemicals in them?" Carson said.

"That would be fucked up if they did," someone answered.

The day before we were told that Sadam's SCUD's had taken out a shopping mall full of people in Kuwait. To be hit with just an explosive ordinance like that would be fine to me because unlike the mall, we have bunkers that will provide sufficient protection against such an attack. It's the chemical and biological weapons that scare the shit out me.

The SCUD's should have impacted by now, but there was just silence and a lot of people looking at each other with eagerness. The silence became a void of information to act upon, now leaving us with the question of, what next?

Finally, over the loud speakers the signal for "all clear" was given. This meant that we could take our chemical protective mask off because the danger had passed and we could all go back to what we were doing, sleeping.

Then, just before I nodded off...

LIGHTNING! LIGHTNING! LIGHTING!

Oh shit, here we go again. Welcome to the job from hell.

CHAPTER TWO

LOBSTER TAILS, AMMO, AND METALLICA

The next morning came way too early, as we were more out of our beds than in them all night long. Sgt Brown's infantry training kicked in as he leaped up out of his cot to be the first one to greet the day. Unfortunately he was bunked next to me and decided to include me in his eagerness to wake up, so he kicked my cot and shouted, "SSG Jenks, time to get your ass out of bed." I looked at him like a sleepy teenager would when it's time to get up on a Saturday morning, but I knew he was right. Today was our first full day in theater, meaning we are in the war zone. An early start to our duties would be a good idea on our first full day.

The local time was about seven hundred hours and we could already feel the heat filling up the tent from the morning sun, even though it was just in the middle of March. Being from the Pacific Northwest, this climate was definitely a shock to my system.

As I sat in my cot trying to gain my composure to get my ass out of bed, I looked around this unfamiliar environment and tried to piece together the chain of events that led me to this moment in time, which was sitting on a cot in a war zone during a hot morning. My mind was now in full swing as I started to focus on the past. I recalled the moment when I first walked into the recruiting station and asked the recruiter how I could get some much needed college money. Without reading the full contract that was presented to me and eager to acquire the promised college money, I enlisted into the Army Reserves that day. Before I had a moment to reevaluate what I had committed to, I found myself doing pushups at Fort Benning, GA. I also suddenly realized I had dedicated myself to the Army reserves for at least six years. One of the positive benefits I realized from joining the Army reserve during this time frame was that I was able to graduate from college debt free.

Then after I completed the first six years, I found myself once again in need of more money. The answer for this was to re-enlist for another six years because the Army had dangled another big bonus in front of me if I did so. Once again, without thinking, I spontaneously signed the papers in order to pay off all the bills that had stacked up on me over time. Now I found myself trying to start a civilian career while simultaneously trying to satisfy the Army.

Being here in this current situation of sitting on this cot in a war zone during a hot morning wasn't a favorite option for me. Not because I didn't want to be here doing my patriotic duty, but because once again I had a lot of bills at home. The Army didn't promise any type of bonus this time because they knew I didn't have a choice in this matter.

Actually this mission would have the opposite effect on my finances because during this deployment, I would not achieve the income that I would normally earn as I do in my civilian job. Eventually, the savings in the bank account will be used to help offset the bills at home, followed by the college fund for the kids that I had saved. My only hope was that this war would get over before that day came.

What I did have going for me was that things always have a way of working out for me and the Army has always provided me with some type of opportunity. What that opportunity was in this forsaken land would remain a mystery to me at this point.

As I was finally standing up from my cot and grabbing my head gear and weapon, I watched other members of our group start to wake up and seize the day. There are a total of fifteen of us in this deployed detachment who came from Washington State. We are a Psychological Operation Company or better known by our acronym,(PSYOP). PSYOP soldiers use persuasion to influence perceptions and encourage desired behavior to a given audience. Our communication skills provide commanders with the ability to communicate information to large audiences via radio, television, leaflets and loudspeakers.

We are going to be assigned to the 2nd CAV[3] during this Iraqi invasion. We are a part of Special Operations so we don't have the traditional Army framework of squads and

[3] 2ndCAV - The 2nd Armored Calvary Regiment based in Fort Polk Louisiana. Its roots trace back to the civil war.

platoons. Instead, we are made up of four separate three-man teams, plus one detachment team consisting of a Sergeant First Class who is the NCOIC[4]. This NCOIC position is filled by SFC Hunter. We also have an Officer assigned to the detachment team and his name is Cpt Barker. Also, a Specialist who actually does all the work for the detachment is assigned and his name is Spc McClure. Our official nomenclature is Tactical PSYOP Detachment 1280 (TPD 1280), and I am a leader at the team level. My team is the second team and we are called Tactical PSYOP Team 1282 (TPT 1282). Our call sign on the radio for the Detachment is Voodoo. This call sign was chosen by SFC Hunter because he always thought that PSYOP messed with people's heads and he called that Voodoo magic. Since we were the second team on this Detachment, our call sign is Voodoo Two.

We are just three average guys who were thrown together to make this team with nothing in common except we all joined the same Army Reserve unit back in Washington State. Having these guys on my team who I just literally met for the first time only a couple of months ago was just fine with me. One thing that I had learned about being in the Army was that you could take a handful of guys from anywhere in the United States, throw them together in a room, and within a matter of minutes, they would all be best friends for life. I don't know if it's because we all have something in common like basic training or belonging to a bigger cause than ourselves, but we always seem to immediately click. Then we would start to share war stories about the last group

---

[4] NCOIC - Non Commissioned Officer in Charge.

of soldiers we shared adventures with. A few years from now, I'll be sharing new stories about this current group of guys to a new group of soldiers.

As with any group of people, each person has their strengths and weaknesses. Talking to people and figuring things out is what I'm good at. That's probably why back in the real world I'm in sales. I get paid lots of money to talk to people and to get them to buy things that they may or may not need. I'm definitely full of useless knowledge just like the character Cliff Claven in the classic television sitcom show called Cheers. Sometimes I joke around with others and make statements as in "you don't know the burden I have carrying around all of this knowledge." I'm thirty-seven years old, six feet tall, and I have always been on the heavier side weighing in at an even two hundred pounds, but I can still run just as fast as the younger kids and sometimes a lot further.

Sgt Brown was my assistant team leader, I always kept him informed with all the information I received and I let him participate in the decision making process so he could step in if something happened to me. I was fortunate to have him on our team because of his combat skills. His skills were sharp since he was just released from active duty as an infantry sergeant. He was happy that I assigned him the SAW[5] because he was the one who wanted to provide a show of force for our team.

---

[5] SAW - A Squad Automatic Weapon used to give infantry squads or sections a portable source of automatic firepower.

When I first met him I had asked why he joined this unit. He said that he originally joined the Army to get into the infantry so he could shoot someone, but after four years of serving, he was never provided with the opportunity. He transferred to the inactive reserves when his contract was up to burn off the remaining four years while he went to college. Then President Bush started making threats to Saddam, so he figured he would get a second chance. He immediately transferred out of the inactive reserves and joined our reserve unit because his recruiter told him we would have the highest probability to be deployed into combat.

He was an average size person of average proportion and was about twenty three years old. He had dark hair with a white spot in the center of the back of his head, which reminded me of a skunk. A fact that I always made sure I reminded him of. He had just married his junior college sweetheart just days before this deployment. They were scheduled to be married after they both graduated from college, but they didn't want to miss out on all the extra pay and full spousal benefits, so they got hitched right away.

Spc Carson was the third person on my team. He was only a couple of inches shorter than I, but about forty lbs lighter. At only nineteen years old, he was just a kid out of high school with no skills except chasing girls and going to parties with cheap kegs of beer. His job was to take care of our HMMWV[6] and drive us around. Spc Carson always wore

---

[6] HMMWV – The High Mobility Multipurpose Wheeled Vehicle (HMMWV or Humvee) is a military 4WD motor vehicle primarily used by the United States military.

the glasses that the military had issued to him while we were at Fort Bragg, the type that were flexible and had a head band that wrap around you head. We called them Birth Control Glasses (BCG's) because they made him so funny looking that if he were in public, there would be no chance of him getting laid if he had them on.

Just a few days ago we were in the cold and rain just outside Seattle working our civilian jobs and going about our business. For me, the weekdays involved playing taxi service for the kids and taking them to Cub Scouts, swimming lessons, and basketball league. The weekend was my time, which always consisted of having a couple of drinks and a cigar.

Now we were in Kuwait waiting on our orders to invade Iraq! We were a couple of days behind the rendezvous with our element the 2nd CAV. They had arrived in theater a few days earlier and were already heading north to Baghdad. We were to leave as soon as we got our shit together and we would meet up with them down range.

Though first things first, you can't start the day or go into battle on an empty stomach. "Let's go and get some early chow men," I shouted out to my team.

"Oh hell Ya Sergeant," yelled Carson. "You don't have to ask me twice."

We slung our weapons onto our backs and headed to the chow hall. One thing that is always consistent in the military is that as long as there is a dinning facility, you took full advantage of it. Everything else can suck, but as long as we got three hots and a cot, we were good to go.

When we were settling in yesterday evening after the welcome orientation, we started talking to the other troops that have been here for a few days. I learned that over in the British sector in this camp they have a Post Exchange that sells Cuban cigars. I thought it might behoove us to go and check it out after morning chow since cigars are a delicacy to me. I also had hoped that they would have some of those English candies called Quality Street since this was supposed to be a British establishment. I had eaten them by the pounds on my last visit to London when I was there on vacation, and I have had a craving for them ever since. Another fun fact that I knew about Quality Street was that Saddam himself was also fond of these candies.

The sun was now at full strength, we started sweating as soon as we stepped out of our tent. We weren't yet acclimated to this new environment. Every once in a while a breeze would blow though the encampment and give us a little comfort, but with the breeze came sand in your face.

Hundreds of tents are all dressed in alignment throughout this camp which are identical, but we are focused on the big white tent that is the size of a football field, and it stood out as the center piece to everything. This big white tent is the prized chow hall.

"Listen up you two, you better eat each meal as if it were your last meal because you will never know when you will get another hot meal or even get to eat again." They both looked at me like I'm some old crazy man lecturing some young kids on a street corner.

As we made our way through the chow lines with our trays, I looked over at Carson's plate and could see that he took my advice to its full meaning. He piled on just about everything the chow hall had to offer. The food was stacked so high, he had to balance it as he walked. Next, he scarfed down his entire breakfast in about two minutes and then said, "I wonder what's for lunch." I couldn't believe my eyes. I wasn't even done jamming my first piece of toast and he was already done.

"Jesus Christ, I didn't mean for you to become a disgusting fat body. I'm going to have to check and see if your boot prints are a little deeper in the sand when we step outside."

After we left the chow hall, we decided to take advantage of our spare time and head over to the British Post Exchange as I had planed. We reckoned that we could grab some of those sought after cigars, figuring we're going to need them when we find ourselves in a combat situation. If I'm going out, I need to go out with a cigar so I can go to heaven with it, I reasoned. As we made our way over, I went on to state to both Brown and Carson some quotes I remembered about famous people and cigars to pass the time. Like what Mark Twain once said, "if there aren't cigars in Heaven, then I'm not going" or what George Washington said, "if you can't send funds, then send tobacco."

"OK, OK, we get it," the two shouted at me so they could get me to shut up.

The walk was a good half-mile to get to the British sector and when we finally arrived there, we were confused about its exact location. Nothing stood out like the chow tent's characteristics that said, "here is the chow hall you are looking for." We decided to ask one of the British soldiers where the Post Exchange was and in his funny accent he told us exactly where to go, but not without calling us a bunch of Wally's first. Not to be distracted by this statement, we focused our attention on the PX as it became visible to us from the directions we received, not because we noticed a sign that said, "here is the PX you are looking for."

The shop was more or less just a tent filled with a bunch of pallets with merchandise on it. Behind a makeshift counter made out of plywood stood a female British soldier who weighed at least two hundred and fifty pounds. Normally I wouldn't care about how a person looked, but this was way out of portion. How could you even get in the military with that physique? I guess the Brits have a different standard, but all I could think about was how it looked like a whole forest was moving when she walked around in her fatigues.

She is very polite and asked what she could help us with. I scanned the pallets of Gatorade, canned food, candies, and beef jerky. All was the standard poggey bait food that you always stocked up on before you went and played your Army games in the field for a few days. However, I did not see any of the desired prized Cuban Cigars, so I figured it was best to just ask about them. "I heard that you have Cuban cigars here and I would like to take a look at them."

What appeared to be the Sherwood Forest, motioned at me and guided me over to another makeshift counter. From behind the counter she pulled out a few boxes of cigars. She had about three different types of Romeo y Julieta Cuban cigars. A few of them are the type that is packed inside their own aluminum tube. These would be perfect because the aluminum tubes would not only keep them humidified but also provide protection during combat duty. They are a little more expensive than I had expected, so I only bought five of them. Also to my surprise after doing another scan of the place, I did notice that they had big bags of Quality Street candies that I could buy in bulk, and they weren't too expensive. I bought a couple of bags of candy so that in the event we came across any kids on our missions, I could hand them out for goodwill or bribes.

On our way back, one of the bags of candy that I purchases from the Post Exchange became an instant casualty because the temptation of the chocolate treats became too much to resist. As I popped the first piece of candy into my mouth and before I could start enjoying it, somehow Spc McClure found us and was eager to deliver some information. He shouted that our containers that shipped with all our equipment from the States had shown up by our tent and was ready for inspection. "Well then, let's head back and make sure we have all of our equipment," I said.

When we arrived back, we threw our purchases to the side and before we could even get started on our inventory,

SFC Hunter stormed in. SFC Hunter was ready to start playing his character of NCO in charge. He was a police officer back in Seattle and there was only two things that interested him, the Army and police work. SFC Hunter was about the same height as me, but his physique was the exact opposite. On a good rainy day in Seattle, he would weigh in on the scale about 140 pounds if he were soaking wet. "Sgt Norby, SSG Jenks, SSG Dumas, and SSG Hogan front and center." With that command, each team leader was now standing in front of SFC Hunter.

"We just got our marching orders and we are to leave for Baghdad ASAP. The 2nd CAV are waiting for us. It's a two-day drive though a combat zone, so we better get a move on it. Briefing in five," he said before turning on his heels and exiting the area as quick as he had come in.

To get ahead of the game, I informed Sgt Brown to start the inventory check without me, and then I ran over to join the meeting.

"Ok, listen up," shouted SFC Hunter. "We will SP[7] out of here at 1900 hours and our final destination will be Saddam City, which is part of Baghdad. I received word that the UN building where Hans Blix had his office is where 2nd CAV has decided to call home for now. We will travel in our team order with the command vehicle between 2nd and 3rd. SSG Jenks, Cpt Barker doesn't want both of us to be in the same vehicle during this travel in the event we are attacked or something happens so we won't lose both of us at the same

---

[7] SP - Start of Patrol.

time. I want you to have your driver Spc Carson swap out with the Captain."

I wasn't pleased with this information because of two reasons. The first reason was that if I don't have a driver and if the Captain is riding with me, then I would have to drive the vehicle. Reason two was I truly believed that Cpt Barker is a complete idiot and he should not even be in this war. I never understood why the Army would even entertain the thought of him participating. He is definitely a broke dick.

Cpt Barker once bragged to us how he could choke to death if he were to ever vomit. The explanation was that his esophagus was wrapped around his windpipe, so if it ever went into a spasm, his airway would be closed off. Chronic back pain was another issue, which led to a physical training profile of no push-ups or running. Cpt Barker reminded me of Hughey the Duck, his belly stuck out like a sore thumb and he would waddle as he walked.

SFC Hunter went on to say, "team leaders take charge and make sure your people are ready to move when it's time to roll."

It was 1100 hrs and I knew we had a lot of time before we were to leave this place and head north. This would give my team and me ample time to get our HMMWV in order. The last thing you want happening to you while you're in the middle of the desert is to have a vehicle malfunction, run out of food, or even worse, run out of water. Carson started to perform some of the basic tasks such as doing a maintenance check, topping up the gas tank with diesel along with our two

Gerry cans. Brown went over to get enough cases of water for us to drink for the next five days and about four cases of MRE's[8]. While they were doing these tasks, I was going to perform a function check on our main weapon system that is issued to a PSYOP soldier, the loudspeaker system.

The loudspeaker's of this system is mounted on top of our vehicle. This structure consisted of six coned speakers connected to an amplifier that is about the size of footlocker. This amplifier sat in the back cargo space of our HMMWV. Some of the interface capabilities that came stock with the system are both a digital player/recorder that allows you to record, and then play a pre-recorded message. You can also speak directly into the microphone for a live message.

My favorite option to plug into the system was the non Army issue MP3 player. This option wasn't for tactical purposes, but more for entertainment. The system took up half of our cargo space so it was a tight fit when we started packing all of our supplies into the vehicle. The best way to test out the system that I knew of was to play some Metallica from my MP3 player at full blast, and so I did. I pushed down on the button and gradually increased the volume louder and louder until I reached its maximum levels and adjusted the speaker position so that the music traveled down range at its maximum distance, which is about two miles.

If there are any soldiers trying to catch a nap in the mid-afternoon heat on this camp anywhere, they are shit out of luck and now awake. After about a minute or so of blaring

---

[8] MRE - Meals Ready to Eat. An army ration.

"For Whom the Bell Tolls," I noticed soldiers coming out of their tents and they looked around all confused trying to find the source of the music.

Sgt Brown was about a quarter mile away at the water depot rocking out. He was giving me the metal sign with his hands as he rocked his head back and forth as if he was at a heavy metal concert.

Out of the corner of my eye, I noticed the various groups of soldiers that started walking towards me as they discovered who was making all the racket. I assumed they were probably pissed at me because I may have awakened them from their afternoon beauty sleep. As they walked towards me, I prepped for their complaints. As they became closer, they cupped their hands over their mouth and tried to holler something to me. They became more determine to communicate with me as I just stood there and gave them the motion that I could not hear them. When they came into actual shouting range, which was about six feet from me, they attempted again to communicate with me. One individual was able to cut through the loud music and yelled, "hey man, do you have any Ozzy?" Another one was able to shout for some Stain, and then a smart ass yelled when the song was over, "I couldn't hear that, can you turn it up."

"Sorry guys, shows over, but look for me down range," I yelled back as the next song cued up.

I eventually shut the loudspeaker down and the music fans headed back to their tents as if the lights just went on at a concert. I went on to check my radio and my GPS. Being able to communicate and know where you're at is always a plus in my book. After being satisfied with my system checks, and having stocked up on food and water, and giving the vehicle a clean bill of health, I informed my guys that we just received our combat load of ammo for the trip and we needed to start loading the rounds into our magazines. Brown had it the easiest because he was carrying the SAW and all of his ammo was belt-fed, so all he had to do was bust open some boxes and he was set. Carson and I each had to pack a butt load of magazines that held thirty ammunition rounds apiece, and we had to load each round into the magazine one by one. We were sitting on the ground facing each other with a pile of bullets in front of us.

"It appears we are in for a long day," said Carson as Brown sat down with us to help load the magazines because he either felt bored or bad about the situation. Carson continued on as he insisted to tell us a story about how he and his friends drank so much beer one night because they were playing Edward 40oz Hands. This is where you tape a 40oz bottle of beer on each hand and you can't remove them until you consumed both bottles. This overconsumption of beer led to one of them pissing their pants in his story. I thought that person was Carson himself, but he of course denies this fact.

When we finished loading the bullets, it was close enough to dinner time so we decided to get some more hot chow before we hit the road. We march back to the large white tent and decided to feast one last time before we made our journey off this base. As we are making our strides toward the big white tent, I noticed that dusk would soon be upon us. I started wondering at what time tonight the SCUD's would make their appearance, but then again we should be out of here before the next attack. That made my thoughts shift to running down the checklist in my mind over and over again because we now were on limited time. I needed to be sure we would be safe on the road. Once we leave, there is no turning back for anything you forgot. My trance was broken when out of nowhere Spec Carson blurted out, "this is going to be like The Last Supper."

(I just hoped our fates would be different from what Jesus experienced!)

If I liked seafood, this would be the most awesome day in my life, but since I don't like seafood, this day did not register on the awesome day meter. Carson however, was ecstatic at what was on the menu and proclaimed this to be the most awesome day in his life. Lobster tails! Not the kind that are frozen and then warmed up, but fresh top grade lobster tails. Since this was war, there was no limit on the amount you could eat. Carson loaded up about five tails and made a beeline for the condiment table to load up on butter.

I, on the other hand received another extra large helping of chili mac. Chili mac is just as it sounds. Taking all the Army chili that no one would eat and mixing it with bland elbow macaroni. Stir it all up in a pot and you've got chili mac. Today, chili mac is the Army's best food choice for those who don't like seafood.

As I was looking for a table for us to sit down at, I noticed SSG Hogan who was in charge of TPT 1283 was standing by. SSG Hogan was considered to be the little Hulk in our Detachment. He's about five feet six inches tall and has muscles on his arms about the same size as my legs. He always had a hard time getting his top garment over his arms because they were so big. He liked to shave his head and he tried to keep his mustache long. The last thing you ever wanted to do is make him angry. He studied the arts of Tae Kwon Do and he would beat you to a pulp if you pissed him off, otherwise he is just a teddy bear. SSG Hogan and his team were already sitting down at a table and they were waiving us over. I motioned back the acceptance and we all headed over to greet them together.

"Shit," said SSG Hogan as we were sitting down, "looks like Carson likes lobster almost as much as Foltz does." Foltz is his Specialist as Carson is mine. "I think they could sit here all night and eat till they puke," he continued to say.

And that kicked off the traditional Army male macho showdown between these two Specialists. They were both bragging about how much lobster they could eat. That's when I stood up and said, "all right you two little shits, why don't you two have a lobster eating contest and see who really can eat the most. Carson, Foltz, looks like both of you have had about three tails apiece so far, so finish off those two remaining and then get some more. We will stay here, keep count, and of course cheer on our guy."

"How do we determine a winner?" asked Foltz.

"When one of you either taps out or pukes, the other person wins."

SSG Hogan butted in to edit the plan, "better yet, you two stay seated. Brown you are responsible for resupplying your guy Carson. Sgt Altman, since you're on my team, you take care of our guy Foltz." SSG Hogan and I looked at each other and we both almost started laughing because we knew where this was going, but we kept our straight faces.

The first few additional lobsters went down pretty easy, but then they started to slow down. After about ten tails apiece, they appeared to be at a crawling pace. "Come on you two pussies, my Grandma can eat more than you two put together," cried out SSG Hogan as he rubbed his mustache.

They were both eating them at the same pace so they were still tied at thirteen lobster tails apiece. I could start to see a little green glow on both of their faces. It was just a matter of time before one of them gave up. But I knew a tap out was not in the cards for either of these two. On the seventeenth lobster tail Spc Foltz stopped eating and had a thousand mile stare on his face. He sat there for a few minutes glaring into space, but Carson didn't really gain any ground because his bites were small and few. I could see the pot was boiling on Foltz and it was about time for the spill.

"Stand back," I yelled to Brown.

I got up from the table and took a few steps back. Foltz had beads of sweat dripping from his forehead and his eyes were glancing around as if he was looking for an exit. He froze for a second and just like that, about ten pounds of lobster tail exploded from Foltz's belly and out of his mouth. Ten pounds of puke can cover a large area. I hastily grabbed

Carson from the table before he got slimed. "You should make a run to the honey buckets and puke it out so you won't have a belly ache when we head out," I instructed to Carson.

Out of the corner of my eye, I noticed the mess tent NCO was on his way over. He didn't look too pleased with the regurgitated mess all over the table. "Looks like my guy wins, so you need to clean this mess up," I yelled to Hogan sarcastically.

I gave Brown the motion to move out as I still had a grasp on Carson so I could guide him in the right direction. As we were heading towards the door for our mad exit, I looked back at SSG Hogan, he was now pissed. Not because his guys lost the contest, but because he was torn between two choices. Either he could chase us and kick our asses in order to bring us back to help clean up the mess. Though, he would then have to leave his guys holding the bag when the mess tent NCO showed up. His other choice was to take responsibility when the mess tent NCO showed up and let us get away. He angrily made his choice. We evacuated the tent before anyone from the mess tent staff could say anything to us. Especially since the mess tent ironically now had a new meaning behind it.

I could only hope that the anger would ware off SSG Hogan before he came back to the residential tent and he transforms back to a teddy bear.

CHAPTER THREE

GOODBYE KUWAIT

At 1900 hours SFC Hunter went down the checklist with the team leaders to make sure we had all of our weapons and equipment in order. The sun had gone down and the temperature was cooling, so this was a perfect time to depart. We calculated that if we left now and drove all night, we could get to the Iraqi border by midnight.

Once we made sure our radios were all on the same frequency and the proper codes downloaded so we could talk with one another, we figured we were ready to roll. I climbed into the driver seat, wiggled around to get situated for the long drive, and then flipped the start lever to fire up the HMMWV. Cpt Barker jumped in the front passenger seat and Brown climbed up to into the turret.

Normally I wouldn't mind driving, but I knew with Cpt Barker as a passenger I would have to endure his endless verbal diarrhea. However, I thanked my lucky stars that at least I get to sit down for this drive. Sgt Brown on the other hand wasn't so lucky. Although he didn't have to listen to

Cpt Barker up in the turret, he would have to stand while manning his weapon for the entire trip. The only piece of equipment he could rest on was a three inch strap that slung across the bottom of the turret, which he could use as a make shift seat. Once he got into position and adjusted his strap, he gave me the thumbs up and shouted out "Ahh, this is going to be awesome!" He's one crazy homicidal bastard but I was glad to have him on my team.

Cpt Barker is in charge of navigation. He's setting up a non-army issue GPS to my surprise. This GPS is one of those fancy expensive rigs that you would buy at Cabela's outdoor store back in the States. I became worried because he kept glancing at the instruction manual as he pushed the buttons. I heard a sexy female voice tell him to turn left in 200 yards. At that point I recommended to the Captain that we should at least use the Army issue GPS as a back up device. Army issue gear wasn't always top of the line and often it was subpar, but at least we were trained on it and have played with it enough times on weekend drills that we knew how to operate it correctly and fix it if needed, often with 4,000 miles of (duct) tape. This was not the time to experiment with new toys. Cpt Barker noticed that I was looking at him with a worried expression on my face so he said, "you stick with the driving Jenks and let me worry about direction."

One by one our convoy rolled by the front gate, leaving the military base that we temporally called home. The guard at the gate gave us a wave goodbye. You could see on his face that he was thinking better you than me. He was almost guaranteed to make it back home in one piece because other than the SCUD missiles that always got shot out of the sky by our Patriot missiles, it was pretty safe around the place. He would always have his three hots and a cot.

There are a lot of concrete barriers we have to weave around to finally get to the main road that will lead us to the Iraqi boarder. Once we all made it out of the front gate, I was surprised at the quality of the roads. The roads were all freshly paved asphalt. The kind of road you enjoyed driving on just after a construction crew finished their job. The lane had no grooves that grabbed your tires and the smoothness of the road allowed you to feel the vibration from the aggressive tread tires as they made their distinctive hum. If the roads were like this all the way to Baghdad, then this ride might not be too bad. Nobody likes to endure rough roads or dodge potholes.

This is actually the first time we were able to get off the secured military base and check out what Kuwait really looked like. As our convoy progressed down the road, we were able to observe our full surroundings. On one side of the freeway was mostly desert and the other side was a densely packed city. All the houses seemed to be square and brown. They were all very large and some even have huge austere columns in the front. Every neighborhood we passed would be considered as upper class or even rich back in the States. Nowhere did we see any middle class houses.

Most of the cars that are on the freeway were either Mercedes or BMW's. You could tell that everybody had money. This exhibit of money is like being in the city of Bellevue back in Washington State where I lived. The only difference besides trying to let everybody know you have money was that there were no women driving with a cell phone in one hand and a Starbuck's coffee cup in the other while trying to put on their makeup. Mainly because women are not allowed to drive and the Kuwaitis do not drink coffee, they drink tea at tea houses. The men did drive with cell phones, but didn't bother with the makeup.

Once the city of Kuwait was behind us, we were in the suburbs. Even half way around the world, civil engineering seemed to incorporate the same neighborhood concept everywhere. The parks, schools, playgrounds, and sidewalks are identical to what I have seen throughout all of my travels.

On a walking path that wrapped around one of the larger housing developments, I noticed a whole bunch of these fully black-gowned figures walking under the street lamps on the walking paths. They looked as if they were Jawas from *Star Wars*. Though instead, they were actually females in their burqas[9] walking to the market with their kids running amok around them.

On the other side of the road which is all desert, I witnessed herds of camels running around. I have never seen a camel before in my life and now I was seeing them by the dozens in the wild.

---

[9] Burqa - An all-enveloping cloak worn by some Muslim women.

As time and miles started to collect and civilization started to dwindle, the moon took over the night and started to provide a little light. Eventually both sides of the freeway turned into desert, with small patches of houses popping up here and there. I shoved in the Big Country song 'We're Not in Kansas' into the portable tape deck. This song took on a new meaning to me as the lyrics from the song played because the sky's color was all wrong and the days were all too long. Yep, this place was definitely not in Kansas or anywhere else familiar.

I grabbed one of my cigars that I had stashed and lit it up. Nothing like driving under the stars in a foreign country puffing on a fine cigar. Might as well try to think of this whole experience as a mini vacation.

The time was getting close to midnight, and sure enough the Iraqi border was just about ten miles ahead of us. SFC Hunter advised us over the radio that there is an Army fuel and ammo depot just one mile ahead and that it would be a good place for us to pull off the road for the night and get some rest. These depots didn't have the amenities like back at the base in Kuwait, but they did provide their own security so we didn't have to pull guard duty at night. This also meant not waking up at four AM and participating in a stand two[10]. When we approached the entrance, we noticed we weren't the first group of people who had made this decision. There were hundreds of vehicles scattered everywhere that must have

---

[10]Stand Two - All soldier present take a defensive fighting position at dawn, when it is most likely an attack will occur.

been part of numerous different convoys. After a lengthy search looking for some real estate, we managed to find a section amongst the crowd that we could call our own and get some rest.

When I turned off the vehicle, Cpt Barker had turned off his GPS and proceeded to start reading his country study, which we were all provided with prior to our deployment. A country study is an in depth document that succinctly describes the most PSYOP-pertinent characteristics of a country, geographical area, or region and serves as an immediate reference for the planning and conduct of PSYOP programs. In addition, this study describes the Iraqi culture along with the do and don'ts. Some obvious pointers on page one describes that on no circumstance would you ever approach a female for discussion, never ever eat with your left hand because it is used for sanitary reasons, or an obscure one was never display the bottom of your shoe because it illustrates disrespect.

With the Captain just now trying to understand the country study, I became a little disappointed in him. These studies are not light in reading and take an enormous amount of effort and time to understand their content. Most people compared the study commitment to studying for an advanced college final exam, and this Captain is treating it as bedtime reading material.

I set up my cot next to the vehicle and tried to get some shut eye, though this proved to be an impossible task. The Captain kept bothering me with his flash light. He kept flashing me in the eyes, as he rattled around with it so he could read his study. "Hey Captain, this is the time for us to get some rest before we cross the border into a combat zone. It's going to be a long day tomorrow."

"Sometimes in war, we leaders just don't get any sleep," he replied back angrily.

"Didn't we get that study about a month ago? I know I did and I already have it memorized."

"SSG Jenks, I'm the Captain here and I advise you to keep your mouth shut, you go ahead and get your beauty sleep, but I'm going to make sure we all succeed here."

What a douche. He has definitely seen one too many war movies. I wasn't going to let him interfere with my rest so I said, "O.K. I'll see you bright and squirrely in the morning." I rolled over, threw my blanket over my eyes, and tried to sleep as well as I could with his search light on me.

At 0600 hours the next morning, Brown and I woke up and jumped out of our cots that we eventually had to move far away from the vehicles in order to escape the Captain's flashlight. Even though hitting the preverbal snooze button sounded as an excellent option, I knew we had to stick to the plan. Our plan was to be back on the road at 0630, this would give us enough time to shit, shave, and eat an MRE.

In the distance I strangely watched a solider walking towards us carrying some papers. I didn't pay much attention to him until he started to get closer and kept leaning over and picking up additional papers. Brown then came over to me and pointed at Cpt Barker and whispered "Check this out, it's gonna be good."

I turned around where Brown was pointing and saw Cpt Barker passed out with a bunch of his sensitive paper work spread around his cot. The wind must have blown some of the pages over to the next camp of soldiers.

The solider finally approached us and I quickly noticed that he was a Private. This made the situation even more embarrassing as not only did he not have the authorization to even touch these classified documents, but he had to return them back to the Captain and I felt embarrassed for the Private because the Captain is suppose to represent command and authority for soldiers and is generally considered to be the highest rank a commissioned soldier can achieve while remaining in the field. Now this Private had to correct the Captain's mistake.

The solider tried to hand me the documents in order to avoid the conflict all together. I almost took them from the Private, but I couldn't let the Captain off that easy. I wanted to see how the Captain would try to weasel his way out of this situation, so I informed the private that the documents belonged to Cpt Barker. I pointed towards the Captain who was still passed out on his cot and said, "I am not authorized to handle those documents. They're classified, you'll have to hand them over to him yourself."

The soldier walked over to where the Captain was sleeping. He then tried to quietly add the papers with the other ones that were scattered around under his cot but the Captain woke up from all the paper rustling.

"What the hell are you doing Private," he screamed as he jumped out of bed.

"Returning your papers sir," said the Private, who was now standing at attention.

The Captain looked around and noticed that there were still some of his documents lying around, so he quickly snatched the papers up from off the ground in hopes that nobody even noticed this situation. "What unit are you from Private?" he demanded to know.

With pride and instinct from his training, the Private yelled out as loud as he could, "3rd CAV, sir!"

"Are you authorized to touch these documents Private?"

This confused the Private because he was just trying to help out and now he was being accused of an unlawful act. "No sir. If I may explain sir?"

Before the Private could start explaining, the Captain interrupted and asked, "should I go talk to your company commander and get you written up for an Article 15[11]?"

---

[11] Article 15 - Nonjudicial punishment in the United States military which permits commanders to administratively discipline troops without a court-martial.

"No sir!"

"Well then you best go back to your unit Private, and forget this ever happened."

"Yes sir," said the Private. You could see that the Private was relieved and eager to leave, but he continued to stand at the position of attention until the Captain properly excused him.

"Well go Private, before I change my mind!"

The Private then executed an about-face and marched back to where he came from as quickly as he could. Both Brown and I had to exit the scene before we started busting up laughing because we knew the Captain would surely take it out on us if he saw us.

After we all quickly consumed our MRE's and shaved our faces, SFC Hunter called for all of us to gather around his vehicle before we departed out of this depot. He wanted to brief us on some updates he had received from the Depot HQ tent. "Listen up," he shouted to us as if we were all his children looking for guidance. "We need to stick close together and keep an eagle eye out for the combative enemies. It has been reported that small convoy units have been repeatedly ambushed by the Iraqi Army. There is even a report of one unit of soldiers who got lost and wound up being taken hostage and they even took a female hostage by the name of Jessica Lynch. This information is now all over the news back in the States. Since we are a small unit ready to depart for our convoy to Baghdad, we need to remember that we are Special Op's. We have the weapons and the attitude to discourage the enemy from attacking us. So you gunners in the turrets need to display your force by putting on your warrior face and have your weapons in full display. The rest of us need to have our weapons pointed out the window at the ready, and remember that we need to be locked and loaded at all times with your weapons on safe when we're on the other side. Now let's get a move on it!"

CHAPTER FOUR

THE ROAD TO NOWHERE

About fifteen minutes after leaving the depot behind us, we finally reached the Iraq border. We knew we had reached the boarder because of what laid before us. The Army Corps of Engineers had arrived earlier in this war and had bulldozed a berm of earth that was about twenty feet high and went on for as far as you could see in both directions. I had always thought The Army Corps of Engineers were a bunch of slackers who spent their time building dams or levies for flood control, but after seeing this new wonder of the world that would be equivalent to the Great China Wall, one had to wonder. I had to look at them different because if you think about it, they were out here building this thing on the Iraq boarder before anybody else would dare show up to this hostile environment. I could only imagine them working in the cover of darkness with their night vision devises on, building up these high berms while relying on a security element to watch their backs. They probably used every sixty-two ton Caterpillar D9 Dozers known to the Western civilization to accomplish the task in time.

On top of the long continuous berm sat numerous MP[12] vehicles that were scattered about every quarter mile or so with their 50 cal[13] guns pointing down range. The road that we were traveling on cut through the berm and it had a Bradley[14] vehicle there waiting at the checkpoint. As we pulled up to the checkpoint, a soldier who was standing by the Bradley stepped out, gave us a quick once over, and then waved us through.

As we crossed the border, I was able to yell out "lock and load," for the first time. I've yelled that command a million times on the riffle range, but this time it had meaning to it for it was the real deal.

When I gave that command, Brown yelled out a big excited groan as he took out a fresh belt of ammo and charged his weapon with it. As he cocked back the charging handle, it made that distinct sound of metal chunking together. I grabbed one of my magazines out of my vest and place it into my weapon, and then I charged it and made sure I had one bullet in the chamber. I looked over at Cpt Barker to see his warrior face as he loaded his weapon and to my surprise, I caught him fiddling around with his GPS instead.

"Don't you think it would be a good idea to put some bullets in your weapon since we are now in a combat zone?"

---

[12] MP - Military Police.

[13] 50 Cal - 50 Caliber machine gun.

[14] Bradley - An infantry fighting vehicles with armor protection.

"Um, do you have any ammo for me because mine is in the back of the vehicle with my vest or maybe Sgt Brown can crawl back there and get it for me."

"No!" I shouted with disgust, "Sgt Brown is pulling security for our front and I will not take him off of it. Those are the kind of mistakes that can get us killed. Didn't you listen to a word that SFC Hunter said? We need to display our force and we need you to have your weapon locked and loaded pointing out the window. Jesus Christ, looks as if we need to pull the whole convoy over so you can get your ammo!" Cpt Barker flashed me an angry look, but said nothing because he knew I was correct.

When I pulled over, I immediately stepped out of the vehicle, knelt down, and pulled security on the left flank just as we have been trained. The other four vehicles pulled up behind us and did the same. SFC Hunter yelled over to us, "everything OK?" I shouted back, "yeah, the Captain is looking for his ammo." SFC Hunter's sudden look of disgust made my day for the moment. Even though I was entertained by this notion, I knew I needed to scan my sector, so I looked as far as I could see on the left side of the vehicle for any possibility of Iraqi soldiers.

Cpt Barker went to the back of the HMMWV and started digging around for his ammo. As I scanned my sector, I couldn't pass up the opportunity to examine the landscape. A big difference was noticeable between this new location and what we saw a few minutes ago on the other side of the border. The land on this side was barren and deprived of vegetation. It wasn't comprised of sand as I imagined it would be, but it was more of dirt and rocks that had been extremely weathered by the sun.

After surveying the landscape with a little more scrutiny, I noticed large holes in the ground scattered around in various locations. These holes looked like someone dug them out to make a hasty fighting position, but burrowed them real deep. Deep enough to make me think that someone could actually hide in these holes if one choose to do so. Looking intently at one of the holes and studying its architecture, I suddenly realized there was something moving around inside of it and my fear came to reality. This motion definitely aroused my curiosity and caught my attention.

I raised my weapon to my chest and switched the safety lever on my weapon to semi. When I focused my site on the moving object, I wondered what I would do if a bunch of Iraqi soldiers come out of the hole? Then my imagination kicked in to full gear with various scenarios. What if I had to kill one of them and what would that feel like if I had to? Would I be a murderer or just a soldier who has seen combat?

I locked on the target with my finger on the trigger, tracking its movements through my sites. Waiting patiently, it finally emerge from the hole and to my surprise, it was just a kid.

All of a sudden other kids started coming out of these other holes. Six kids in all came out as they exposed themselves. They are all filthy and wearing torn clothes, but they're smiling from cheek to cheek. They started walking slowly in my direction with their hands out, some of them are pointing to their months indicating that they want food. I lowered my weapon and flipped my firing lever back to safe. Although the kids are harmless, I imagined scarier thoughts that they could be a decoy for some Iraqi Soldiers, so I yelled over to the Captain to get him to hurry up. "Captain, you need to grab your shit so we can get going."

"Got it, found my vest and ammo," he yelled back from the back of the HMMWV.

While I waited for him to lock and load a magazine, I grabbed some of the candy that we had purchased back at the Post Exchange and tossed it to the kids. They all made a beeline for the candy and started wrestling over it. I gave the hand and arm signal for everyone in the convoy to get back in the vehicles because we were ready to roll.

Then the Captain noticed the wandering kids and decided that he had a bright idea. He decided this would be a perfect opportunity to gather some intelligence from the kids. "Hold on SFC Hunter and SSG Jenks, give me a minute with these kids," he yelled out. He held up a bunch of our MRE's to the kids. "If you can tell me if there are any Iraqi soldiers around here, I'll give you some food," he hollered to the kids.

The kids looked up at him with confusion, so he shouted even louder, "hey! if you can tell me if there are any Iraqi soldiers around here, I'll give you food!"

The kids just stood there chewing on their candy.

The Captain turned and looked at me and said, "I think that there may be an ambush ahead because these kids are not saying anything when I ask them a question."

"You have got to be shitting me," I replied, even though I knew he could be right on the ambush part. "What country are we in," I continued?

"Iraq," said the Captain with confidence.

"Do you think maybe that they don't understand English, maybe they speak Iraqi? And besides, what kind of propaganda do you think the enemy could create if they found out you tricked these kids into eating pork products from those MRE's you're trying to offer?"

"Watch it Jenks, nobody likes a smart ass," the Captain responded back.

"Let's go," I yelled to the rest of the convoy. Once again, Cpt Barker flashed me the angry look but said nothing.

We all got back in the vehicles and started heading towards Baghdad. The Captain became silent for once as he went back to reading his GPS manual. Figuring this would be a good opportunity to enjoy another one of my cigars in order to release some of the stress caused by the Captain's stupidity, I retrieved one of my aluminum tube cigars and lit it up as we continued our travels.

A few hours had gone by as we made our way north and we were all taking in the sights of the landscape as we sped by. This was soon broken up when we noticed a lot of black smoke coming from the roadside just ahead. As we came closer to the smoke, I could see that this smoke was coming from a few Iraqi military vehicles that had been demolished by our troops. This was a horrible site to view. The bodies were still smoldering inside the vehicle as it burned. You couldn't help but stare at the wreckage and observe the scene as you do when you pass an accident on the street with all the ambulances around. After we passed the scene, it was only a matter of minutes before we forgot all about it. As long as they weren't our boys, it didn't bother me I reasoned to myself.

On this drive we would pass other battle scenes that were similar to the first one, but they varied in the type of vehicle that was damaged and the amount of dead bodies inside. As we got deeper and deeper into Iraq, there were more signs of intense battles that had taken place and the landscape looked even more burned with black residue from the battles. (Also the more time we spent in Iraq and the more we saw these disasters, the more we became desensitized to the violence and blood.)

Markers had been placed on the side of the road by the Army EOD[15] indicating that the outlying fields are full of mines. I had confidence in knowing the EOD had done their job correctly and cleared the road for travel. If I just stayed on the paved road, we would be relatively safe. But then again, I also knew that the Iraqi's could at anytime replace the road mines, so I still paid attention to what might be in the road at

---

[15] EOD - Explosive Ordnance Disposal.

all times. My mind played its chess game about what could be waiting for me around the next corner for quite a few miles.

CHAPTER FIVE

STRIPPERS, KEGGERS AND THE VOODOO CONVOY

We were making good time, but the sun was starting to set and we all agreed that it would not be a good idea to travel in the dark too much. According to the map with our route plotted on it, there was another refueling station about twenty miles ahead. This would be a good place to not only gas up, but to spend the night inside their secured perimeter so we could try and get a good night's sleep. This depot also had their own defense system with MP's and all, but what could they do about Cpt Barker and his stupid flashlight?

Just as the last rest stop, we had to search for a patch of land where we all could be grouped together. When we were all situated, Cpt Barker exited the vehicle and checked into the depot HQ tent along with SFC Hunter. Carson jumped in our vehicle and immediately doled out the MRE's because he was famished. After we all made our selection for dinner, the three of us sat together as we chowed down our food and talked about the day's events. There is nothing like a good MRE (Menu #3 – Beef Ravioli) after a long day of driving.

Half way through my pasta, SFC Hunter came over and informed us that there was a safety briefing in ten minutes in the main tent for convoys that are traveling this route to Baghdad. I quickly finished my ravioli so I could get to the best part of the MRE before I headed over to the tent to see what was up.

The best part of any MRE if you were so fortunate to posses was the Jalapeño cheese spread with vegetable crackers. The deli shops in the States have nothing on the MRE cheese and crackers, it's a delicacy to me. Two kinds of cheese packs are available in an MRE if you are lucky enough to get one. One is the regular processed cheddar, the other is the jalapeño and cheddar. This is my favorite and luckily, is currently in my possession. I always made sure to squeeze out the last bit of the processed cheese food onto the stale crackers no matter which one it was. When you opened up an MRE and discovered either the peanut butter spread or the grape jelly, you always felt a little empty inside and disappointed because you were denied the treat.

A short and stocky MSG[16] appeared out of nowhere and started to lead the briefing. You could tell he has been in the Army forever and a day (a lifer). He had the traditional crew cut hair that was all gray in color and his expressions were as if he hoped this would be his last war. "You are going to see a lot of destroyed Iraqis vehicles out there and every

---

[16] MSG — Master Sergeant - A noncommissioned rank in the U.S. Army that is above sergeant first class and below the position of sergeant major.

once in a while you might see an American one too. Do not tinker around with any doggone vehicles or any doggone objects because they could either be booby trapped or just ready to explode. The shoulders on the roads have been cleared all the way to Baghdad, so feel free to pull over and take a break if you need one, but make sure you always pull 360 degree security."

Looking around the room and seeing the blank stares on everybody's faces in this briefing confirmed my thoughts that this really couldn't be everything he wanted to mention to us. Why would he make me rush through my delicious MRE to tell me this? Then the answer suddenly came to me, as I realized there had to be a fucking idiot that did all of those things he was telling us not to do. Now we have to sit through this safety briefing because of their stupidity.

Finally, the MSG concluded his safety briefing and started to provide us with some useful information concerning the war. "Two more things, Donald Rumsfeld has requested that everyone keeps an eye out for Weapons of Mass Destruction as you journey up north. He reports that they're in the areas around Tikrit and Baghdad; east, west, south and north somewhere. For those of you who are traveling north, we have good news for you. Operation Thunder Run conducted by 70th Armored Regiment was successful and An Najaf has been under the control of the Coalition Forces for some time now. We are getting reports that Baghdad may now also be under Coalition control."

We broke from the meeting and I started on my walk back to my guys so we could get ready to rack out and inform them of the good news. Sgt Brown seemed to be a little disappointed when I provided him the updates on the war. Probably because he realized his chances of combat were now slipping away. I for myself, was happy of the news.

The wind had started to pick up a little. Actually, it started to pick up a lot. All the green Army tents started to sway with each gust of the wind that blew through camp. The wind was exceptionally warm because it was blowing over the hot ground and cooling it off.

When I arrived back at my HMMWV, I was standing next to Carson and a big gust almost knocked me over, and with it a bunch of sand sprayed my face. "Holy shit, who turned on the blow dryer," I said as I spitted out some dirt from my mouth.

The moon was full, allowing me to see quite far into the desert, which permitted me to see what was coming. But what was coming no longer allowed me to see far into the desert and it darkened the sky.

"Guys, better grab all of our shit and put it back into the vehicle, I think we will be spending the night in this shit," I screamed.

As soon as those words left my mouth, a big blast of sand and heat hit us and almost knocked us over. We grabbed everything that we had out and threw it into the vehicle, and then we jumped in immediately afterwards. Luckily we had the windows already in the up position, because we could see the sand hit the window like a mini tornado.

The night sky no longer existed and you could not see more than three feet in any direction because of the sand storm. The wind howled and rocked the vehicle while the fine dust seemed to find its way through the cracks and around the doors, filling the inside of the HMMWV. This provided us with a thin vapor of powder for us to breath. We grabbed our t-shirts from our packs and tied them over our faces to filter the dust and sand.

Cpt Barker knocked on the window as I watched the sandblaster try to remove his face. He yelled through the window that he was going to jump in with SFC Hunter and go over some planning, so Carson can stay put for the night. A sand storm in exchange to be rid of the Captain was not a bad trade.

The evening came early and we couldn't fall asleep, so we started telling stories to each other about our wild partying back in the States. Carson told his stories about going to High School keggers again and Brown told stories of how he and his buddies would still be drunk the next morning for physical training and still have to run their 5k. I finally butted in with one of my wild stories. As with any Army story, it started out with "no shit, there I was…"

"Me and a couple of guys were over in Honolulu, HI on some Army maneuvers and we had some time off so we decided to hit the town. Now you need to know that before I went over there, my wife suggested that I should visit one of her best friends whose name is Karen who lived and worked in Honolulu. You also need to know that her friend was a stripper working at one of the joints there."

"Yesss!," said Brown.

"I had never met this person before and I did not know what she looked like, but my wife was very insistent that I visit her, even if it meant going to her work to find her. So before we hit the town, I called her and of course the timing worked out. She wanted me to meet her during her work hours at the club. So I had it all set up with the boys that we were to go and party with some strippers."

"You the man," said Carson.

"This joint was a bring your own bottle establishment, so we paid our ten bucks each for the cover and toted in a cooler full of beer. We sat at a table close to the stage and the boys started pounding the beers and tossing dollars on the stage for the ladies. I started asking around for Karen, but no one seemed to know who she was.

The beers were going down nicely and after a while I started to stumble around. I was starting to get a little worried because I was getting low on beer and I knew that my wife was going to kill me if I didn't visit Karen. One of my buddies finally came up with a brilliant idea and suggested that I find out what her stage name is, which of course made total sense. So as drunk as I was, I went up to one of the naked strippers and said, "I don't know her stage name, but there is this stripper who just moved here from Seattle. She has blonde hair and is about medium height."

"Oh you mean Emerald?"

"Yeah, I don't know what she looks like so can you tell her that her best friend's husband is looking for her."

"You can do that yourself because that's her on stage."

And there was Karen, in the buff dancing provocatively on the stage. After the set was over, she started walking off the stage.

"Karen?" I yelled.

"James!" she yelled back.

Then she ran over and gave me a big hug with her boobs squishing up against me. Now during this hug, my instincts almost kicked in and I almost grabbed her bare naked ass, but at the last moment, I caught myself and just patted her on the back. That was the first time I had a naked lady in my arms while I was drunk and didn't get laid."

"That's the most awesome story I have ever heard," said Brown through the t-shirt that was draped over his face to protect him from the sand that was blowing through the vehicle.

I had left off the part of the story when I called my wife from the strip club payphone to tell her that I loved her, and missed her and the boys. They just wouldn't understand that kind of thing at this stage in their life.

The next morning when we woke up the sand storm was still blowing, but it had tapered off a little. The sun was out, at least I thought it was because it was daylight, but you still couldn't see more than a couple of feet in front of you.

With the sun trying to make its presence and with all the sand blowing around, everything appeared to have a reddish glow.

Cpt Barker once again decided to stay up most of the night working on his GPS and map skills during the storm and continued bragging about how he can stay awake for endless hours while in a combat zone. And once again because of his habits, he was the last person to step out of the vehicles and greet the day.

Even though the sand storm was pretty intense, I was able to sleep like a baby because I knew the soldiers guarding this gas stop had my back. It also helped that Cpt Barker decided to do his bragging in his own vehicle with SFC Hunter that night. SFC Hunter on the other hand, appeared to be little slower than usual this morning. One could only assume he had to endure the long night of pointless bragging from the Captain.

The sand storm finally broke enough to be able to safely drive before nine hundred hours. Ironically, even after with all the sand blowing everywhere, the roads were still halfway clear. Even though SFC Hunter seemed a little impeded this morning, he was ready to get back on the road and I would have to agree with his enthusiasm.

Our intentions are to make it to Baghdad before nightfall and hook up with our supporting element, the 2nd CAV. We figured that if we drive hard and don't take too many breaks or get into a firefight on the way, we should be able to make it in time.

Without all the sand blowing everywhere, we were able to top off our tanks and resupply ourselves with water before we hit the road again for Baghdad. Carson proceeded to do a quick maintenance check on the vehicle to make sure there was no damage or clogged vents. Cpt Barker took it upon himself to go ahead and take his position in the passenger seat while we prepped for the ride. SFC Hunter waived his arms in order to get our attention and in his cocky attitude gave the order. Satisfying his command, we all climbed back into our perspective vehicles and started to head towards Baghdad. Hopefully this would be the last day I had to drive with the Captain. I knew war was hell, but spending three days straight with him in a vehicle was pure torture.

There were definitely more burned up vehicles as the MSG had said there would be as we drove deeper into Iraq. The engineers had come through and plowed the shoulder of the road with their dozers. I thought to myself, maybe that's why the roads are clear. These guys must have been keeping up on the sand removal like our snowplows do back in the mountains at home on the pass when there's a snow blizzard.

A few more hours into the drive I started to get bored with looking at the same repetitive landscape. The landscape reminded me of the Flintstones, where you see the same palm trees pass by, as if they were on a continuous loop. I decided to go against my better judgment and try to pick up a conversation with the Captain. Listening to him tell his non important stories that never amounted to anything would be better than counting the white lane strips on the highway. At this point, any type of distraction would be welcomed. As I looked over at the Captain to initiate the conversation, I was truly shocked and surprised at what I saw. Cpt Barker was passed out and fast asleep like a baby!

You fucking dirt bag, I thought to myself. How dare you fall asleep and make our right side vulnerable to attacks. The Captain was a sad sight to look at. His head was slumped forward, bobbing around to the motion of the vehicle. His arms were relaxed to his side while his M-16 rested across in his lap. The worst part was that he had a little drool coming out of the corner of his mouth and it started to drip on his precious map that was folded out over his weapon. I was just about to yell at him to wake him up, and then I came up with a much better plan.

I picked up the radio mic, "calling Voodoo Convoy, this is Voodoo Two." (Our sign on the radio was Voodoo.)

SFC Hunter responded back on the radio, "this is Voodoo Actual, go ahead."

"I am going to pull over for a second on the shoulder, but no need to get out because we will take off immediately," I whispered.

"Why, what's up," SFC Hunter asked.

"I will explain in a few minutes, just keep your distance."

"Roger that, Voodoo Actual out."

"Voodoo Two out."

I looked over at the Captain, he was still asleep.

I tugged at Browns leg and pointed at the Captain, he shook his head in disbelief. We were going about fifty miles an hour when I veered over onto the graveled shoulder of the road. A big dust cloud immediately kicked up and engulfed the HMMWV. As soon as I was all the way over on the shoulder, I purposely locked up the brakes and we went into a skid. This broke the Captain's siesta, his eyes popped open and he looked over at me. His face was a blank stare because he wasn't all the away awake and he still had some drool on the corner of his mouth. When he made eye contact with me, I looked back at him and yelled at the top of my lungs "AAAAGGGHH!!!"

I gave the Captain my best war face as I kept screaming. When we finally came to a complete stop, dust filled the inside of the vehicle. The Captain was still trying to figure out what the hell was going on as I kept on screaming as loud as I could. Then I stepped on the gas and I took off again, kicking up more dirt and dust.

The Captain went into a panic. He grabbed his weapon, pointed it out the window and started firing rounds into the desert.

"Cease fire! Cease fire! What the hell are you firing at?" I screamed.

When the Captain came out of his daze, he started to realize what had just happened. "Goddamit SSG Jenks, I'm the Captain here and you can't pull shit like that on me. I'm going to write you up on an article 15 you for what you just did." He was so pissed that his freckles on his face started to turn red. He finally decided to wipe the drool from his chin as he gave me the evil eye.

I couldn't decide whether to burst out laughing or call him a complete idiot. Since calling him an idiot would get me into trouble for disrespecting an officer, I decided to play it safe and go with my first option.

"You go ahead and do that. Just remember to write in your report how you fell asleep while you were supposed to be pulling security on the right side of this vehicle," I responded as I was laughing hysterically.

Then SFC Hunter came over the radio, "Voodoo Two this Voodoo Actual, what the hell just happened, is everything all right?"

I picked up the mic and said with most of my hilarity under control, "everything is fine, Voodoo Red just wanted to do a weapons check and fire down range because he was afraid that his weapon may jam up in this weather." I handed the mic to the Captain with a big shit eating grin.

"Everything is fine here, weapons check is successful, this is Voodoo Red out."

CHAPTER SIX

KILLING AN ARAB

Jesus Christ I need another cigar. This drive is mentally killing me. I only had two left and I'm saving at least one for my arrival in Baghdad. To smoke or not to smoke a cigar had never been such a complex issue with me before. It was still a long way to Baghdad and to smoke the one reserve cigar would leave me with many of miles that still needed to be traveled before I could celebrate with the final cigar. The miles seemed to be getting longer and longer and the heat from the desert kept getting hotter. The palm trees that I was enjoying were long gone. We were now deep into the desert and there was absolutely nothing to look at to keep me entertained. A cigar would at least keep my mind off the drive.

"How you hanging in there buddy?" I yelled up to Brown in the turret to keep my mind occupied.

"Doing fine," he yelled back down.

Well that didn't help. Not much conversation there to distract me from the drive. Then I remembered what my Drill Sergeant used to always say when I was in basic training, "smoke em if you got em." That was good enough logic for me, so I pulled out my reserve cigar and started puffing away.

Looking back up at Sgt Brown as I puffed on my fine cigar, I noticed he had a towel wrapped around his face along with the big ass ski goggles they issued to us in order to protect our eyes from all the sand that was in the air. The temperature up in the turret definitely has to be hot and being exposed to the sun for long durations in these conditions had to be brutal. If he has any sun screen on, it is probably SPF nuclear.

Since the conversation with Sgt Brown did not work out, I once again went against my better instincts and started a discussion with Cpt Barker. The question of why he was accompanying us on this deployment still needed to be answered. So, I simply asked him and waited for his response. His response, needless to say, was very interesting. He went on to explain that he was not here for the adventure, experience, or even the opportunities one could gain from a combat deployment. No. The main reason he was here was because of his wife. His wife is the type that would nag at you all day long. No matter what you did, you would still get in trouble and be the bad guy. She would always bust his balls. So he figured that if he was going to have his balls busted on a daily basis, then he might as well have the Army do it and get paid for it. This deployment would at least allow him the opportunity to take a break from his nagging wife.

I didn't know if he was pulling my leg or if he was trying to open up to me. The fact of the matter is, I didn't want to know either way. Not wanting to carry this conversation any further, I kept silent and re-focused on the road.

Every once in a while we would see Nomads trekking across the desert with their herds of camels carrying all of their belongings. The landscape kept changing from burned ground with little shrubs and rock piles to nothing but sand dunes. Eventually, we found ourselves in a full bona fide desert. Seeing nothing but sand everywhere with the heat waves dancing around on the horizon made me think I was seeing a mirage when I noticed something that looked like a large mountain started to appear in the far distance.

As we drove closer to the mirage, I realized that it was not an optical illusion, but an actual mountain. I could see that the road ran into this mountain and zigzagged up the side and over the top. The part that caught my attention was that at the base of the mountain, palm trees were growing and someone had actually landscaped the mountainside.

We finally made it to the base of the mountain and started to ascend the hillside. As we traveled up the road, the palm trees provided us with some relief from the sun. The landscape on the side of the road then changed to an agriculture style. The primary crop appeared to be tomatoes growing in the fields along with some other vegetation I could not indentify. Exposed everywhere was all the viaducts they had built throughout the years in order to get water flowing universally, so the crops could get the precious soaking. It kind of looked liked Napa Valley with all of their vine grapes, but this place was Iraq style with vine tomatoes. Every once in a while I could see a farmer in his palm tree shaded field waving at us as we drove by. Eventually we made it to the top of the mountain where the city of An-Najaf resided, a major metropolitan city had been built here.

Normally (Stateside) I would just read the sign that says, "welcome to our city," but in Iraq everything is in Arabic. I had to rely on the Captain to provide that information from his map, which took a few moments. We went through a couple of stop lights trying to figure out how to get out on the other end of this city. "Captain," I shouted, "why don't you just have your sexy voice GPS tell us where to go?" I was trying to be witty, but he must have took me seriously, because he went on to explain to me that he lost service a while back, and he's been using the map ever since. This piece of information made me nervous because I trusted his map skills less than the commercial GPS. My only hope is that he has been tracking our map location with the government issued GPS, since I was not able to do so as the driver. Then to my surprise, as I tried to figure out where the Captain has led us, we hit a road stop check point that was set up by our boys, the US Army.

We had to maneuver around a few cars that had been destroyed and burned. They were being used as barriers when we arrived at the security check point which was a good quarter mile up the road. This road block turned out to be more of a makeshift check point hastily put together, because it was really just a couple of GI's with a radio. They had no back up protection like a Bradley or anything with serious fire power.

Cpt Barker snatched the radio and said, "all units pull over so we can get some instructions from these soldiers on how to get to the other side of this town and continue on to Baghdad."

We all pulled over in a large space next to the checkpoint. Everyone got out of their vehicles and pulled their normal security positions while Cpt Barker and I addressed the soldiers at the check point. The soldier manning the checkpoint looked as if he was no more than nineteen years old. His buddy seemed to be about the same. The soldier who seemed to be in charge immediately started the conversation on why they had set up this check point. We both had to stand there and listen because we couldn't get a word in at all during his speech.

"This check point was put up because there are some militias that were not in uniform trying to take advantage of the situation. It's all gangsters like around here, so we need to check everybody out for weapons in their cars. We got this whole place cordoned off and nobody is getting in," he said in his southern drawl. He was definitely from Arkansas or parts around. He must have been asked this question a million times, so now he just has a speech memorized.

As soon as he finished the last word in his sentence, an old white Toyota with orange doors came speeding through the make shift barriers of blown up cars. This vehicle obviously had no intention of slowing down to chat. The other soldier guarding the check point made sure that he was visible to the speeding car. He waived his arms to indicate that this vehicle needs to stop, but for some reason his message was being ignored. "Holy shit, he's passed our point of the no return marker. The other vehicles have always stopped before they passed our marker. My Sergeant told me if any cars sped pass that marker, we need to light them up."

The first soldier we were talking to, raised his weapon and pointed it at the speeding vehicle. Without hesitation, he pulled his trigger. Unfortunately, when he pulled the trigger, all you heard was a metallic click. "Shit! My weapons jammed, somebody stop that son of a bitch," he yelled.

The second soldier who was still trying to waive at the speeding vehicle to stop, raised his weapon and fired some shots towards the car. All of his shots missed his target because the car was weaving all over the place.

All that ran through my mind was that this vehicle was probably loaded with explosives and he wanted to blow up the check point along with us in it. I realized that the only thing that was going to stop the vehicle at our disposal was an M-203 round, which I conveniently had on me. I took one of the rounds from my vest and chambered it into the cylinder and flipped off the safety. I knew this was going to take some Kentucky windage to get this shot in the sweet spot. As I looked down the aiming sight, I realized I couldn't get a clear shot because of all the vehicles in the way. "Crap, I can't get a shot because of my angle," I cried. Then I heard Sgt Brown shout, "throw your weapon up to me, I can get the shot." Without hesitation, I tossed my weapon up to Brown and watched him catch it in mid-air. He took steady aim at the speeding car's windshield and then pulled the trigger. A big thump sounded off as his shoulder took the blow from the force of the round being released. The gold colored round traveled through the air and then broke the windshield as it entered the vehicle. Then all of a sudden there was a loud explosion as the grenade detonated. You could see the bright flash and the concussion wave rip through the vehicle and then onto the ground. This made the dirt ripple with waves.

The explosion forced the car to come to a sudden stop. "Holy sheep shit," I heard Sgt Brown yell out with excitement.

We all looked at each other with amazement as to how the car annihilated itself. "Hold you positions and keep a tight security, there may be more," screamed Cpt Barker. Then he yelled, "Jenks and McClure, go check out the vehicle and let me know what the situation is!"

Spc McClure and I ran to the demolished vehicle that's about a hundred meters down range and we looked inside. All that is left of the driver is half a torso still sitting in the seat with blood and guts splattered everywhere. "Looks like you got your first confirmed kill," I shouted back to Brown.

"Dog, this dude's toast," McClure replied.

The trunk was halfway popped open. I went to the back of the vehicle, carefully inspecting all the hinges and gaps for any trip wires. Then I slowly peered inside the trunk. I could see that the driver was carrying at least five 105mm Howitzers[17].

---

[17] 105mm Howitzers - High explosive ammunition used in artillery.

Seeing those Howitzers in the trunk made me want to get away from the vehicle as fast as possible. McClure and I are both in agreement and ran back to the checkpoint.

"What is the story SSG Jenks?" Cpt Barker inquired.

"Well, you better call this one in," then I went on to explain the situation to him.

Less than a half hour after Cpt Barker called it in, the Engineers from the 7th Engineer company in Fort Drum arrived to defuse the bomb. We were now all cleared to leave this situation and continue our mission. Before we all could get back into our vehicles, Cpt Barker wanted to make a statement to all of us. He said with all of his pride, "good job Brown, I'm glad we have you to cover for Jenks." Satisfied with that jab at me, he then gave the command for us to load up and we started to head out of town.

As we took off from the check point site, I leaned over to the Captain and asked, "did you get the correct directions out of here?" The panic look on his face made it clear to me that he did not like my question.

CHAPTER SEVEN

ZOMBIES IN BABYLON

As we finally figured out how to exit the city and continue our travels to Baghdad, there started to be large groups of people walking on both sides of the road. As we passed them, they waved back at us with big smiles on their faces. They seemed to be very pleased to see us. It almost looked as if they were on a pilgrimage. Some of them had big flags that they were carrying, but they appeared to not have any military significance. They seemed to be peaceful so we just left them alone.

Then we drove through the historical city of Babylon. I remember reading about this city from biblical stories and how king Nebuchadnezzar built a magnificent city, including the Hanging Gardens. I had imagined it to be something special. It turned out to be a big shithole with garbage and sewage everywhere. The houses were just old clay and brick buildings that they've built throughout the centuries. I'd seen better neighborhoods in Tijuana. This is what must have happened after Isaiah, son of Amoz received his message concerning the destruction of Babylon. When God decides to smite you, it appears he really does a bang up job.

Eventually, we made it to the outskirts of Baghdad. The vehicle traffic started to get thick like molasses. Pedestrians were everywhere traveling in every direction as if a sporting event had just finished. They were mobbing through the traffic with no regards to the vehicles. SFC Hunter's voice crackled over the radio and said, "let's keep these vehicles real tight so no one can get in between us." Even though we were almost bumper to bumper, every time we stopped somebody would try to weasel their way through the tiny space between the two vehicles.

Some of the people tried to get close to your window and they would wave and yell to us with sayings like, "mista mista what's your name" or "Bush good Saddam bad."

If it wasn't for some of the burned up Iraqi army vehicles lying around, you would have never guessed that a war was going on. The people seemed to go about their business as if nothing ever happened, and even more surprising was they are being nice to us.

Once again, SFC Hunter's voice came over the radio. "I know these people are acting friendly, but we need to keep our eyes peeled for the bad guys. I have no doubt they are mingling in the crowds."

Slowly but surely we moseyed through the packed streets and eventually made it to our destination. The UN building is barricaded with a very large brick wall all around it. An M-1 Abraham tank is standing guard at the front gate to greet any guests who want to enter. All around the wall I can see the muzzles of our soldier's weapons peering over as they manned their post.

When we approached the gate, a guard peered into our vehicle just to make sure we were really US soldiers, and then he waved us in. The tank paid no attention to us.

You could tell that the 2nd CAV had been staying at the UN building for a few days with how entrenched they are. They weren't kidding around when it came to protecting themselves, because not only do they have a well fortified machine gun's nest about every 30 feet, they also have M-1 Abrams Tanks strategically placed around the perimeter. They have it so well secured you could walk around in confidence without your armor vest on, as long as you are inside the UN building or behind your vehicle. This was going to be a relief for us because we still hadn't acclimated to the weather all the way and the body armor was brutal to wear.

We finally found a space within the compound so that we could park our vehicles and get out of them in order to stretch our legs from the long drive. I ripped off my vest that contained the body armor and a pool of sweat that had been swashing around in my mid section splashed on the ground. My blouse was soaking wet too and when I rung it out, about a pint of sweat also splashed on the ground.

"All right, everybody needs to gather around," yelled Cpt Barker. "Hunter and I will go inside and check in with the Battalion Commander, the rest of you should spend some time and give your weapons a good cleaning and then eat some chow."

As they went inside, we stacked our weapons to the side and we dug into our MRE's. As we looked around our surroundings, we noticed that there was a lot of garbage and junk everywhere. The surrounding buildings seemed to be made from cheap brick and what little mortar they used to hold it together seemed to be disintegrating. The cars owned by the locals, who were driving next to our protective wall, all seemed to be pieces of junk. They were all rusted with dents all over them. Having tread on the tires seemed to be not a popular option. We then looked at each other and we all came to a quick agreement, this place was a shit hole. About an hour later after I finished taking in all the scenery, both SFC Hunter and Cpt Barker came back out of the building and gave us the news.

"This is where we all go our separate ways," Cpt Barker said, "first thing in the morning 2nd CAV HQ will be moving to a new location just down the road a couple of miles. This is where SFC Hunter, Spc McClure, and I will go."

They divided our four teams up with the four different CAV squadrons. All the squadrons are to take responsibility of different sectors of Baghdad. Sgt Brown, Spc Carson, and I are now attached to the 2nd squadron of the 2nd CAV who is now responsible for Saddam City.

This was essentially East Baghdad, the slums where all the Shiites are forced to live. We were briefed that Saddam City is one of nine administrative districts in Baghdad. A public housing project neglected by Saddam Hussein and where Baghdad's urban poor decided to call home. Saddam City holds more than three million Shiite residents, all in about a six square mile area. In this area, there is a cigarette factory that was used as a base by Saddam's elite forces (the Republican Guard) during the invasion, which the Marines eventually kicked ass on and took over. We are to go there and relieve the cigarette factory from the Marines. Then we will establish a FOB[18] for all of our future operations. The name that was assigned to the 2nd CAV, 2nd squadron new headquarters and what we would call home was Camp Marlboro.

After a full day of briefings subsequent to meeting the 2nd squadron commander, we figured we didn't have much left to do except wait for the "move out" order tomorrow morning. This would definitely be a good time to kick back and smoke my last cigar and enjoy the company of my team.

The evening was upon us and it was starting to get dark. We were all sitting behind our vehicle leaned up against the building's wall relaxing, eating more MRE's, and smoking cigars. Sgt Brown was telling one of his "how it sucked to be in the infantry" stories when out of nowhere, Cpt Barker came over to us and said, "when you are outside, you need to get on your body armor vest and Kevlar helmet." Then he turned around and went back inside, and of course, he did not have his on.

---

[18] FOB - Forward Operating Base - A secured forward military position that is used to support tactical operations.

"Ah screw him," I said to my guys, "we're relaxing and tomorrow is the start of a long adventure in Saddam City."

As the night started to draw in, I noticed there was more gunfire in the background, but I knew we were safe where we are. We somehow got on the subject of zombies. As I was explaining the different classes of outbreaks, we heard a loud explosion in the background. We all looked at each other, grinned with satisfaction because we all thought the explosion sounded cool, and then went on with our discussion.

"What freaks me out about zombies is how they all stick their arms out and crawl out of their graves," Brown said.

"That is only possible with Hollywood zombies," I butted in. "Real zombies don't have the coordination or the strength to dig themselves out of the ground, especially if their muscles have deteriorated. Think about it, even if you were buried alive and you had all of your current strength, you couldn't dig yourself out."

We all heard another loud explosion in the background, but this one seemed to have multiple explosions.

"That was kind of fucking cool," said Brown.

Once again we looked at each other with a grin, but this grin was a little different. This grin was the, this is still exciting, but it's starting to get a little too close for comfort.

"Now look," I continued. "The only way for a zombie to animate is through the virus Solanum. The Solanum virus was first discovered by Jan Vanderhaven during his leprosy research in South America. The only way for the virus to spread is by traveling through the bloodstream, from the initial point of entry to the final destination of the brain. While not only is it impossible for this virus to pump through a dead corpse veins, but who would want to bite a dead corpse? Zombies never attack dead corpses. The infection attacks the frontal lob in the brain and kills the host and then within 24 hours, re-animates the host. That's why the only way you can kill a zombie is with a headshot, because the virus can't survive if the frontal lob is damaged."

This time there are five consecutive explosions that rocked the ground.

"Jesus Christ," I yelled. "I'm trying to educate you two about zombies so you will be prepared if you ever find yourself in an outbreak and I keep getting interrupted with these explosions. Now if you ever find yourself in an outbreak, there are certain things you need to take into consideration if you want to survive. First thing is a weapon of choice. A crow bar is good for close quarter combat because you don't need any room or aiming skills to give them a hard blow to the head to kill them. A high-powered assault riffle is good for open space warfare because it can carry a massive amount of ammo while a single bullet to the head will terminate the zombie. The next thing you need to consider is fortification. You will never know how long it will take for the Government to take control and it usually takes about five years for a zombie to completely deteriorate where they are no longer a threat. And of course you need to think about food, water, and what to do if you need to reintroduce civilization if the outbreak goes global."

This time we heard the explosions start again, but this time they didn't seem to stop. One explosion was followed by another and they kept getting louder. Then the ground started to shake like an earthquake and the explosions continued to get louder and louder and we felt as if they were getting closer and closer.

We all looked at each other wide eyed because we didn't know what to expect or do at this point. These explosions seemed to go on for at least two minutes, or at least it seemed to be that long of time. It could have only really been just a matter of seconds. Then all of a sudden, the explosions seemed to have arrived on our front door step which caused all of the windows in the UN building to blow out and glass went flying everywhere like a bomb just went off inside.

We all hit the ground flat on our bellies and covered our heads with our hands. It seemed like the thunderous explosions were never going to end and the strength of the explosions kept intensifying as every second passed by. Out of the corner of my eye, I could see the night sky burst into an orange glow.

Every possible scenario went through my head at a hundred miles an hour. a) What if Saddam decided to use a nuclear bomb this time? b) What if he called an air bombing campaign on us? c) Am I going to die? d) Am I already dead?

Then the explosions finally decided to stop, and we looked at each other in disbelief because we're still in shock as to what just happened. My ears are ringing from all the loud noise and it was hard to hear what all the other people were shouting. Even though the silence had set in because my eardrums are numb as if I just attended a heavy metal concert, I knew my voice was still functional and I could still shout out commands to my guys.

I jumped up, dusted myself off, straightened out my blouse, and looked directly at my team. "Carson and Brown, you heard the Captain, so get your God damn armor vest and Kevlar on!" I yelled.

CHAPTER EIGHT

WINDOWS XP

The next morning we were getting our shit together to make our journey over to Camp Marlboro in order to relive the Marines. Part of this planning led me to be standing in a small room with SSG Hogan from TPT 1283. It was a good thing he was no longer angry about the mess tent incident, at least I hope he was over it because no one was present to protect me if he decided to go berserk on me. We were looking over a large map that was laid out over a table, trying to get a feel of our newly assigned sector. While I was studying the map, he started explaining the information he gathered about the explosive event from last night to me.

Apparently, the Engineers had been gathering all of the large ammunition rounds that were left lying around Baghdad after the invasion and they proceeded to stash them into a depot for safe keeping. Over time, so much ammunition had been collected that numerous piles had been formed and they needed to eliminate the excessive stock. The best way to dispose of this ammunition and keep it from the locals for future use, especially using it against us was to mark it for destruction. The Engineers intentions were to clear these piles of explosives with a controlled blast one at a time in a proscribed fashion. What happened was one pile of explosives got out of hand during its demolition and some hot fragments found its way into the neighboring piles. This accidently ignited the other piles. A chain reaction took effect from there with the remnant piles, and then eventually there was no longer a cache of ammunition.

During the end of his explanation, SFC Hunter suddenly stepped in and asked SSG Hogan to excuse us for a minute. He also commanded that he would need to close the door on his way out. With SSG Hogan out of the room, I no longer had to worry about his retaliation but now I had to prepare for a battle of the wits with SFC Hunter. I knew right away that this wasn't going to be a social call by that look of disgust on his face. SFC Hunter and I never saw eye to eye on military manners back in the States. He was one of those individuals who always thought his way was the best way, and it was the only way. I, on the other hand, always looked for the most resourceful way to get things done, even if it went against conventional thinking. You couldn't find two people who are more extreme on the opposite ends of the poles with their viewpoints.

Our standard normal operating procedures during these confrontations would always be SFC Hunter pointing out all things he felt was wrong with me and then I would rebuttal with witty comments that would make him infuriated. The final result always ended in him needing to excuse himself from the situation. This was accomplished by me possessing the knowledge of how he behaved during our debates. I knew his logic was controlled by his emotions so I always tried to get him emotional so he would become illogical. For me, my emotions are controlled by my logic. As long as I stayed logical, I could keep a cool head.

SFC Hunter got close to my face and I could tell he was already geared up with something to say while trying to remain calm. "Jenks, I need to talk to you before you leave because it could be a while before we see each other again."

"What's up?" I replied in a casual tone, trying to take a step back because my nose processed a pungent smell from his mouth when he delivered his word.

His lip started to quiver a little bit. He looked as if he was trying to fight back some emotions, and then he responded with, "first of all, I'm an E-7 and you are an E-6, so you better give me some respect. If I don't see you standing at parade rest in two seconds, I'm going to bust your skull in."

Knowing that a verbal assault was on its way from SFC Hunter, I needed to knock him off his game so I just stared at him and causally went to parade rest while remaining calm. Apparently, this seemed to work because I could swear I almost saw an eye pop out of its socket.

"I never wanted you to come on this mission in the first place," he continued. "I figured that we all would be together where I could keep an eye on you. With us separating like this, I know you will pull some stupid ass stunt and get us all in trouble. I'm going to be riding your ass and as soon as you mess up, I'm going to request that you get relieved of duty and get sent home. I never liked you in the first place because you always think you're smart and try to find the easiest way of doing things. You know there is only one way to do anything and that is the Army way, by the book. When I was in Bosnia, I was a PSYOP god."

Oh no, I thought to myself. SFC Hunter always goes on with these 'I was in Bosnia' tirades because he did a tour of duty there. What slipped his memory is that just about everybody else had done this tour also, including me. When he went on these tangents, he would get all animated and become a spectacle. Then his eyebrows rose to his forehead and he got close again to me, pointing with all four fingers at my chest as he was the only authority around here on this subject.

"I know how to get things done around here, therefore you will always need to listen to me. You are just like everybody else who was in Bosnia, not knowing what was going on and I had to correct everybody. If it weren't for me, we would have had our asses handed to us in Bosnia."

He appeared to run out of steam and that was his final statement. With his long pause, I started to relax because I figured I survived another one of SFC Hunter's scoldings and I wouldn't have to retaliate by being too canny. That hope faded when he took another deep breath that seemed to recharge him.

"Another point I need to make is that I know you have your own personal laptop that you brought with you. The Captain and I have decided that we need you to sign over the

Army laptop that was assigned to you before you head out to Camp Marlboro. The Captain and I will both need a computer so we can get our important work done and we were only assigned one computer, so we need yours." He stepped back and relaxed a little thinking he made his point and I might have understood him fully.

I could see the look in SFC Hunter eyes that he thought he was going to get away with this statement and not deal with me being a smart ass. What he didn't realize was that this was the calm before the storm and this seemed to be a proper time to display my astute skills that he despised. "But if we go by the book, it clearly states that any classified information is not allowed on any computer that hasn't been certified by the communication personnel, and I know everything that we will be dealing with will be highly sensitive material," I said mockingly. "Besides, my laptop is on Windows XP and all the Army computers are running on Windows 2000."

(I knew that I could easily save the files in the older format with backwards compatibility, but I knew he didn't have a clue as to what I was talking about and this was a chance to confuse him.)

"Listen here SSG Jenks, everyone here is using their personal laptops, and so you can too."

As I stood there taking his continuous verbal beating about turning over the laptop, I realized I could use his lack of knowledge regarding computer formats against him. I decided that I would have a change of heart and turn over the

Army issued laptop to him. I didn't do this because I'm a nice guy, but once again this provided me an opportunity to mess with him in the future. My plan was to simply create my reports with my laptop utilizing Office 2003, which was produced in a XML format. This way he wouldn't be able to open up any documents generated on my computer because his laptop was loaded with Word 2000 which operated on a binary format. Until he figured out that I could simply save with backwards compatibility, I could continue making him infuriated. These future lashings were a risk I was willing to make for my own entertainment.

When SFC Hunter thought I was throwing in the towel by agreeing to turn in the laptop, he decided to capitalize on my assumed demeanor and lash out on other subject as he continued with his arrogant scolding. He determined his next topic would be him bragging about being promoted before me and made the statement, "I'm the E-7 here, I got promoted for this tour and not you."

This was the opportunity I was waiting for, when his emotions took over and made him compose these types of statements. Besides, when someone makes a statement like that, you have no choice but to be a wise ass and luckily I was good at it. "True, but did you know the Commander back in the States asked me if I wanted to be promoted into your position? Though, I turned it down because I didn't want to be a desk jockey like you're going to be. I like to be in the field and get real work done."

SFC Hunter's head looked like it was ready to explode and I could have sworn that steam was coming out of his ears this time. The best part was I could see that he knew I was right.

"Go and fucking turn the computer in to the Captain now!" Then he left the room, slamming the door behind him. I knew he left the room not because he was done with me, but because he knew he had to leave before he went all ape shit on me and it would be him who had to be sent home early. I always had fun with these discussions with SFC Hunter, especially when they ended this way.

CHAPTER NINE

BASE CAMP

We are one of about thirty vehicles that are in the convoy on its way to the cigarette factory in Saddam City. By participating in this large convoy and having the fire power of 2nd CAV with their weapons pointing in every direction, I was finally able to relax my guard just a little and actually look around a bit to take in my surroundings. After about a minute of taking in my surroundings, I decided I had enough taking in because the surroundings looked like a shit hole. Apparently, Carson had the same attitude with the scenery and decided to make a change by requesting we blast Metallica over the loudspeakers as we plowed through town. With him being so young and inexperienced, I had to take a deep sigh and explain to him that wouldn't be such a great idea. Especially since we're making our first impression to 2nd CAV and pissing off the locals on day one wouldn't go over too well.

On the positive side though, Carson was my driver, Brown was in the turret, and nobody was going to mess with us. I was glad to have my team back and to be ditching Cpt Barker and SFC Hunter.

A few miles later after driving through what appeared to be the shit hole of shit holes, we arrived at the cigarette factory. The gate at the entrance is fortified to prevent anything shy of a tank from getting through, mostly because there are two M-1 Abram tanks playing the part of fortification, not to mention there's a ten-foot concrete wall surrounding the entire factory.

As with all factories, there is a building designated for doing the business and the administration end. This particular business building on this particular piece of property is six stories tall. A building six stories tall provided plenty of sniper positions for defense, particularly in a neighborhood of buildings no taller than three stories. I could see why they chose this as our FOB. The whole establishment is about twenty acres, which included the business building, the factory, and about fifteen or so different warehouses. The business building and the factory are in good shape. There is even a functional decorative water fountain out in front of the business building. The warehouses are a different story, more than half of them are crumbled and destroyed from the war.

As soon as we entered the establishment, the Marines started their exit and they were gone within a matter of minutes. Then we noticed the ground guide who was in charge of this particular convoy waiving his arms and directing vehicles where to go just like a traffic cop in a busy street intersection. We parked our HMMWV where he specified us to be and then we all exited the vehicle.

Looking around and seeing the poor condition of this establishment required us to come up with a new measurement system for shit holes. This new system would be reminiscent of Sgt Brown's various levels of 'this sucks,' which he continuously applies in the infantry. We would need to utilize the criteria that he used to rate suckiness.

On the high end of 'this sucks' scale is when your weapon jams in combat during a firefight or if you're at Ft. Lewis Washington doing your Army weekend bivouac and it rains the entire time. A mid-level 'this sucks' is like having to endure Cpt Barker on a convoy from Kuwait to Baghdad or having to hand over your assigned computer when you actually need it. At the low end of 'this sucks' is when your watching a football game and the cable goes out or if you arrive at the mess tent in Kuwait on lobster night and all the lobster is gone because a group of soldiers before you had a lobster eating contest and devoured the entire supply.

This place wasn't too bad, so I would have to rate it a category one shit hole because as messy as it is, we are going to fix it up. The UN building is more like a category two shit hole because it's filthy and covered in garbage, but it too could be fixed. The ride through Babylon and parts of Saddam City were category three and four shit holes because there was massive amount of filth and garbage that stunk up their neighborhood and no one would even try to clean it up, that's just the way they lived.

The worst we had seen so far was having a dead horse decaying on the side of the road in a garbage filled neighborhood. This earned a category five shit hole. I hope a

Voodoo Gold by James H Jenks

category five shit hole would be the worst we would have to endure because I couldn't see how much worse it could get. I told my guys to hold fast, while I went to go track down the Sgt Major in this category one shit hole to see where we're supposed to set up camp.

After about twenty minute of dodging other vehicles and trying to avoid all the dust from their movement, I eventually found the Sgt Major. He was more than happy to inform me that the one warehouse in the far left corner all by itself would be the Special Operation barracks. At first I was delighted to not be grouped in with everybody else, but then a funny feeling sank in as I took a second look at the building. Comparing our assigned building to all the other ones that 2nd CAV had claimed for themselves, I could tell that we were being assigned the one building that nobody wanted. I wanted to demand that we be provided a better living quarter, but making those demands to the Sgt Major would be political suicide. The Sgt Major is at the top of the food chain and his word is always final, even if it's wrong. I would just have to say "thank you" and make the best of it. He then continued to inform me that there are some Civil Affair guys that we will be bunking with. (This made sense as PSYOP and Civil Affairs were both under the same command back at Ft Bragg.)

Civil Affair units act as a liaison between the civilian inhabitants of a warzone or disaster area and the military presence. Informing the local commander of the status of the civilian populace as well as effecting assistance to locals. Either by coordinating military operations with non-governmental and international governmental organizations or by distributing aid and supplies directly to the populace.

"After you get settled in, I need you to attend our 1700 hours TOC brief on the first floor in that building over there with the fancy fountain in front," said the Sgt Major as he pointed to the business building.

"Roger that, see you at the brief," I replied.

I walked back to my guys and then escorted them over to the building that was assigned to us for our living quarters. When we got there my suspicions were confirmed and I could see why they assigned this building for us:

1. The roof is littered with bullet holes, so this was going to be a problem if it ever rained.

2. There's a big hole in the concrete slab where an artillery round had exploded.

3. There's a big hole in the side of the wall where the artillery round came through that caused a big hole in the concrete slab.

4. A half an inch of dirt covered the ground because all the doors were left open and the sand storms had their way with the place.

5. A set of railroad tracks that went straight down the middle of the building. I assumed this was for loading and unloading boxes of cigarettes, but on the outside of the building the tracks did not exist.

All the fully intact buildings were saved by the Sgt Major for their own people. I knew complaining would not produce any positive results, so I stuck with my plan to make the best of it, and that's we did.

I looked at my team. "Boys, say hello to our home for the next year."

"With a little TLC we can make this work," Carson said as he looked around trying to figure out exactly how that could be possible.

"All right," I said, "the first thing we need to do is scavenge the entire place and see what we can come up with. I'm sure there's a lot of hidden treasure throughout this cigarette factory. We need to build this bombed out warehouse into a place we can call home. Let's do this before everybody else gets the same idea and the good stuff is gone. So let's all head out in different directions and meet back here in about an hour."

When we all returned from our reconnaissance mission, we had appropriated some good items to use. Carson found a frame from a futon couch, some pots and pans, a campfire style coffee pot, and a hot plate that may or may not work. Brown took three business chairs from the main office building that had wheels on them when nobody was looking. He also brought over a ten-foot table, along with a lot of little end tables. I dragged over a six foot metal shelving unit and a metal wall locker.

Brown also informed us, "I found where they boxed up the cigarette cartons and there were bundles and bundles of six cubic foot boxes. They're all flat and need to be folded into boxes, but never the less, we had boxes. I also found barrels of glue over in the factory that we could take."

"Shit, are you serious? Boxes are building blocks and with the glue, we can build a house in here. The Three Little Piggy's aint going to have shit on us," I said with excitement.

"That sounds awesome, why didn't I think of that?" Replied Brown.

"Let's go and get a whole bunch, you lead the way," I commanded to Brown.

We drove over to the factory building and loaded our vehicle with as many boxes as we could pack into it. We decided after about five trips, that we had enough to build a mansion. Then we concluded that we had to make one additional trip because we also needed the fifty-five-gallon barrel of glue, and that was a task on its own. A fifty-five-gallon barrel of glue is not only heavy, but awkward to move. The last thing we wanted was spilt glue all over ourselves. When we were all done, we had hundreds of flat boxes that would have to be folded into shape one by one in order to make our house, but we had the whole year to do it.

"Why don't we make a three bedroom rambler, that way we can all have our privacy. We can also have a large living room and maybe even a kitchen." I looked at my guys and I could see a glimpse of excitement in them as they were anxious to get started on their new project.

As we started to fold our boxes into shape, another HMMWV's rolled up to our building and three soldiers got out, baring the same unit patch on their left shoulder as we do. The United States Army Civil Affairs & Psychological Operations Command (USACAPOC) patch. This patch that we shared had a sword pointing up and two lightning flashes running through it. These must be the Civil Affairs guys the Sgt Major was talking about.

They walked over to us and stood there for a second as they gave us the once over. "We are CA (Civil Affairs) and we will be rooming here with you per the Sgt Major," the one whom appeared to be in charge said with a smile, and then he extended his arm out for a handshake.

"Welcome to the neighborhood," I replied, and returned his gesture with a firm grasp for a proper handshake.

"My name is SSG Cole," he replied back.

He was a slender fellow with a fragile frame. He was about five and a half feet tall with brown hair. His face was narrow and he wore round glasses that slipped down to the bottom of his nose. "This is SSG Vanscoy my partner in crime," he continued.

Vanscoy looked like Mr. California. He was at least six feet two inches tall with blond hair. If he weren't in the Army, he would be the type that would be at the beach on a surfboard all day long. The last person he introduced was Sgt Butkus who looked like a bulldog with his crew cut hair and a flat but round face. He was about five feet ten inches and weighed a good two hundred and seventy pounds. After looking at him for a bit, I concluded that the name Butkus means you carry a gene that makes you look like Dick Butkus, the famous foot ball guy. If you put the two together in the same room, you would swear they were twins. I don't think this Butkus was teased a lot when he was a kid. If he was, then I don't think the teasers are around to talk about it.

Then a soldier from the 2nd CAV approached us as we were making our small talk with our new friends. "The sit-rep[19] briefing has been moved up to 1630 hours over in the main building where we are setting up the TOC[20]." He waited for my confirmation and then left as rapidly as he appeared and moved on to the next group to inform them the message.

I looked at my watch and it was already 1500 hours. "Let's get gluing and build our house." Also as a friendly idea to my new neighbors, I informed them about the box location. They were very appreciative of this information and they too sprung into action of building a house with boxes.

All the Squadron leaders, the S shops, the XO[21], the Sgt Major, and the SCO[22] are seated around a big table in the

---

[19] Sit-Rep - Situation Report - The Who, What, When, Where and Why.

[20] TOC — Tactical Operations Center - A command post where officers communicate information between each other.

[21] XO - Executive Officer of an army unit who is responsible for the staff, logistics, maintenance and basically making sure everything runs smooth for the commander.

conference room. These folks have trained together and have known each other for a long time. I was meeting the leaders of 2nd CAV for the first time. Also in the room was all the additional leaders from other elements: the engineers, the MP's and SSG Cole for CA, and then there was me representing PSYOP.

The XO kicked off the meeting by introducing the SCO, and then having each of us introduce ourselves and explain who we are and what we would bring to the table for 2nd CAV. He then went on to explain that we would have a sit-rep everyday at 1630 hour in this room until otherwise instructed.

The purpose of the sit-rep is to inform everybody else what you know or discovered because they may need to know what you know or discovered. They usually went in numerical order of the S shops and then followed up by each leader of each detachment.

The S-1, which is personnel, just wanted a roster of all the people who are on the FOB.

The S-2, which is intelligence, went on to inform us how the locals were reacting to our presence since now we are living in their neighborhood. Their reaction is more of curiosity which entailed watching and calculating if they should like us or not.

---

[22] SCO - Squadron Commander, usually a lieutenant colonel.

Next in line was the S-3, which is training and operations, he went on to explain how all operations would come from his desk.

The S-4, which is supply, said if you need anything, just let me know. I of course, immediately thought to myself that I need to get on this guys good side.

Each of the four different Squadron leaders which were all Captains, made their introductions and explained what sectors of Saddam City they would be responsible for.

This was finally my opportunity to introduce myself to the SCO and the rest of the crew. As a PSYOPer, it is crucial to win over the unit we get assigned to so they believe in our capabilities. This will then allow us have the freedom to run our own show so we don't end up being tasked with guard duty or other meaningless task. I had prepared my speech in advance and rehearsed it many times. All eyes were on me and I could see them awaiting a response. I took a deep breath, cleared my throat, and dove in head first.

"My name is SSG Jenks and I'm from the 361st PSYOP unit out of Bothell, Washington. My main weapon is my loudspeakers, which gives my team the ability to do surrender appeals, public broadcast, and deception missions. We can design and distribute any information that you want to get across by means of media or leaflets. We can also help out with intelligence gathering because we are experienced in conducting face to face operations with the target audiences. All we require is security in this fine establishment we now call home along with some ammo and beans."

The SCO sat there for a few moments as he processed the information that I just gave him. I could tell he was a man who would be confident in his final decisions. I stood there and watched his facial expressions display his thought process. The long pause made me nervous as I started to think I may not come out on the right side of his preference.

"Excellent," replied the SCO. "What I envision you doing right now is getting out to Saddam City and finding out what the people are thinking and see if you can have them point out where the Iraqi military soldiers still may be hiding out at. Just make sure you adhere to my two vehicle convoy rule. If you need an escort to accompany you, just let the S-3 know and they'll set you up."

"Yes Sir," I replied. I now felt relieved, knowing we would be gainfully employed doing the fun stuff that PSYOP's likes to do.

The XO went on and gave us updates about what other elements are doing and how the war is going so far. One thing that caught my attention during the briefing was the information about the two tons of gold that was seized at the Turkey border.

Saddam had various stashes of gold placed around Iraq for emergency funds. If he ever had to make a run for it for any reason, at least he would have several tons of gold to finance his lifestyle. I assumed this gold that he had stashed everywhere from his personal wealth was the result of numerous crooked deals he performed with the Soviet Union and other WARSAW[23] nation.

Eventually, the meeting came to a close and I was able to head back and check on the progress my guys were making on our new digs. They were busy at work. I had them take a break in order so I could explain everything that went on at the sit-rep meeting. I informed them what our mission is going to be and that I already had an escort lined up for us. Now we can do our first mission in the morning. I also told them about the gold because it was kind of cool.

"Can you imagine finding a bunch of gold like that? I for one, would figure out a way to get that shit home. I would consider it my bonus from the Army to compensate me for all the shit they've put us through," said Carson.

"Fuck yah," said Brown. "I would have never turned the gold over. You know it's just going to go straight to the crooks, I meant to say the politicians. They'll take all the gold for themselves and come up with some excuse of why they need it to pay for their pet projects. That gold will never make it to anybody who deserves it."

"Now listen you two," as I injected my opinion to this conversation. You both have valid points, but let's be realistic. There is no way in hell you will be able to smuggle gold out of this country. This report is proof that it can't be done. Don't

---

[23] WARSAW - A mutual defense treaty subscribed to by eight communist states in Eastern Europe and the Soviet Union.

think about taking any home because you know we have to go through customs on our exit from this place. There is no secret spot to hide the gold like in a shipping container. You couldn't even cash it in while we're here because if you did, you would get Iraqi Dinars in return. The Western worlds don't even recognize the Iraqi Dinar, it would be worthless outside of Iraq. Though it is nice to fantasize about having that much gold and what we could do with it."

CHAPTER TEN

ROMEO AND JULIETAS

As we started our day at 0700 hours in the morning, we could already start to feel the weather get a little warm. The guys started to gather around for our pre-mission briefing of the day. Luckily the electric burner that Carson had found worked, so we were able to use our electric converter and plug it into our vehicle battery for a power source. With the coffee pot that we also found, we were able to make some tarnished coffee with our fine Army issue coffee grinds from the mess hall that we had appropriated back in Kuwait. This made my briefing more tolerable for the guys.

Our first mission of the day would be to ease into the population and start forming relationships as the SCO had requested. We would start with the tea shops and just start shooting the breeze to see what we could possibly find out. But first things first, we needed to head over to where SFC Hunter was residing and have him supply us the interpreter we requested. Providing that SFC Hunter accomplished his duties and he actually had them ready for use.

If we went into the city now, without an interpreter and someone started yelling at us to "go fuck off", or even worse, if we encountered some bad guys who are not cooperative, we wouldn't be able to instruct them on what to do to avoid any harm. We would wind up shooting them. We are all eager to meet our new interpreter so we could go into the city and hopefully not shoot anybody. Well, at least Carson and I felt that a way. Sgt Brown, on the other hand, was itching to pull his trigger on somebody. We all grabbed our gear and rushed to the front gate where our escorts were waiting to escort us over to SFC Hunter location.

During an earlier briefing before we departed our ways with SFC Hunter back at the UN building, we were informed that the interpreters we would be able to choose from would be paid out of USACAPOC funds. We could then use them as we saw fit, twenty-four/seven if needed.

I had put in a request for a Shiite interpreter because Saddam City is about ninety percent Shiite and I don't think they'll open up to anyone other than their kind. Luckily, these interpreters would come from a local pool, I had a good feeling about getting what I wanted. What I requested was someone who not only spoke the language, but one who the people we were going to meet could trust.

After taking a couple wrong turns, we finally arrived at the 2nd CAV HQ, which was where SFC Hunter and Cpt Barker now resided. The HQ location was an overtaken Iraqi military training facility. It appeared to be in good condition, except for a couple of buildings that had one side or the other demolished from US military missiles. The size of the establishment was also quite large with numerous buildings spread out everywhere. Not knowing exactly where they were, we spent close to an hour tracking SFC Hunter and Cpt Barker down. Luckily the PSYOP vehicle is very distinctive with its loudspeakers on top. We were finally able to find them by locating their vehicle which was parked out in front of their new quarters that they had claimed for themselves. They were some lucky sons of bitches because they were able to get a small storage building as their billets and it came with air conditioning and electricity.

Not wanting to invest into any small talk with SFC Hunter, I brought up our need for the interpreter immediately. The good news was that SFC Hunter said he was already on top of it. He instructed us to head over to a near building where they had the interpreters lined up and waiting for selection. While we reversed our steps to walk back out of the building, I noticed Cpt Barker sitting at a nearby desk with his feet kicked up. What I was witnessing I couldn't believe. He was using the canned air spray that was intended to be used to dust off your computer as his personal cooling element. He was pushing down on the nozzle and spraying himself over his head and neck with the cool air exhausting from the nozzle, enjoying the cool breeze it created. I looked at the almost empty case of the canned air spray that was rationed for everyone's use and noticed the trash can next to it full of empty cans. I wanted to grab the can out of his hands and tell him how much of an idiot he was, but escaping the room before SFC Hunter could pin me down for another lecture was more important. I needed to choose my battles wisely. We raced over to the other building to escape the stupidity, though SFC Hunter was in tow.

Arriving at the building with SFC Hunter for our interpreter draft pick, we noticed he had arranged ten different locals for us to choose from. SFC Hunter had informed us that all had been scrubbed by intelligence, and they all passed the background checks. With not having to worry about their backgrounds, the pick all came down to just finding a right personality match for us. The first interpreter who we talked to spoke English well and appeared to be pretty cool, but he turned out to be a Sunni so we had to turn him down.

The next one was a Shiite, but he looked like an Iraqi General that was on the most wanted poster and we couldn't understand a word he was saying due to his heavy accent. He was definitely not acceptable for us.

We went through a few more that had the right qualifications, but for some reason or another, they just didn't seem right for our crew. We needed someone who wasn't a diehard Shiite, one who would be more secular so we could ask him to run errands for us like going to the liquor store. Yes, the liquor store. I knew that somewhere they had these liquor stores and I was going to find a way to break the Army rule about no liquor for soldiers.

Finally, we found one who was not only a Shiite from Saddam City, but one who liked America's capitalism and he wanted in on it. His name was Milik Hussain Al-Qure. He said he had learned how to speak English by watching

American movies, and one day he hoped to make it in the United States the way Arnold Schwarzenegger did who happened to be his favorite actor.

"This is the one I want," I told SFC Hunter as I pointed at Milik. He stood there with a grin on his face as if he was the first person to be picked while the captains took their turns selecting their teammates. We quickly filled out some paper work and Milik was hired. I was shocked that he was so excited to be making ten U.S. Dollars a day, but I guess to him that's a lot of money.

Before we left HQ, SFC Hunter pulled me to the side once again as I was not able to escape without a lecture. "If I ever catch you abusing your interpreter for any reason, I will have your ass!"

When SFC Hunter launched into these types of quick lectures, I would stare at his unibrow and imagine that he was Bert from Sesame Street yelling at me. I didn't pay attention to any of the words he would say, I would just have a secret laugh to myself that I was getting chewed out by a puppet. When he was finally finished speaking to me or should I say shouting at me, I turned to my guys after I was done with my internal laughter and said, "let's roll."

We left the HQ building in a scuttle and quickly jumped into the HMMWV. We then drove to the other side of the base where SFC Hunter could not bother us with his shenanigans. Once we were in the clear of his micromanagement, I turned to Milik who was sitting in the backseat and stated my first request from him.

"We want to get into Saddam City and start meeting the people."

His response was casual but to the point. "First of all, since Saddam is no longer in power, the people have decided to call their city Sadr City after the late great Imam Sadr, but not to be confused with the current living son who ran off to Iran. Second, since the afternoons are when the heat is most intense, most people go inside by two o'clock and don't come out again until dusk. If you want to meet people, you must go early in the mornings and drink tea with them."

"Shit, another day down the toilet!"

We were being delayed another day before we could even start working on the requirements that the SCO wanted us to do. It was only mid-day and we all were still eager to go into the city and be productive. Then I had a sudden flash on what to do. If I couldn't accomplish the SCO's objectives, then I could at least accomplish one of our provision objectives. I recalled how I always saw Saddam smoking a cigar on TV during the news. If Saddam had cigars, then there had to be a cigar shop in Baghdad somewhere. This revelation gave me an idea and a new mission.

I looked around to make sure SFC Hunter didn't follow me and wasn't trying to eavesdrop on my conversation. When I knew the coast was clear, I asked Milik if there are any cigar shops in Baghdad?

"Yes, I know of a place where it is believed that Saddam purchased his cigars for his personal use and it's not too far from here. It's in the Christian district of Baghdad, next to where all the Western style restaurants are."

"There's a Christian district of Baghdad? I thought you were all Muslims?"

"Yes most of us are, but we also have Christians, Hindus, and even Jews."

"You have Jews here? That's impossible, I thought you hated the Jews?"

"Yes that is true, but we cannot fault God's will to have all the different groups of Dhimmis[24] here. We must allow them to practice their religion, Insha'Allah."

"Wow, I guess you learn something new everyday. You can explain more on our way to the cigar shop, so start giving directions."

We took a tour through the part of Baghdad that was not a shit hole and wound up in a shopping district that looked similar to any strip mall in the United States, complete with beauty salons, restaurants, coffee shops, women's clothing stores, and of course, the prized cigar shop.

In big bold brown letters on the front outside wall over the front door of the shop read Zanobia Tobacco. I was starting to get excited like a kid on Christmas Eve and I couldn't wait to get inside the shop.

---

[24] Dhimmis - Jews and Christian's subjected to Islamic rule in order survive as non-Muslim entity in an Islamized country.

When we walked into the cigar shop, not only were we surprised that this place actually existed, but I was shocked to see actual humidors with various Cuban boxes of cigars on display. This cigar shop is identical to any other cigar shop where I could buy individual sticks or by the box. The part that blew my mind is that this shop displayed the seal on the window that it was certified by La Casa Del Habano's. This means that all these Cuban cigars were guaranteed to be of the best quality from Cuba.

I found places like this in Paris, London, Munich, and many other major European cities, but to find one in Baghdad took the cake. Their selection wasn't as robust as some of the other shops I have been to, but they still carried enough to make me happy. The other astounding fact is that these smokes are priced just slightly above inventory cost. This means they are inexpensive, and those prices caught the attention of Brown and Carson too!

Luckily they accept American money, so I spent a couple hundred dollars. I walked away with a little more than a box and a half of various brands. These cigars are definitely worth it to me. I may get blown up or shot tomorrow. I might as well enjoy a few quality cigars before I cash in my chips. Besides, isn't this what the extra danger pay is for?

After we purchased the smokes, we decided to head back to the FOB to celebrate our find. As I grabbed one of my prized cigars and lit it up, I instructed Milik to be back tomorrow at 0700 hours so he could take us into Sadr City. Puffing on my cigar as I watched Milik exit our billets, I started to ponder a question. Do I report this cigar information during the sit-rep and then watch the cigar shops inventory get wiped out by everybody else or do I keep this information to my team so only we have an ample supply of smokes while we're here?

CHAPTER ELEVEN

THE TEMPEST IN THE TEA POT

The next morning we acquired our escorts, we had our interpreter, and we were ready to converse with the local populace. Milik had suggested a few tea shops that we could visit and we plotted them on our map with the grid coordinates.

We left the front gate and headed toward Sadr City. As soon as we traveled a few blocks into the city, I was overcome with an effluent stench. I looked over at Carson who is driving and noticed that he has a puzzled look on his face as to what to do about the smell. I looked up at Brown who was mounted in his turret, his war face disappeared quickly because he didn't know which "this sucks" category to place this experience in. I also noticed that there was a four-inch thick layer of black mud on most of the streets. I could see women in their burqas walking around with either baskets or propane tanks on their heads trying to avoid the mud.

The horrible smell finally got the best of me. I looked over at Milik and for some reason this smell did not seem to bother him so I exclaimed to him, "what is that awful stench?"

"Many years ago Saddam paid the Germans to develop a sewage system here to appease us, now it is old and broken," said Milik with a grin because he has adapted to all of this.

"You mean that this mud is nothing more than shit?"

"No it's a combination of dirt, garbage, water, and sewage overflow."

"Like I said, shit! This place just expedited itself pass a category five shit hole. I didn't think it could get much worse than a rotting horse carcass in a neighborhood. This place has definitely gone to the top and earned the honors of a category ten shit hole! It's not like this everywhere is it?"

"No, just in certain spots like here."

We drove deeper in the city and the shit streets became intermittent. At one point we became caught up in a crowd of people and traffic near a busy street market. Most of the people waved and smiled at us as we drove by. Some flashed the peace sign and some gave us the thumbs up. I constantly heard a certain phrase being shouted to us. The people shouted it to us in a heavy Iraq accent, but always delivered it in English and with a smile on their face, "Saddam gone." Though, I didn't know if this was a statement or if they were asking?

We suddenly found ourselves in the middle of a very large street market. The market had all kinds of food available for sale. Many various types of fruits and vegetables are on display in their baskets. Some you could recognize right away like tomatoes or onions. A lot of the other stuff was a mystery that I have never seen before, not even at one of those fancy organic food stores we have in Washington. This market also has all different kinds of fish being displayed on ice. Big bubbled eye fish, long boney fish, and funny colored fish with big teeth where readily available. Not anywhere was there any salmon or tuna on display. Butchered goat hanging on hooks seems to be the other staple food available. All the food is covered with flies and the merchants are trying to fan them off with newspaper, but it appears to be a hopeless battle. The market also has other goods for sale such as stereo systems, satellite TV dishes, leather goods, blankets, and clothing. You name it, they seemed to have it. This part of the market reminds me of the swap meets that my wife always dragged me to back in South Seattle.

I then noticed that what started out as a few kids chasing us, because they were curious as to whom we are, turned into a massive crowd. Around every corner we turned, the herd of children would follow. They had to run their little hearts out in order to keep up with our moving vehicle that we were in.

We were starting to create a distance between these children and ourselves when Milik sprung out of his seat. "There is the tea shop," Milik said as he pointed to it.

Carson pulled up next to the curb, making sure we weren't parked in any street shit so we could avoid getting it on our boots. As I stepped out of the vehicle, Carson followed by walking behind me and watching my back. His job is to keep watch for me so I can concentrate on my conversation with the tea shop owner. Brown pointed his SAW forward to take the front, our escorts stepped out and took up positions for the left flank, right flank, and their gunner took the rear. As soon as we were all in position, the children caught up with us and surrounded the vehicle. They're all out of breath, but between gasp, they were able to continue screaming with joy and shouting different phrases at us like, "mista mista what's your name" and "America good-number one."

Milik told us not to worry about the children, that they would be harmless and are just curious as to whom we are.

I was more than ready to go into the tea shop and start performing the task that was issued from the SCO and do my job as a PSYOP Soldier. This consisted of gathering a solid understanding of this target audience, what motivates them, its leadership, what are their influences, and what are the best ways to appeal to this audience and convince them to behave in a desired manner that would help the SCO accomplish his mission.

We all walked inside the tea shop and I was introduced to Zenab Al-Jifar, along with his two other brothers, Nearan and Amira. They seemed pleased to meet me as each shook my hand, followed by placing their hands over their hearts. As they spoke, Milik translated their words for me.

Zenab handed Milik, Carson and I a transparent glass cup that was about triple the size of a normal shot glass that he just poured some hot tea into. He then tossed in four tablespoons of sugar into each glass as we held them. He put a small silver spoon in the glass so we could stir. When he gave us the nod that it was OK to drink, we sipped the tea graciously.

Zenab then pointed to the rest of my crew who is standing guard outside and I knew he was trying to ask if they wanted some tea also.

"They would be happy to have some."

Zenab shouted some words in Arabic to his two brothers and they ran outside with a tray full of tea for the crew to enjoy. With the pleasantries out of the way, Zenab got down to asking very direct questions.

"What are the Americans going to do now that Saddam is no longer around?" Before I could even answer him, he immediately asked another question. "Do you intend to capture him?" Being new to using an interpreter in a real life situation, revealed that I didn't have the rhythm down yet. Zenab continued on with, "as long as Saddam is on the loose, the Shiite people will live in fear of his revenge if he comes back."

Then there was a pause from Zenab's statement. This was my chance to answer, "Saddam will never be back in power and your people have nothing to fear. Now is the time for you to start a new Government and you should start enjoying your new freedoms."

"Only time will tell," Zenab said. "An order from our Imam was put out to watch you and see if you are really here to help or to take the land from us."

"Zenab what can I do to help out, to prove that we are on your side?"

"We would like to have enough security where we are free to roam the streets without worry. We need you to bring more electricity to the city so we can run our businesses, and fix the sewer lines. When Saddam was in power, we at least had these utilities working." As Zenab informed me of his wishes, I thought to myself why can't you do this on your own? Has Saddam dictatorship been so brutal that these people can't solve their own problems? I couldn't respond with that answer so instead I said, "I cannot make any promises of these things happening, but I will take this information and present it to my people who can make things like that happen."

"Yes, Yes," said Zenab. "I would expect this not to be a problem for you since you are America. You have built many great cities and you have even put a man on the moon. Rebuilding our power and sewer lines should be really easy task for you."

"Let's not get ahead of ourselves Zenab. Like I said, I will report this and see what I can do. Thank you for your time and for the tea. Let me know if it would be O.K. for me to drop in every once in a while to see how things are going and to give you updates on any progress with your concerns?"

"I will always have a fresh cup of tea waiting for you."

We shook each other's hands again and then I yelled to my guys, "let's roll."

We maneuvered around the swarm of children as we came out of the tea shop. We jumped into the HMMWV's, and headed back onto the road like a well choreographed dance movement.

In another part of the neighborhood outside from a different tea shop, I noticed there numerous people coming out of a shop with bags of flat bread.

Milik explained that this was from a bread shop that made the very staple of their daily meals, and it was very delicious.

"Excellent, I love bread."

We pulled up next to the bread shop and we all got out and our escorts did their security drill. The children who had been chasing us caught up with us again. They began to surround our vehicles once more. I felt as if I where Britney Spears being chased by the Paparazzi!

Milik, Carson and I walked into the shop to buy some bread and establish a relationship with the owners. I was introduced to Amira Farque.

"It is two hundred and fifty dinars[25] for five pieces of bread," he informed us.

Luckily I exchanged some of my American Dollars for some Iraqi Dinars earlier that day. I slapped down about two grand in Dinars for some bread, which was about two American Dollars.

Amira smiled as he was please I was going to do business with him. "If you can wait for a moment, I will bake a fresh batch for you."

"Absolutely," I replied.

"Are you the boss, because if you are I will make you a special treat?"

"Yes. I am in charge of this group and I am talking to people in Sadr City to see how we can help."

Once again, Amira started to put a big grin on his face as he grabbed me by the elbow, indicating that he wanted to give me a tour of his bakery. He showed me the mixing room where he made large batches of bread dough with his 50 Kilogram bags of flour. He demonstrated how he kneaded the dough and then formed little pieces that would sit on a baker's sheet that would allow it to rise from the yeast before he went to the next step which is to place them into the oven. He explained how his firebrick oven worked and how it has been in his family for generations. He then took a wooden

---

[25] Dinar - Iraq Currency - 250 dinars is worth about 20 cents.

peel that was about nine inches wide and about six feet long and placed about ten bread pieces on it from the baker's sheet and prepped them for the oven. In one jerking motion he slid all ten pieces in and they formed a perfect column on the brick oven floor.

Within about two minutes, they were done and he used the same peel to scoop them all up in one motion and pulled them out of the oven. He put half of them into a bag for me take later and put the other half on the table. Then he took a small iron skillet and cracked two eggs in it and stirred them up with some spices. Then he slid that into the oven and a minute later he pulled them out and then he split open the bread and filled them with the scrambled eggs. He offered me the first one and waited in anticipation for me to eat it. I thanked him for the sandwich and took a big bite. The cuisine was actually delicious, the savory spiced eggs mixed with the uber fresh bread combination was very tasty.

I told him how much I enjoyed it. Our discussion then turned to what the people of Sadr City thought of the Americans and what we could do to help out. Amira's responses were similar to my last conversation with Zenab. After about a half hour of talking back and forth, I decided we needed to get rolling for security reasons. I thanked him for his time and the bread and then we proceeded to leave.

We visited numerous places of business throughout the day and gathered some useful information, but at this point in the day the sun was really heating up, the people were leaving the markets, and the streets were becoming vacant. I figured this would be a good time to call it a day and head back to the

FOB and report what information I gathered for the daily sit-rep.

CHAPTER TWELVE

OPEN FOR BUSINESS

A few weeks went by as we were getting into the swing of things. We had established numerous intelligence gathering points at various local establishments. I was even embraced by a restaurant owner named Jassim who said I was his new adopted son and he wanted me to stop by at least once a week so he could serve my crew and me a nice meal. He wanted to ensure that I knew how much he appreciated being liberated from Saddam Hussein and the efforts I was putting into place to improve his city. He also wanted to make sure I knew he used to have one of the largest construction companies in Baghdad, but business was slow because of the war. You can't blame the guy for trying to get some business out of me because the Americans now had the construction dollars.

Through our intelligence gathering efforts, the 2nd CAV was able to start addressing the needs of Sadr City. My three new friends in Civil Affairs were also busy at work writing contracts with local business and construction firms in order to fill these needs. I just needed to figure out a way to introduce them to my friend Jassim.

Our living quarters are now complete. We had managed to build the three-bedroom rambler out of our cardboard boxes, but our house was a shed compared to SSG Cole, SSG Vanscoy, and Sgt Butkus our Civil Affairs counterparts on the other side of the warehouse. They had organized an Iraqi construction crew who came to the warehouse and built them a wood house out of plywood and two-by-fours. They also had a big dish satellite TV installed. They started to make jokes about us living on the other side of the tracks because of the old rail track that ran down the middle of the warehouse that divided our living spaces.

We got along very well with the Civil Affairs guys, especially on Thursday nights. They even helped me out on my quest to break rule number one applied by the Army. SSG Cole always seemed to have a few bottles of the good stuff readily available like Johnny Walker Blue or Grey Goose Vodka. They made sure that I knew my crew and I could make ourselves at home anytime we wanted to. Thursday nights are our designated drinking nights, and we always made sure we took advantage of the Civil Affair's hospitality. Since Fridays was the day Islamic people went to the mosque all day, we knew we could take the day off to recuperate. I even arranged it with the SCO that Friday's are to be our day to get personal stuff done and our day to recover.

I continually wondered how Civil Affairs was able to afford construction of their house, have all the electronic luxuries, and always possessed the expensive merchandise, while never worrying about the price. They even had an ice cube making machine in their possession in order to serve a proper cocktail.

One Thursday night when we were all watching their TV and drinking their booze, I sat down next to SSG Cole as we both enjoyed our beverage. With the alcohol already loosening up both of our gossip, I became bold and blurted out the question of how he could afford all of these luxuries. The response that Cole returned to me was very interesting.

He took a big puff off of his cigar and said, "kickbacks dude. It's all about the kickbacks. You see it is Iraqi culture to give presents when work is granted to the other party. So every time we grant funds to these construction companies to rebuild their city, they insist we accept a present from them. Now of course as you know we are not allowed to accept these gifts, but me and my guys say fuck that. We never asked to come over here, we only joined the Army for the college money. But here we are! So our attitude is why not profit and make our lives a little more enjoyable while we're over here in this hell hole. Besides, there are a shit load of corporations back in the States making money off of this situation just as I am. If there was a way I could send any of these kickbacks home so I could enjoy my efforts at a later day, I would. I know that is not possible though, so screw them and enjoy it while you've got i!." After he made his statement, I could see the look on Cole's face that maybe he shared too much information with me. I actually admired his attitude and wished I had the same opportunities. Then he leaned over to me and tried to whisper in my ear as if he was giving me a secret. "This is just between us, no need for anybody else to know what's going on. If they do, we could all lose our luxuries and be brought up on charges."

I then took a sip of my drink and a big puff from my cigar as I gave a dramatic pause, "and give all this up, never." Then my entrepreneurial skills kicked in and I came up with an idea that would not only benefit me, but put Cole at ease. I continued on to say, "actually I think the best thing to do would be let me and my guys write a contract so we can get a kickback. This way, we'll be in bed with you."

"Sneaky, sneaky Jenks, I'm impressed with you craftiness. Not everybody can come up with a plan like that. You must have that ability to be creative, and that's a gift. I think I just might let you do that. The first thing you need to do in order for you plan to work is that you need someone who you can write a work order and hand it over to you. Do you have anybody in mind?" he said with just a little slur to his words.

I informed Cole about my relationship with the restaurant owner Jassim who adopted me, and how he also owned a construction company. I also went on to explain that I was working with the DAWA party and they were requesting a lot of different projects so they could look good in font of their constituents.

"There you go. Get a statement of work from your friend at the construction company and then I'll go and get the funds requested for you."

We both toasted our glasses and drank to our new partnership. Cole's resources seemed to be better than any supply sergeants ability, and he was a cool guy on top of that. I hoped this new relationship would be the type that we could look back on in our later years and have a good laugh about being in combat.

When I finished my drink, I went over to the bar to refill my glass. As I was pouring myself about two fingers of fine scotch, I could see Carson was standing just outside the Civil Affairs' front door. I could only imagine he was trying to eavesdrop on my conversation and he was now calculating in his head how he would spend any proceeds from Cole's offering. That is when I noticed out of the corner of my eye, a bug about the size of a sand dollar flutter through an open door on the side of the building and its flight pattern flew directly at Carson and smacked him on the side of the head. The bug fell to the ground and started slowly crawling around. Carson went running in the opposite direction, screaming like a little girl who just saw a snake for the first time. After he gained his composure, he grabbed a broom and started to beat the bug to death. Everyone in the room busted out laughing as they watched him panic. After Carson was done whacking the bug to death, he stood back to observe the dead bug and contemplate his next move. "It's time to burn the motherfucker he exclaimed."

Carson ran over to our stash of Gerry cans that we lined up against the wall next to the exit door where the bug flew in through. He proceeded to grab a five gallon diesel can that was full, and ran back with the can, ensuring to pour about a quart of its content all over the bug. Then he grabbed some matches that he saved from an MRE packet, lit the match and threw it on the diesel soaked bug. As soon as the match hit the bug and the flame was fully ignited, the bug became reanimated and took off running. There was this big fireball running across the floor and this fireball decided it wanted to head straight towards all the Gerry cans that are full of diesel. Luckily the flame was able to consume the bug and kill it before it reached the cans. We all stood there staring at the burning flame that eventually burned out, and then we looked at each other and started laughing real hard, again.

CHAPTER THIRTEEN

KICKBACKS AND SHEESHA

During that Friday's sit-rep, I didn't have anything to report because we were still taking Fridays off, but that didn't relive me of attending the sit-reps or any actionable information. In the course of this particular sit-rep, I was informed that my team would be doing a loudspeaker broadcast for a surrender appeal mission because intelligence was zeroing in on the location of someone who was on the "top ten list[26]" who may be residing in Sadr City. More details were to follow once the operation had been approved, but for now we were to start prepping for it and to be ready to roll when it pops.

Also during the sit-rep, there was more news about semi trucks full of gold being discovered and confiscated at the Turkish border. I presume the reason these people all head to Turkey is because that is the only State that has a

---

[26] Top Ten List - The top ten Iraqi bad guys wanted by the US ARMY.

banking system recognized by the West and coincidently boarders with Iraq.

When I made it back to my guys, I informed them with the information about the surrender appeal mission and about the gold. They thought the new mission was going to be cool, but they immediately concentrated on the elusive gold and the large bank accounts that must be sitting in Turkey, for surely some of that gold must have gotten through. Since I couldn't get them to focus on the new mission and it was just really a warning order at this point in time. There would be no harm to let them discuss what they would do, if we had access to one of those bank accounts.

Spc Carson immediately wanted us all to know what he would do. "Limousines would take me to the finest restaurants everyday and I would drink magnum sized bottles of champagne with gorgeous women. I would also have a house in the Hills and throw kick-ass parties to whoever wanted to show up. I think I would try to emulate the life of Hugh Heffner. Yeah baby, party like a rock star!"

Sgt Brown chimed in with his list. "I would take a minimum of two luxury or adventuress travel vacations per year for the rest of my life with my spouse. Then I would have a Hall built at my wife's college named after me, so I would become a legacy. That way everybody would have to remember me."

Listening to them day dream about the gold activated my imagination into full gear, but I had to be a realist. "Like I said before, there is no way in hell we could ever get any gold out of this country. But since we are just fantasizing, then here is what I would do. First thing is first, I would make sure the Karma of acquiring that much money continues. I would donate a large amount of the gold to some kind of September 11th fund for all those families who lost their livelihood. After satisfying the Karma gods, I would then pay off all those nasty bills I have at home. Then I would purchase that dream house for my wife. Next I would help out all my family members, like setting up college funds for my nieces and nephews and paying off everybody's mortgages. Finally, I would splurge on myself by doing some world traveling for the rest of my life, which would consist of smoking a cigar in every country. And sorry Brown, I won't be traveling with you."

"The best thing about getting rich on Iraqi gold would be that the Civil Affairs guys on the other side of the tracks would then become the lower class compared to us. They would have to come over here and ask to drink our booze, said Carson."

"Now we need to get back to reality and start planning what needs to be done in order for us to be ready for the new mission." Both Brown and Carson hesitantly shifted their focus away from the gold.

The next morning after being well rested with our day off and not doing any missions, we were ready this Saturday morning to get back to work. Just as most days, our plan was to go into Sadr City and see what kind of intelligence we could gather. Today was a special day though because I could line up some work for my friend Jassim and get some kickbacks.

We left the front gate with our escort from 2nd CAV and headed into the city. The markets were full and the people were going about their business as usual. Then just like clock work, the children started to chase us through the streets again.

First thing we did was to go over to the DAWA party to let them know we could help them out with one of their projects. Visiting the DAWA party was always a pleasure because their intentions are always good and they treated us with kindness. They knew that it was in their best interest that we succeeded in our missions. Mainly because they're Shiite and they concluded that as long as we were successful, the Sunni's could no longer control them.

When we arrived at the DAWA party headquarters, we were seated in a conference room while their guards went to go fetch Hassan al-Zamili who was in charge of their operations. I was always a little nervous about this guy, not because of anything he has done or said, but simply because he looked like Charles Manson, it was kind of creepy.

On the other hand, Sheik Nabil al-Maliki who the guards also went to go fetch, is the main religious sheik for this DAWA party's location. He's a counter balance to the looks of Hassan al-Zamili. He is a short pudgy little guy who always wore a white gown with his white turban and sported a long gray beard. He almost looked like Papa Smurf, just without the blue skin or a red hat.

Once they entered the room, we immediately got to the business at hand, but I always kept one eye on Hassan just in case a carved swastika appeared on his forehead. Our main subject that we discussed was how to deal with the violence in their sector. They suggested that the way to get rid of the violence was by getting rid of the Bathist who lived amongst them. They explained that these are low-level Bathist and they should not be rounded up in raids. So we came to an agreement that the DAWA party would start a de-Bathification campaign by going door to door and giving them the opportunity to swear on the Koran to denounce the Bathist party and convert over to the DAWA party. Part of this process would be to hand over their weapons that were used in the old regime.

I absolutely knew that these people were playing politics and trying to establish themselves in the new free Iraq as a party who would eventually step up and try to take power. Since they always seemed to help me with accomplishing my missions, why not help them out a little. Besides, this party was banned under Saddam Hussein rule and they had to go underground during that time frame. They even help out with the rebellion back when Bush number one was in power.

Once the de-Bathification process was agreed upon, I told the Sheik, "today I bring good news. Please tell me of a construction project that you are in need of within reason and I will be able to fund that project. This will be a gesture of goodwill from me because of all the good work we have done together."

Sheik Nabil al-Maliki eyes lit up a little and a small grin started to form as Milik translated the words. He immediately responded with a request for us to build a mason wall to wrap around their entire HQ building that would be ten feet tall and it would also require a security gate. The wall was to protect them from the nightly attacks from Saddam's extreme loyalists who were not too pleased that the Shiites are working with the Coalition Forces.

"I think I should be able to get enough funds to cover your request," I told the sheik.

After a couple glasses of tea and a lot of cordial pleasantries, I explained that I had to leave so I could go and line up the contractor to do the work. After a solid handshake and a quick pat to the heart, we set off to go visit Jassim Al-Mohammed at the restaurant.

On the way to the restaurant, we weaved through all kinds of traffic, and dodging kids as they darted out in front of us. Some of this traffic consisted of either a horse or a donkey pulling a cart. At this particular moment, we had to pass a horse pulling a cart that was on the street. This horse must have been curious about who was going to overtake him because as we passed by, the horse swung around to see what was behind him. By doing so, his head smashed our driver side mirror clean off.

Carson leaped out of his driver seat about two feet and acted as if the boogey man just jumped out of a corner. I looked back out of my window and could see the horse wobbling around as if he were ready to pass out. Then when the horse started to gain consciousness, he got pissed and started bucking around. The driver was holding on to the reins for his dear life. The cart was actually jumping up and down behind the horse like a pogo stick. Then all of a sudden the cart broke in two, so the rider finally let go of the reins and the horse took off down the road pulling half of a cart.

Carson sarcastically said, "looks like I get my first kill." My first response was to give him a nice kick in the head for that statement, but then I calmed down and realized he was just a kid who hasn't put the bigger picture together yet. I took this opportunity to educate him.

"Spc Carson, that person was probably using that horse and cart for deliveries, meaning this is how he is gainfully employed. Without his ability to deliver, he may not be able to earn a living and may resort to other tactics to earn money. For example, he may start planting bombs on the side of the road. He may also now go and tell everyone how the Americans destroyed his livelihood. This is the exact opposite of what we are trying to do. Now I know this was an accident, but let's not be a smart ass about it. We should at least go and see if he is all right and apologize for this situation."

When we slowed down to a stop and looked out the window, we watched the man get up and brush himself off. The gesture of stopping was sufficient for him as he gave us the wave to keep going, and so we did.

A few minutes later we pulled in front of Jassim's restaurant and parked our vehicles. This time we let the 2nd CAV Sgt stay behind and relax in their vehicle because we didn't need the added security inside the restaurant. I just had Carson go inside and visit Jassim with me. This didn't pose a problem for the security Sgt. He preferred to just hang outside and not be bothered with all the questions I normally ask when I make my visits.

Carson and I weaved our way around the tables as we walked to the back of the restaurant, which was where his office was located. His office wasn't actually an office, but more like his personal table that he always sat at so he could keep an eye on everybody. Jassim was a chain smoker and he always had a cigarette in his hand, as he did right now. His fingers were stained yellow, but that was a badge of honor to him.

We sat down at his table and he motioned over a waiter to take our order. He always made sure we had some type of food any time we stopped by for a visit. He then told the waiter to make sure that the soldiers pulling security outside were also provided for. I offered to pay him for the meal but as always, he would never accept my money. He would always remind me that I was his adopted American son and he would always take care of me. The nice thing about Jassim was that he spoke English very well. He had studied in both England and Germany. After we went through all of the formalities, I asked Jassim to explain the reach of his construction company.

He took out another cigarette and lit it. Then he took a big puff from it as he was contemplating what to say. "My major concentration is here in Sadr City, but I have family and friends that go all the way to the Turkey border. I use to have to drive into Turkey many times a month and I always stayed at various villages who hosted me along the way because of my many family connections."

"Why do you go to Turkey?" I asked as my curiosity grabbed hold of me.

"I keep my major investments there because it is a stable market there. I used to do a lot of work for Saddam's government and when I received payment, I would take a major portion of that and drive over the border. I love my country, but I'm not stupid enough to keep my money here. I hope that one day Iraq will be like Turkey and I can bring my money back. Lately though, the construction business has been kind of slow and I have not made any trips to Turkey."

"Today is your lucky day," I exclaimed as Jassim sat across the table curious to my statement. "I need you to go over to the DAWA party HQ and write up a statement of work for a concrete block wall they want built around their compound. You can deliver that statement of work to me and I'll get you paid. I can only pay contractors that are registered in our system, so I need you to go over to the Green Zone and register yourself. You can expect more work once you're in the system and have been used a few times. If you do good jobs, then all the NGO's[27] will utilize you."

Jassim was enthused by my information and just as Cole described, he wanted to display his appreciation. "I would like to buy you a present to illustrate my gratitude," he said delightfully.

---

[27] NGO - Non-Governmental Organization.

Not wanting to seem to be too eager to take advantage of this situation, my response was humble. "No, that is not necessary, the hospitality you provide me and my men is good enough."

"Mr. Jenks, it is a custom of ours to bestow a gift upon one who is so generous, a refusal would be an insult."

Wow, this actually works I thought to myself. "Well, just so you know, the contract that I will grant to you has a twenty thousand dollar limit. My intention is not to insult you, but grant you my goodwill. If you must offer me a gift, then so be it."

"I know you like cigars, so I will buy you two boxes of the finest cigars that you choose. I request for you to go to the cigar shop in Baghdad and tell the merchant which two boxes you wish to own and have him reserve those boxes for you. Then I can send Milik over with the funds needed to purchase the boxes and he can deliver them to you as soon as my company receives the finances."

"Excellent, once I receive the statement of work from your company, I will get the funds over to you."

"Yes! Yes! This is all good, I knew I adopted you as my American son for a reason, Insha'Allah."

"Insha'Allah," I responded back.

We shook hands and then placed them on our hearts as we have done many times before.

When we arrived back at our living quarters, the Civil Affair guys were already there watching satellite TV and enjoying their down time.

I was excited to go over and interrupt their TV show and tell them the good news. I shouted through their front door, "hey SSG Cole, I lined up a contract today and I should have the statement of work by tomorrow."

The lock on the front door made the clicking sound that it was being dismantled and the door flung open with Cole standing there with a smile. "No problem," he replied, "getting the funds will be easy since the Army feels that spending money on the local population is the answer to winning their hearts and minds."

I escorted myself in and was on my way over to the hidden bar to pour myself a celebratory drink when suddenly SFC Hunter, Cpt Barker, and their escorts pulled up in their vehicle. Luckily I hadn't made it all the way to the bar yet. I would have been caught red handed violating rule number one, which specifically stated no drinking. I could see Spc McClure rolling his eyes as SFC Hunter and Cpt Barker pushed their way into the room where SSG Cole and his guys were sitting in order to get at me. SFC Hunter got in my face while Cpt Barker stood next to him with his arms crossed, looking as if he was encouraging SFC Hunter with this inquisition.

"Jenks, what is up with your sit-reps? Just because I am not on you all the time since we are staying in different locations, doesn't give you the right to leave out any details in your sit-reps."

I was struck by how much SFC Hunter reminded me of Barnyard Dog, Foghorn Leghorn's canine nemesis from the Warner Brothers cartoons. He is always trying to chase me down and catch me until he gets to the end of his leash and can no longer get me and is reduced to lame barking. This image was making me laugh but I knew that would just upset him so I bit my lip, which was twisting into a kind of smirk.

He continued to explain how I need to learn the English language because he found numerous grammar errors in my sit-reps. He then started to blab on about how he once took a college level English class so that makes him a master of the English language. He also went on to say that he doesn't get the chance to go out and perform missions like our PSYOP teams do. There for he needs to know every detail of what is going on.

"How come you haven't mentioned anything about you supporting the mission of capturing one of Saddam's henchman listed on the wanted poster?" He demanded to know.

"Well, because these orders are coming down from your HQ through our SCO, therefore you should already know about it. Now when the event goes down, I'll write a full report and make sure you get a copy. But I can't do that until it actually happens."

"You smart ass! I need to report this up to his HQ."

"There has got to be some kind of miscommunication going on here I told him. The people at your HQ are the people who crafted this information. Maybe they forgot to tell you about it." I was actually thinking they purposely did not inform him. "Like I said, when I have information that you don't already have, I will definitely get it over to you."

This response must have resonated with him because instead of vaulting towards me and trying to wrap his fingers around my throat, he instead picked up one of the glasses that was sitting on one of the Civil Affair's bamboo tables. He flipped it over, took a long look at it, and realized that it was real crystal. He glanced around the room and noticed the satellite TV, the leather couch, and the glass coffee table.

"What the hell are they doing?" SFC Hunter yelled and demanded to know from me.

"They're just relaxing and flipping through some TV," I replied.

"What do you mean, they are just relaxing and watching TV? Nobody in this war has a set up like this. They must be stealing this shit. If I ever find out you are up to any kind of bullshit like this, I will personally make sure you get court marshaled and that you get sent home in shame. You'll be the first PSYOP team chief to lose his team. I'm going to keep my eye on you, because I know you are up to no good. All it takes is one slip up and I'm going to nail your ass," Hunter yelled.

SFC Hunter went on to say as he pointed his finger at me, "the second you get back from your mission, I want a full detailed report." Before I could respond to his request, he did a quick about face, motioned for Spc McClure to get the vehicle for departure. Cpt Barker unfolded his arms, gave me a look over as if to say he was disgusted, and then followed SFC Hunter back to their vehicle. Their departure was quick and welcomed.

SSG Cole started to bust out laughing, but was still able to state the obvious, "that guy is a dick, now pour yourself a drink."

"No shit! You know what's worse than a know it all? Someone who thinks they know it all. One thing for sure is that asshole doesn't get any of my free cigars now," I responded back with my signature smirk.

CHAPTER FOURTEEN

PSYOPING A PYSOPER

A few days later the DAWA party appeared at the front gate of our FOB unannounced early in the morning while prepping for our day's missions. They arrived with a truckload of AK-47s, RPG launchers, and various other weapons that they wanted to deliver to me. Apparently, these were the weapons they collected while they conducted their de-bathification campaign. Now it was my responsibility to take inventory of the weapons and figure out what to do with them.

Before I could even scratch my head to help myself think of a solution, the SCO suddenly appeared and recommended that I take the weapons and assigned them to the new Iraqi Army recruits that are being trained by the 2nd CAV. This way the new recruits would have a weapon at their disposal to help bring peace and provide their own security. He went on to explain how this could have easily saved many US Soldiers life because the weapons are now off the streets. The SCO then patted me on the back and thanked me in advance for my efforts to ensure I followed his request. Then he excused himself and quickly vanished.

The SCO's request was against my initial idea that popped in my head, which consisted of selling them to my friends for souvenirs and trying to make a profit. I would have never thought of handing the weapons over to somebody for free.   I guess that's why he is in charge and I'm not.

Not wanting to go against the SCO wishes, we transferred the weapons over to the training NCO as he suggested. After this welcomed delay, we finally headed out to the city to perform our missions. It felt good to get back into Sadr City, over the last week we had been tied up rehearsing the surrender appeal mission with the 2nd CAV. Today though, we were able to get out and visit some of our usual spots to see what kind of intelligence we could find, and of course re-thank our friends from the DAWA party for their efforts. I also wanted to check on the progress of their fortification project that we funded.

We rolled up to one of our regular tea shops and of course, we had about a hundred kids in tow. The neighborhoods seemed to be accustomed to us by now and they had no problem letting their kids chase us everywhere. I guess this was now part of their daily exercise routine. Now when we made our stops, we would have to take the kids into account. We always made sure we parked in a safe place where traffic wouldn't hurt the kids and if we needed to make a getaway, they wouldn't be blocking us.

The shop owners quickly poured us some tea and made sure that we were comfortable. Then they went on to ask their standard question that every shop owner asked when we did our visits of when will the electricity and sewers be fixed? I was about to give my standard answer about the electricity of how it could have been fixed a long time ago but you idiots keep stealing the copper. Then a man we had never seen before approached us and asked if I wanted to know some crucial information. He spoke English very well and there was something about him that captured my attention. I excused myself from the current conversation and told Milik to enjoy his tea because I would be handling this one solo, but stay nearby just in case.

We both stepped outside of the tea shop so no one could listen in. In order to break the ice and to get him talking about himself so I could analyze his personality and intentions, I proceeded to ask, "where did you acquire such a proficient knowledge of the English language?"

He stood there for a moment in his well pressed dishdasha[28] and I could see that he was putting some thought behind my question as if he were trying to win a chess game. After he decided on his best response to stay in control of this conversation, he replied with "I studied at the University of London, but my education is not the subject at hand here."

He wasn't much for small talk, he wanted to get straight to the point of why he was here. Remembering back

---

[28] Dishdasha - An ankle-length garment, usually with long sleeves, similar to a robe.

in my civilian sales job, I encounter many people with different types of communication skills. Some like to have small talk all day and only talk a little about the product while others only had a few minutes and wanted just the facts. Either way, the end result was always the same with me walking away with a new contract. I kicked in my skill set for the later as I prepared to listen to his facts.

He continued on with his factual inquisition, "I know you are the person who gathers information and can make things happen. I have some information I would like to sell to you. The posters you place everywhere states that you will give cash rewards for the capture of certain people. The information I have is not a person, but it is something you Americans have been looking for."

"Go on, I'm listening."

"I need a cash advance before I tell you what I know."

I now had the same feeling as when certain customers of mine would try to beat me up on price or get something more than I could offer out of me. Luckily I had a skill set for that too and a response. "Well," I replied. "It doesn't work that way, besides I'm not the man with the money. Here is a suggestion, why don't you tell me what it is we are talking about and you can withhold the details. That way I can see if this would be something I could take to my commander and then get you the requested money if approved."

"Fair enough. First, my name is Maqtada. I am acting as a middleman for my brother-in-law who brought me this information. He served in the Iraqi Army under a special command from Saddam. His job was to transport the chemical weapons to various places so no one could keep up with their current location. He informed me where he buried them per Saddam's orders."

"What type of payment are you looking for?"

"A sum of ten thousand American dollars would be sufficient. I would need that payment upfront before my brother-in-law will tell us where the chemical weapons are buried."

My bullshit sensors started to go off a bit. Now I was having that feeling I get back in sales when I know the customer is just trying to get a quote from me so he can then take it to my competitor and get a better price from them. Therefore this was something I would mention in the sit-rep verbally to the SCO, but not to SFC Hunter until I had some proof that this was legitimate information because he would be all over this without question. I didn't need him jumping in and trying to take over my job for his benefit. I decided to further listen to his story, but with caution. First thing I needed to do was respond to his outrages financial demands and see how desperate he was to make an agreement.

"That is a lot of money especially in Iraq. I think something more in the line of about five hundred dollars upfront to get the information and the rest payable upon securing the chemical weapons."

"Think about the fame and honors you will receive when you are the first American soldier that will find the chemical weapons. You will be able to validate George Bush's war."

Bullshit sensors were now on full alert. The time had arrived for me to end this conversation because I was almost certain he was full of it, but you never know so I responded in order to at least leave the dialog open for another day. "Yes, I understand what you are saying but that's not the way the Army works. If you do produce the chemical weapons, you will get far more than ten thousand dollars, but for now the five hundred upfront fee stands."

"I will ask my brother-in-law and let you know."

"How do I get in touch with you?"

"You can ask the shop owner here to set up our next meeting."

"Give me at least a week to set this up," I said, but not really having those intentions.
"Insha'Allah," he replied.

Then we shook hands and he took off without delay.

As I was heading back to the HMMWV, the escort Sgt turned to me and said, "wow man, we're going to be heroes."

"Sorry to burst your bubble Sarge but that guy is full of shit. He was too focused on getting cash up front. If he is as smart as he says he is, then he should know there is a hotline he can call into. By doing so, he would get a tremendous amount of cash for that kind of information."

The escort Sgt rubbed his chin and then said, "you are great at reading people. That's probably why you are in Special Forces and I am humping this rifle around. I hope you put those smarts to good use and get rich someday SSG Jenks."

"I'm working on it. Believe me, I'm working on it."

We then jumped back in to the HMMWV and headed back to camp Marlboro as the day was getting close to being done.

During our sit-rep that evening, the SCO was focused on our mission to capture our target on the most wanted list. He was focused on this mission because the order to capture him had been approved. After the sit-rep was adjourned, he recommended we all get a good night sleep tonight because in the morning we will be busting the bad guys. As the SCO was collecting his papers, I approached him and brought up the information I gathered from Maqtada just to be on the safe side.

His response was quick and to the point also. "Yep I know of him. He approaches everyone and tries to sell classified information. You are right, he is full of shit," the Commander said. Then he smiled at me, informed me I was doing a good job, and excused himself for another meeting.

That was the end of that and now it was time to focus on more important issues like preparing for the mission in the morning.

We didn't get much sleep that night since we're so high on adrenaline thinking about our mission. We rehearsed our part a million times before we finally hit the sack for the night. The morning came pretty early because I have learned that at five AM, it's pretty damn early. The first thing I desperately needed to do in order to overcome the fact that it was five AM, was to make the coffee. We have a great supply of quality coffee from all over the world to choose from. Our families sent them over in care packages. Washingtonians takes their coffee seriously. Starbucks was started in Seattle! We had ample supply of that brand on hand, but our favorite coffee was the Java Java coffee company. We loved this coffee not only because it was from my hometown Maple Valley Washington, but also because my wife sent it over to us in bulk.

While we waited for the coffee to come to a perk on the electric one-eyed burner, we distracted our craving by lubing up our weapons for combat. This burner was amazing as it was always working overtime for us heating up our coffee and top ramen noodles.

Milik arrived looking more tired than usual. He had no idea why we asked him to start work this early, or what we were up to that day. We never informed him about any of our missions beforehand to ensure he never had any information to sell to the other side. It wasn't a matter of trust, it was because if he knew the information, he was being exposed to the possibility of being captured and tortured for that information. We could never be too cautious with Milik's safety.

The coffee started to percolate madly to inform us it was ready. We always poured the coffee into our aluminum canteen cups and then cooled it down with ice cubes that we acquired from the Civil Affairs guys ice machine the night before.

We then gave our script to Milik to translate. The message was a basic surrender appeal. It consisted of who we are, who we wanted, and what we wanted to be done. We recorded it as Milik translated the message onto our digital recorder so it would be readily available when we were down range.

Finally, when the time came for us to roll, we threw on our gear and we all climbed into the HMMWV. I could tell that Brown was excited as he quickly climbed into his manhole with the SAW. He was ready for some action. Carson was at the wheel and I was riding shotgun. Milik had the whole back seat to himself. I was proud to go into battle with this solid crew.

When we arrived at the start point and joined the rest of 2nd CAV on this mission, I had my guys stay put as I proceeded to go report to the Lieutenant who was in charge of the convoy. This Lieutenant was easy to find since he was the only individual who had the distinguished mustard stain on his helmet and collar, ready to impress other people with his ability to give orders. With great pride and authority, he told me we were slated to ride with the 2nd platoon and we would be the second vehicle in their convoy line up.

When I walked back to the HMMWV, I directed Carson to our place in the lineup. Once there in our position, all we had to do was wait until we got the signal to go. During these long waiting periods was when we always started telling each other stupid stories and jokes. Milik always took these opportunities to raid the MRE box and have a smorgasbord. Obviously he tossed any meal with pork in it to the side since that was against his religion. The Spaghetti with meat sauce or the ravioli with meat sauce seemed to be his favorite. It made him feel like he was having a fine Italian dinner. There was also only one restaurant in Baghdad that served Italian food, and only dignitaries could eat there. This MRE's made him feel as if he was actually a patron at the fine establishment.

After about twenty minutes of waiting with our engines running and watching Milik stuff numerous MRE down his face, they started the roll call over the radio. Finally, the SCO called out, "Voodoo Two."

"Voodoo Two operative with three plus one," I replied. Meaning there's three soldiers and one other individual in the vehicle.

After the last team reported in with their operative, the SCO gave the command for the convoy to move out. Simultaneously all the vehicles engine came to a loud roar and set everyone in motion. As our convoy rolled through the front gate, we charged our weapons with a round in the chamber. We made sure our select levers were on safe. Once again, Brown started to get excited.

The sun wouldn't be up for at least another hour so it was still very dark outside. There are fifteen vehicles in our convoy that was making its way down the streets of Sadr City in the still of the night. The convoy traveling next to us consisted of four Bradley's that would provide heavy combat support if things got ugly. Providing the air support, there are two Kiowa[29] helicopters hiding in the night sky. As we approached the target, the vehicles started peeling off in their synchronized manner and took their positions as they had practiced over a dozen times back at the FOB. The different positions of the vehicles are designed to cordon off the area. This kept it so no one who we were after could slip through. Next, the Bradley's took their designated outer ring position. Our position was in the middle of the street right in front of the suspected target's house. Once again, everything was going just as we rehearsed, except this time our adrenaline was so high and our heart rates were racing.

When we moved into our position in front of the designated house, I jumped out of the HMMWV, gave the area a quick scan for any signs of trouble, and simultaneously took cover by the front hood. This strategically placed the vehicle between the house and my team. Brown had his head down to his weapon looking through his aiming pins and was zeroed in on the house as he crouched down in his turret. I could see the coolness he poised while he too was scanning the area looking for any signs of trouble. The only difference

---

[29] Kiowa - Single engine, single rotor, military helicopter used for observation, utility, and direct fire support.

between the two of us is that Brown wanted trouble so he could go all Rambo like. Carson crawled out from his driver's seat and took cover by the rear wheel well. Looking around in all different directions, I could see the entire 2nd CAV behind me. I knew that whatever Brown couldn't handle, they would be able to jump in and deal with the rest. I stayed knelt down in my position with the start button for the loudspeaker in one hand and the headset from the communication radio next to my right ear, while waiting for the OK from the SCO who was in charge of this mission. Crackling over the radio headset, I finally heard the anticipated go ahead command. I firmly pressed down on the button with my thumb and started the broadcast. We had the loudspeaker unit volume set to full blast and whoever was in the neighborhood of around a square mile or so, would definitely be able to hear the message. The only problem was that when the message started, it woke up the whole neighborhood in a square mile radius and fostered their curiosity.

The hissing of the speaker started with the amplified white noise, and then in a loud and thunderous tone, Milik'e voice came over the speakers. "Attention, Attention, Attention, this is the United States Army."

In mid sentence, I noticed the lights in the third story bedroom instantly flickered on.

"We are here to arrest Kamal Abdallah Sultan and you should come out the front door with your hands in the air. We will not arrest any family members as long as they do not interfere."

Then all the lights in the house came on and we could see people scuffling around inside.

"There is no other option except surrender, we will use force if you do not comply."

While the message was on auto play, I went back to scanning my sector. I then noticed that there are two individuals on the roof who looked as if we had just woke them up from their nap. They were rubbing their eyes and scratching their faces as they stood there. They didn't appear to have any weapons, but you never know. I yelled over to Brown to keep an eye on them. He responded with a smirk that represented, 'I dare you to try something, I dare you.'

"This message will only be played a total of three times before we use force."

A ten second pause was created before the message started over again. During this ten second pause was when I noticed two things happening. Nobody was enjoying the crackle and pops the speakers were making at a loud volume for ten seconds. The other thing I noticed was the one thing that gave me a paralyzing sensation. I realized that while the rest of the 2nd CAV was taking cover behind brick walls and other buildings while trying to ignore our noisy message, the three of us along with Milik who was still sitting inside the vehicle, were in the middle of the street fully exposed. This seemed to work out on paper much better. I started to become conscious that if I were a bad guy, the first thing on my list would be to shoot the loud and annoying speaker that was in the middle of the street and was waking up the whole neighborhood.

The message started again for the second time. This time the message seemed to take forever to play because I was still really conscious of being in the middle of the street. I thought about moving to a new location, but then a chain of events that was probably not going to be in my favor would start if I did. I would just have to hope that the neighborhood and Kamal Abdallah Sultan were enjoying my message. Finally, the message was done playing for the second time and during the scheduled pause, we could here a female's voice yelling at someone inside in what I assumed was an Arabic bitching! Even though I didn't understand what she was saying, I did understand her tone and that tone was one of panic and being pissed off! I quickly turned to Milik and asked what they were saying. After not hearing a response from him, I peered in the vehicle to see if he was all right. I had to laugh when I saw him hunkered down inside the vehicle with his eyes looking left and then to the right in a rapid fashion. "Did you hear what I said?" I shouted again to get his attention.

He paused for a second and then finally responded with an answer. "It sounded as though his wife was telling him to go outside and take care of this situation." Then Milik slipped down a few more inches thinking the lower he was, the safer he would be.

The message started for a third and final time. "Be prepared for some action," I yelled to my team.

We all had our weapons pointed at the house ready to take out anything that posed as a threat. Brown was gleaming with anticipation, but that suddenly vanished when the front door opened and a man came out by himself with his hands up. I could see the female in the background with her arms sternly crossed. Carson and I kept our aim with our weapons on the target while Brown kept his eyes on the rooftop, waiting eagerly for someone to flinch. The subject was taking small and methodical steps toward us. As he got closer, we could recognize that his appearance seem to be the same guy in the picture that we all had viewed during the briefings. This was no surprise when we realized his appearance was an exact match since he was the reason for all of this fuss in the first place. Then eight soldiers from the 2nd CAV came running out from behind their protected positions and tackled the target. They zipped tied his hands behind his back and escorted him to the extraction vehicle.

"All right guys let's wrap this thing up," I yelled. A sense of relief came over me. No one got hurt during this exercise, especially since we stood out like a sore thumb.

We powered down the loudspeaker and Milik rose up from the floorboard of the vehicle. Now he appeared to be fully energized and ready to do his job. We're now all standing together in front of the vehicle looking at each other with a quizzical look of, what do we do now? The adrenaline and excitement of this experience was still elevated. We needed and we're looking for a way to exhaust it. The only thing that came to our minds to answer that question was it's now time to give each other high fives, and maybe smoke a cigar.

We started our high five celebration and I started to reach for a cigar, but before I could get to my stash that I kept in the vehicle, the S-2 Captain came over and addressed us. Apparently, he wasn't there to receive a high five from us or to secure a cigar from me. He was there to keep us gainfully employed with a new request.

"We have a new mission for you. Can you take your interpreter and go in and see if you can interview some of the people inside. See if you can uncover any information or documents as to maybe where some weapons of mass destruction might be."

The Captain already had a Squad at the ready for us and he waived them over. He had assigned one guy to stay with our vehicle to guard it from any locals who may decide to see what's inside, and three guys to go into the building with us to provide security while we conducted any interviews.

Brown, Carson, the three soldiers from the 2nd CAV, and I went into the building with our rifles at the ready. We took caution not to point our weapons at anybody in particular. I had Milik speak to the lady who seemed to be the head of the household and to "ask permission" to be here. (As if they had a choice.)

She invited us in, walked us through the living room, and escorted us back to the kitchen. As I looked around the house en route to the kitchen, I concluded that these people enjoyed the same things as we do here in the States. They had a nice overstuffed leather couch sitting in front of a 53 inch HDTV with a full surround sound system. Not to mention all the delightful nick knacks in the various hutches. When we approached the kitchen, I could see that they also had all the modern appliances that any suburbanite would be proud to own.

Our captured target's wife sat down at the kitchen table with the two other men who were on the roof earlier. She motioned for me to sit down. I made eye contact with the soldiers that where with me and we gave each other the secret nod that we were in agreement. That they are to keep an eye on the two guys while I concentrated on my business with the wife. She waived to her daughter who was also nearby and shouted out a command that apparently turned out to be an order to fire up the stove and make some tea. I laughed to myself as I imagined they should instead make me a caramel macchiato cappuccino, a pleasure I use to enjoy back home. That is what I would serve if they were visiting me. When the tea was served, we all knew it was time to get to business. I had Milik ask her about Kamal Abdallah Sultan's involvement with Saddam. She ran on and gave me a sob story that when Saddam was in power, they had no choice but to work for him. They always thought they were helping to better Iraq.

As the wife was talking and providing all the excuses of why she was innocent, I noticed one of the men at the table who kept looking over at a messy office desk with a bunch of papers stacked on it. They gave us training in conducting interrogations before we deployed and I could tell something was up with this guy. I kept an eye on him to see how he would react when I decided to walk closer to the desk. When I was in the vicinity of the desk, I noticed three paperweights resting on top of the paper stack. The paperweights appeared to be about six inches long, three inches wide, and about a half inch thick. They were gray in color and had an Iraqi eagle stamped on the front. Picking one of them up to inspect it a little closer, I was surprised at how unusually heavy the bar was. These bars probably weighed around six to seven pounds each. Was it made out of lead? Tossing the weights off the table and onto the floor so I could rustle through the documents on the desk, I started to filter through the papers. The man at the table was watching my every move and he was getting uncomfortable with the situation. Milik provided his assistance in reading the documents on the desk since they are all in Arabic. Though after studying most of them, he informed me the documents are mainly just bills and non-sensitive paperwork that wouldn't be of any use for intelligence gathering.

"Listen up, 2nd CAV you stay down here and watch the mother, the daughter, and this guy," I said as I pointed to the non-nervous guy.

Then I pointed to the nervous guy and said, "Milik, tell this gentleman to escort me through the house so we can search the place. If they are hiding anything, it is best to come clean now because we will find it. If they try any funny business, we will shoot to kill."

Milik translated this to the group and the one individual stood up from the table and followed Brown,

Carson, Milik, and I upstairs. We went into various bedrooms and performed a thorough but not too intrusive search. When we got to Kamal Abdallah Sultan's office, I made sure we went through everything. The office had files upon files stacked everywhere, too much to filter through in our allotted amount of time, so I decided we should take it all back to the FOB.

We all went back down stairs and I had the suspicious guy sit back down at the table. I still had a feeling that there was something here, but I couldn't put my finger on it. The daughter had some more tea ready and insisted that we all have another cup. So we all sat back down at the table and drank more tea while I had Milik ask more questions about what they knew about Kamal Abdallah Sultan's involvement with Saddam. Once again, I got a bag full of excuses and not much information that I didn't already know. Not being able to gather anything useful, I concluded it was about time to call in the professionals to interrogate these people. I was only good enough to a certain point and that point has arrived.

As I was starting to get up and leave, I caught the nervous guy eyeing the three paperweights that I threw on the ground. This definitely confirmed my suspensions that there was something here they didn't want me to find. I followed my instincts and walked over to the three paperweights again. The guy started to try to pretend not to look at me but at the same time, kept a keen eye on me with a nervous twitch. With my curiosity getting the best of me, I picked up one of the paperweights and started tossing it up in the air and catching it as if I would do with a tennis ball. After a few pitches in the air, I noticed that my hand was turning all gray from residue. Great, the fucking lead from this weight is wearing off on my hand, now I'm going to get lead poisoning.

As I stood there looking at the paperweight trying to figure out why the lead was rubbing off so fast, I suddenly noticed in one of the worn down corners, there was a little glimmer of gold color. This is definitely weird. I took an M-16 round out from one of my magazines and started scratching the surface of the weight with it, using the brass casing end. After a few scratches, I could clearly see that this was no lead paperweight. This was a gold bar that had been camouflaged with massive amounts of pencil lead. I looked straight at the nervous fellow, he knew they had been busted.

Frozen in a moment of time, all kinds of thoughts ran through my head. How much is a gold bar like this worth and would it be enough to solve most of my problems back home? If I took these gold bars, could I get away with it, would the nervous guy just sit there and let me walk out with them? What about Sgt Brown and Spc Carson, should I share with them and if I do, would they want to share in the risk of taking these gold bars? Then I started to imagine different scenarios on what to do next in order to get away with the gold. I'm sure this was a once in a life time opportunity because it's not every day that you hold a gold bar in one hand and an M-203 rifle in the other.

Looking at the two guys at the table and the wife, while they were looking at me to make a move, which made me run the scenarios one more time in my head just to make sure I had taken everything into consideration. Then the obvious and most practical choice came to my head and I decided to act upon it. I yelled to the 2nd CAV escorts, "I need for you three to go and grab all the files from the office upstairs so we can examine them back at the FOB."

Once they scurried upstairs, I showed the gold bar to Carson and Brown. This at least answered one of my questions when they responded, beside I could never hold any opportunity or information back from my guys. "Holy fuck!" Exclaimed both of them. "Daddy is getting some new shoes."

"Keep it down," I whispered back as if we were in a library. "Let's see if we can find out if there is any more of this lying around. Maybe if we find enough, we can upgrade our barracks and outclass Civil Affairs like we've always been talking about, along with more cigars for everybody."

Sitting back down at the table while the 2nd CAV guys continued scuffling around upstairs gave me an opportunity to address some of my other questions that I proposed to myself with this find. Not having any creditable witnesses around gave me some time to interrogate the group and see if there was more gold and if we could have some. With time being the essence, I had Milik ask the nervous guy, "where did you get this?"

"I don't know, Kamal Abdallah Sultan brought them home the other day."

"Don't give me that shit, where did you get these?"

"I don't know, Kamal said that he knows where there's a whole bunch of these gold bars and he had a plan to get them soon. With no opportunity for an income since Saddam has left, he wanted to use these gold bars to survive. Please let me keep at least one of those, one gold bar can feed us for a year and we have no income since you came here, we will starve without them."

"Who else knows that you have these?"

"No one, like I said, Kamal just brought them home the other day and that is all I know."

"So what you are saying is that Kamal Abdallah Sultan is the only person who knows where there are more of these?"

"Yes."

"I tell you what, you tell no one and I mean no one about these gold bars and you can keep two of them, I will take this one for evidence. If you tell anybody anything, I will come back here and arrest you as a field combative and have you sent to Abu Ghraib, understand? And that goes for the rest of you," I said as I gave everyone in the room a stern look.

"Yes!" everyone in the room replied back simultaneously.

"If I can get your friend to tell me where the rest of these are located at, I'll make sure you get a fair share. Once again though, if you tell anybody, nobody gets anything except a one way trip to the prison."

I heard the guys from 2nd CAV walking down the stairs with the files, they had a couple boxes worth of paperwork. I quickly pocketed the gold bar and yelled out to everyone, "let's get out of here, I'm not getting anything from them."

We left the house and headed towards our vehicle with the 2nd CAV guys in tow. As soon as we approached our vehicle and before we could even discuss our next step, the S-2 Captain whisked over and asked us if we found anything other than all these files. Carson and Brown glanced over at me and I gave them the confident look back that I would respond with something clever.

"All of these files we secured are Kamal Abdallah Sultan's personal files. If there is something to find which I'm sure there is, we'll definitely be able to accomplish it back at the FOB."

The S-2 Captain appeared to be pretty happy now since we explained who the rightful owner of those documents were, I knew he was excited because now he had something to do for the next few days, even if there may or may not be a needle in the haystack.

I knew I needed to get in front of Kamal Abdallah Sultan in order to get the location of the gold and I needed to do that immediately. I also knew the only way to do that was through the S-2 Captain, so I came up with a witty excuse to see him.

I approached the S-2 Captain and asked, "is there any chance I can have a few minutes with Kamal Abdallah Sultan in order to see if there is anything I can get out of him?"

I was trying to leverage his excitement with our finding the documents into a favor.

"Like what?"

"Nothing in particular, I would just like to practice some of my interrogation skills. Maybe I can cut to the chase with him and have him point out what we need to know in this stack of paperwork."

The Captain thought about it for a second and then replied, "I think I can get you in front of him for a couple of minutes, but I'm sure the SCO would want me to be there in order to make sure everything goes well."

"Not a problem, when we get back I will track you down for the meeting. I'll bring Milik as my interpreter, so you don't have to worry about any of that."

CHAPTER FIFTEEN

THE INTERROGATION

Brown, Carson, Milik, and I sat around back at our pad on our overstuffed homemade couch that we made by stuffing cigarette filters from the factory into sandbags. We were trying to come up with a plan for the interrogation. After much deliberation, we finally came up with a plan. This plan was a crazy plan, but at least it was a plan and it just may work because it was so crazy. We decided we would create a list of questions on paper that I could display for anybody to see, particularly the S-2 Captain. These would be legitimate questions one would ask about the documents for intelligence gathering. I would ask these questions in English to Kamal. This way the Captain would think I was addressing the matter at hand as he listened to my questions. Milik would then pretend to translate those questions, but instead he would ask a list of questions we came up with about the gold. Obviously we didn't make a list for these to be displayed. Milik would try to write down anything important in Arabic and he would translate it to us later. He was also instructed to translate back his fake answers in English, but they need to be gibberish so the Captain would think we were not getting any useful information. The whole key to us pulling off this stunt was to come up with an offer that Kamal could not refuse, and that we did. Milik would explain to Kamal that his wife had asked us to help them retrieve the gold. We would convince him that we would assist her in that endeavor and we would ensure his wife and family would get their fair share. We would also explain that the family was about to be arrested too, but I put a stop to that because of their information. If the information he provided proved to be false, then they would be arrested and sent to a military tribunal camp.

Once we had completed our list of questions (the bogus and real ones), the four of us headed over to the TOC to find the S-2 Captain. When we arrived at the TOC, I had Milik wait outside the building because our protocol called for no one but US military personnel to be allowed in the TOC.

The Captain told us they're waiting for us in building G by the front gate and he'll meet us there in a few minutes. This building was the security compound where we had meetings with the locals who we invited on the FOB and also where we interrogated people. We grabbed Milik who was patiently waiting outside and we headed over to building G which seemed to be quite busy today. Obviously we weren't the first group who wanted to ask the new prisoner some questions, so we had to wait for our turn to interview him.

After the guards were done parading Kamal Abdallah Sultan around like a prized trophy after they extracted him from one room, they locked him in a different interrogation room where I was to question him. I'm sure the last group was raking him over the coals as they tried to collect information from him. I just hope that they didn't beat him down too bad, as I still had to find the whereabouts of the gold from him.

When we walked down the hallway of building G, Kamal Abdallah Sultan was waiting for us in the special room. We walked in and we all stood there while we waited for the Captain to arrive. As we stood there and waited, we gave the subject a good stare down. I could tell he was getting worn out. The look in his eyes was hazy and his facial expressions were long. I could only imagine the other interrogators who were professional probably kept asking the same questions over and over, expecting different answers each time. I hope their verbal beatings would be a benefit to me by taking the fight out of him.

The Captain finally showed up and he locked the door behind himself as he entered the room. I had Brown stand by the door with his SAW and I had Carson stand behind him with his M-16 at the ready for intimidation. The Captain and I sat across the table from Kamal and Milik sat down at his side. I had a file folder with me that was full of blank paper. I opened it and then inconspicuously placed the gold bar that was still painted with lead onto the folder as a paperweight. I wasn't too worried about the Captain paying any attention to it or even figuring it out because it did look just like a paper weight, and it was functional because the fan in the room was set on full speed.

Kamal Abdallah Sultan looked pissed off when he saw the paperweight. I gave him the look back that he needed to keep his cool. The Captain started off with the introductions and started in with some of his own questions, which Milik translated truthfully. This went on for about ten minutes or so and the Captain wasn't getting anywhere. Then finally it became my turn to ask questions.

"O.K. Milik, lets ask him our questions," I said as I wiggled my eyebrows.

I started my act and asked the first pretend question of where his subordinates are and the location where they are hiding their weapons caches. Milik went on and then asked Kamal where the gold was and after a few attempts at this question, it seemed that the subject was cooperating and we could continue with the rest of the questions. Sometimes Milik translation was intense and at times it didn't seem to jive with the questions I was asking, but the Captain didn't know what Kamal was saying because he didn't speak any Arabic. On a few incidents, Kamal's answer would go on for quite a while, and then Milik would quickly inform us that what he said was "I don't know." I was starting to get a little nervous that the Captain might catch on to our poor performance.

After about fifteen minutes of bantering back and forth, Milik gave me the nod that we had the information we were looking for. I then turned to the Captain and said, "it looks like I need to stick to the PSYOP stuff and leave this line of work for the professionals."

"OK then let's wrap it up," he replied. Brown then went and retrieved the security guards and we handed Kamal

Abdallah Sultan back over to them. They jerked him back out and started the parading process again as they moved him to the next room for the next group.

Then we thanked the Captain for the favor, escorted ourselves out, and starting walking back towards our pad to find out what information Milik gathered. When we were in the clear, I asked Milik if he got the location of the Gold. "Yes," he replied with a smile.

We all wanted to break out in a victory dance, but that would have to wait. SFC Hunter vehicle was parked in our driveway. "Fuck! Dick Head is here to give us some shit for some reason. Let's go and find out what his problem is this time. Milik, hang outside until he leaves."

The feeling I had when I walked into my barracks was the same type of feeling I always get when I have to confront my wife after staying out a little too long after a night of fun. When you're excited about how the night unfolded, but now you have to explain yourself to her and probably be punished for it from her. Will I have to explain my interrogation reasons to SFC Hunter and will I be punished?

"How's it going," I shouted to SFC Hunter, acting all casual as to not alert his sensors. Cpt Barker was with him too, standing next to him with his arms crossed as usual.

"Get the fuck over here!" he shouted at me. Knowing the routine now in order for him to not go all berserk, I stood in front of him at the position of parade rest. He continued, "why in the hell would you give all of those classified documents over to 2nd CAV?"

Normally, this would be a fantastic opportunity for me to wear SFC Hunter down with my quizzical answers, but I had other thing on my mind and I wanted him gone as soon as possible. I decided to answer his questions and act in a way he would appreciate. This would speed up his inquisition and let himself feel important and allow me to get back to my business. Just as I do with my wife as I previously described. Just say, "yes dear," and thing will move along pretty fast.

"What do you mean?"

"When you cleared the house today, didn't you have a couple of file cabinets of documents that you seized and then handed them over to 2nd CAV?"

"Yeah, that's right."

"That is what I'm talking about. You had no business handing them over, if you had any brains you would have called the Captain and me to meet you there and we could have secured them."

"I gave them to S-2 who deals with intelligence, they have a whole network of people behind themselves that specialize in these type of things." Even though I was trying to get through this as fast as possible, I had to throw that one in.

"Yes," SFC Hunter replied. "But we are PSYOP's. I could have made a significant impact on the intelligence report to HQ if I had my hands on those documents first."

"S-2 has the manpower and resources to thoroughly go through those documents."

"That not the point! We need to prove our worth to everyone and you passed up a perfect opportunity. We could have scrubbed those documents and took any credit they may have produced. You need to start thinking about the PSYOP team first. Next time you get any kind of intelligence like that again, you deliver it to the Captain and me first. You got it?"

"Sure, no problem," I replied as I swallowed my pride for not challenging him on his logic.

"I want you to write a complete report on what happened today and get that to me by morning."

"What happened today will be in the daily sitrep and that will get reported to you," I explained.

"That's not what I fucking asked for, I said I want a complete report from you by morning! Now I have to go and visit some of the other PSYOP teams. When you are writing that report, think of a reason why I should let you stay in charge of this team because I don't think you have what it takes."

SFC Hunter and the Captain excused themselves from me by walking over to their vehicle with their chest pumped out as if they just won a championship fight. They finally climbed in their vehicle and drove away.

"What a douche," I said to Brown and Carson who were standing nearby. "Only in the Army do I have to listen to self conniving idiot like that and have to agree when they tell me what to do. Milik! Get in here."

We all sat down around our homemade coffee table made from a crate and a slab of plywood with anticipation. "Spill it," I said to Milik.

"Do you have a map of Baghdad with the Tigress River?"

"Yep."

Brown pulled out a huge 6'x12' map and taped it onto the side of a concrete wall at eye level. Milik walked over to the map and started to point at the Tigress River, moving his finger back and forth a bit until he finally pressed it on a location on the map.

"There, I believe it's right there. The gold is in the river, at the bottom, and locked in a cage. Uday Hussein hid the gold there a few months ago before he was assassinated. Kamal was one of the select few people who helped with the operation of hiding the gold there.

The problem besides being under water and under lock and key is that there are guards around its location twenty four-seven. Only a few people know about the location of the gold, but each individual who does know the location, is waiting for the right moment to take it. These select few people are watching each others moves and are planning their own strategies to get it. None of them want to share and if one takes the gold and draws attention, they will be massacred by the others. So before anyone attempts to take the gold, they must have a solid plan to retrieve it under the radar in order to not be detected.

Kamal was one of those people who had a plan to retrieve the gold and he had a plan to do it with out anybody noticing, but I think today spoiled that. He now agrees that you helping in getting some of this gold to his family before the other people who know about it takes off with the entire loot is currently his best option. Leaving his family out with nothing is not a good option."

After listening to the details in order to get the gold, I butted in and said, "I don't know guys. If we wanted to throw our hat in the ring to take this gold, we would need to move fast before the bad guys take it. This is where mistakes are made. The more I think about this, the more I have my doubts. Sure it was fun to play a con game on the S-2 Captain during the interrogation and sure it was kind of cool to get a bad guy to confess where some gold might be, but we have to considered the consequences of what might happen to us if we fuck up and get caught? SFC Hunter would not only get his wish to send me home early, but he would get the extra bonus of sending me to the stockade, and this goes for all of us. We also need to consider the fact that the other people who want the gold and are guarding it will probably want to shoot us. I know if we could confiscate this gold, it would be like the equivalent to finding a drug dealers stash of money and keeping it. I just don't think the risk is worth a few bars of gold so we can upgrade our living quarters to tease the Civil Affairs guys. Look, we have this gold bar and it's worth about $35 thousand dollars. That's enough to buy a shit load of cigars and party like a rock star for a while. Why don't we call it good and quit while we're ahead?"

Carson jumped in and said, "I agree with SSG Jenks, how can all of us drive up to the access point with the guards all around, load up a truck with God knows how much gold, and then drive away with no one getting hurt? Not to mention, what we'd do with the gold once we have it. If we try to cash the gold in, other people will notice, especially the bad guys who are tracking this gold. We can easily just mail this one bar home that we have in our possession. We can have either one of our wives deposit the cash from the sale of the gold bar into our accounts and then we can start doing large cash withdrawals from Army Finance on pay day. No one would be able to connect those dots, so let's do that and call it good."

"You are all a bunch of pussies," Brown shouted at us. "If the Army has taught us anything, it is to adapt, improvise, and overcome. I didn't hear any of the like in your speech, besides Carson asked a great question and we should know the answer before we make any rash decisions. How much gold is there?" We all looked at Milik who was all relaxed on the couch and demanded an answer.

"Yes, yes, yes, the amount of gold. I think he said in the amount of around two to six tons of twenty four karat gold."

I couldn't tell if Brown tripped on his foot or if he lost his balance as he went stumbling back. Luckily, Carson was able to catch him before he hit the ground.

"Holy sheep shit!" I said, "at least two fucking tons of gold. I was thinking more like a couple dozen bars or something. This changes everything because two tons of gold is a lot of fucking gold. The risk factor just changed on us. I think Brown is right, we need to buck up and figure this shit out. This can make a difference in our living standards not only here, but definitely back in the States too with that kind of money."

After we all regained our composer, I continued to gather the rest of the information from Milik. "Did he really buy off on our offer to not prosecute his family and share the gold with us? And if so, what are his demands?"

"Yes, he knows that his days are limited, but he wants his family to have a cut of the findings. He agreed to keep silent as long as he was informed that we kept our end of the bargain of giving his family their fair share. He knows that if he spoke out against us before hand, then his family could be tied to terrorist dollars through our doings. He also wanted to remind you that if they did not get their share after we recovered the gold, then he would definitely blow the whistle on us."

"Well no shit. Whatever happens, we need to make sure the family gets their cut so they will keep silent. And Milik, this goes for you too. Don't fucking say a word to anybody, especially your family. I know you are required to share this type of information with you family, but if you peep one word, you will have a wrath to pay. All we would need now is half of Sadr City racing after the same gold. I need you to go back to Kamal's family right now and make sure they do keep their mouth shut and let them know we'll get the gold and give them a fair cut."

I was dreading the fact that I had to not only write the sit-rep as I normally do, but I also had to create a detailed report for SFC Hunter. I just wanted to concentrate on getting the gold and live on easy street, but I knew that I had to bide my time and to take all of these micro steps to pull off a detailed plan and not get caught. I figured the more business as usual around here, the less attention I would draw on myself, but then again, time is of the essence right now.

CHAPTER SIXTEEN

GOLD RECONNAISSANCE

The next day we had to get back to the real PSYOP work. Our mission for the day was to make a public broadcast about the upcoming provincial elections. Once again we're to record a message that was handed down to us from HQ and play it over our mounted loudspeakers. We had to make sure all of the residents of Sadr City knew about the election and that they knew where to go in order to vote. Milik and our escorts from 2nd CAV showed up and we were ready to roll with our mission. We are all pretty tired though, we all had to have an extra cup of coffee because we had been up all night with "gold fever." A condition that was to get worse as each day passed.

I advised our escort that today we had a full schedule, but the first half was going to be pretty boring. All we were going to do during this period is drive around in circles and broadcast our message, nothing too exciting. To start the day off right though, we planned to have breakfast with the locals before we started our boring broadcast mission. Next, we wanted to go into Baghdad today after the broadcast and get more cigars. The reason for the cigar shop visit was not only to stock up on more smokes, but also to start the planning session for retrieving the gold. The gold location so happened to be in the same neighborhood as the cigar shop and this would allow us to reconnaissance the situation under the disguise of a cigar visit, our escorts wouldn't have clue.

We finally arrived at our broadcast mission start point, the bread shop. Having a good breakfast before you start your day's mission is always a good idea. We went inside Amira Farque's bread bakery to get some of his delicious bread and egg sandwiches. When you added the jalapeño cheese spread from the MRE packs that were inside, they were simply the best breakfast sandwich you could ever taste. Amira had his traditional two cigarettes and a cup of tea as we enjoyed his delicious sandwiches. After breakfast and some updates to Amira about the progress of the city's electrical grid and sewer reconstruction, we were ready to start our mission.

Next, I had Milik translate the script that was previously prepared into the DVR so we could just put it on loop for replay. With our bellies full from breakfast, we were ready to start blaring our speakers. Our mission is to drive up and down the streets until we cover the entire city with our message. This was always a good time to light up a cigar and people watch as we drove around. We still had to keep an eye out for the bad guys in the crowd, because if we didn't they would take advantage of the situation. They always used the crowed as a way to conceal their movement so you had to be on high alert. If you didn't act as if you were ready to use extreme force, then these bad guys could expose themselves and try out their skills.

The time was about eleven in the morning and the heat was already dialed up to about a hundred and twenty degrees. I was keeping myself hydrated by drinking large quantities of Crystal Light. Pink Lemonade was my favorite flavor to mix in my liter of bottle water. These drinks where more effective than water because warm pink lemonade was a million times tastier than plain warm water, so you would actually drink a lot more and keep hydrated.

When we exited from the giant roundabout that was in the middle of Sadr City (where there was a big graphic painting with three Arab figures depicturing a battle scene) and while I was enjoying my warm crystal light pink lemonade, two MP HMMWV merged besides us as they too departed the roundabout.

Our speakers were too loud to even try to talk with them, but they still attempted to shout something at us. I think they were trying to tell us to play some Rock and Roll. This is the normal request that is always demanded from other US Soldiers when they hear us. After a few attempts of them thinking I understood what they were saying, we both smiled and waved at each other and continued on with our mission.

After about a half mile of cruising along the side of them, all of us enduring our long and boring message that was in Arabic, they decided to pull in front of us to gain some distance away from the noise. When they were about a hundred yards ahead of us, something appeared that at first I thought was a mirage. It looked like a sea of people gathered on the right side of the road. As we got closer, I concluded that it was not a mirage and in fact it was a very large crowd of Iraqis gathered on the right side of the road. We were close to the Sadr Burrow HQ, so at first I thought that maybe they were having a gathering to address some of their political concerns.

As we got closer to the crowd, I realized that they weren't addressing some political concerns, unless those concerns were my crew and me being here at this location right now. I recognize that they were starting to move and come towards us very quickly. This was not a Sadr City greeting committee, but an angry crowd who was about to make their point. This sea of people reminded me of the scene in the movie *Gremlins* where right after the Gremlin monster named Spike jumped into the swimming pool. Then you saw an infinity amount of gremlins marching towards you as they started jumping up and down. It looked as if there were at least five thousand of these Iraqi Gremlin impersonators and just as in the movie, they were headed straight towards us with one thing on their mind.

I noticed in the distance the MP's hit the gas pedal and made a dash for an exit on the right in an alley just before the advancing crowd. They had the right idea, to get the hell out of there. I yelled over to Carson to also step on it and follow those MP's. Carson hit the pedal without reservation as the HMMWV engine slowly decided to kick into gear.

Next I grabbed the Speaker controls and killed the broadcast while I pointed my weapon out the right door window in order to cover the right flank. Sgt Brown was ready at the turret, I didn't have to explain anything to him. Carson floored the gas all the way and we headed toward the exit that the MP's discovered. The big cloud of dust that was hovering in the exit ally informed me that they had already made it through. This also provided the mob with the same information, that we too had our eye on this exit.

The crowd was surging towards the exit to choke us off and the channel was getting smaller by the second. I told Carson that if anybody jumped in our way, don't fucking stop and just run them over. Our security escorts were in hot pursuit behind us. The crowd was getting close and I could start to make out some of the faces in the crowd. Some of the foremost groups that were actually close to us who were in shouting distance started yelling anti American sediments like, "Death to America" or "Fuck you Yankee, go home."

"I see weapons!" Brown yelled out.

Two seconds later I heard Brown open up the SAW with controlled three round bursts. The escorts behind us who had a M60 machine gun also started to open fire.

We made it to the turn that would allow us into the ally just in time before it was fully choked off with people, but the crowd was upon us. I could hear zingers cracking by my ears from the enemy trying to shoot at us. Carson and Brown were blasting right back at the crowd on the left side, zeroing in on the Iraqis who had weapons. About seventy-five meters on the right side of the vehicle, an Iraqi popped up from behind a building corner. He had a Rocket Propelled Grenade that he was pointing straight at us. My training kicked in and I pointed my barrel straight at him and fired two quick rounds. I paused before pulling the trigger again to check my aim and ensure my two rounds had hit him. Even though both rounds hit his chest as it exploded, he was able to gain enough composer and strength to pull his trigger and shoot off a Rocket Propelled Grenade at us. The Rocket Propelled Grenade round was able to launch out of the tub. "RPG!" I screamed, as the attacker fell over and went lifeless.

The whole thing took two split seconds, but it seemed like two minutes as I watched every foot the RPG covered as it traveled towards us. The round was going straight for Sgt Brown. I looked at him and before I could say anything, the RPG flew right over his head. It missed decapitating him by a matter of inches. I don't think he even knew that he had just escaped death because he kept firing off his three round bursts without missing a beat. Then the RPG hit a parked car about two hundred meters away. The car exploded and shrapnel went everywhere.   This explosion startled Brown, but only for a second.

Finally, we all made it all the way into the alley and the buildings provided us cover. There was dust everywhere from the MP's vehicles that was traveling before us and when I looked at Carson, I could tell he was having problems driving because he couldn't see more than a foot in front of us because of the dust. We didn't want to slow down because we knew we had to get the fuck out of there before they launched a crew after us or even worse, more RPG's. At the same time, I knew from past experience from driving around these parts that there were abandoned vehicles everywhere and I didn't want us to have a head-on collision with one. I was going to need to put my weapon down and help watch for Carson.

The alley was more like a two lane road and I knew it had an exit. With our HMMWV engine screaming at full power as we raced through the alley, I started looking for the dust hidden obstacles in the road. Suddenly, a broken down car appeared right in front of us with about a second to spare before impact, I yelled out "car!" and pointed it out to Carson. He torques the wheel to the right and we all went flying to the left in the vehicle, barely missing the car. As we regained our alignment I could see a donkey cart in front of us, I yelled, "cart!" and pointed to it. We all went flying to the right this time as Carson turned left. We went through a very large puddle of sewer water and it splashed not only all up our windshield, but over the vehicle itself.

"You Fucker," yelled Brown because he got doused in the sewer water from being exposed in the turret. Looking over at Carson, I could see Sgt Brown trying to kick him in the head, he was extremely pissed because of his sudden category ten shit hole tsunami. Carson was having a hard time driving with Brown trying to kick him in the head and dodging dust hidden obstacles in the road by weaving left and right. We finally made it to a paved blacktop part of the road and when the dust cleared, we could see once again, and Brown was tired of kicking Carson in the head. I looked back and thank goodness our security vehicles were still in tow.

I knew exactly where we were, so I told Carson to take a left. The tires barked as he took the turn at a high speed. We very rapidly traveled about a mile when we noticed the MP's that we previously encountered were pulled over on a median. This would be a perfectly safe place to stop and perform an after action check.

When we pulled up next to them, I could see that two of the MP's were huddled against the first vehicle's driver side, so I figured they were already calling the incident in to their HQ. The remaining three MP's were busy going through their security fire drills as they were trained to do so. I even caught a glimpse of one MP taking an M-203 round and chambering it, which reminded me that I should do the same. I jumped out of the HMMWV and ran back to our security guys and did a check on them to make sure they were OK. They gave me the thumbs up.

As I was running back to my vehicle so I could report this incident to my HQ, I became curious as to why the two MP's were still huddled against the driver's door and not paying attention to their surroundings. Instead of picking up the radio, I approached the MP's vehicle. I could hear the driver who was still sitting behind the wheel screaming at the top of his lungs to the other two MP's. "Just take the fucking door off man, just fucking get rid of it!" He repeated this demand numerous times in a hysterical tone.

I approached the two MP and asked if there was anything I could help out with? With that question, the two took one step to the side and opened a gap so I could see what the situation was. My heart stopped beating for what felt like about thirty seconds and I stopped breathing as I rationalize what I was witnessing. There was the tail end of an RPG sticking out from the middle of the driver's door. I took a step closer, peered over the door window section, and observed the other half of the RPG pressed on top of the driver's leg. There was no physical harm done to the driver's leg. Though, he did have an unexploded ordnance sitting on top of his lap, and if we didn't do something quick, he may not have a leg to complain about.

The driver looked straight at me and I could see the fear in his eyes as he repeated his demand, "just take the fucking door off man, just fucking get rid of it!"

I took a few steps back as I tried to keep my calm, glanced at the two standing MP's and said, "looks like you got no choice but to comply with his demands. I don't think it makes a difference if it was a dud or if it didn't travel far enough for the fuse to ignite, it could explode at any moment. You two need to slide the door of its hinges and place it over there next to that building's wall. Before you two do this though, my team and I are going to back up about fifty meters and take cover. This is the luckiest son of a bitch I have ever seen, but with my last name being Jenks, I don't want to break his streak of good luck by hanging around."

I returned to my vehicle, informed my team of the situation, and placed our vehicles out of the perceived blast zone. Then I jumped on the radio to call the episode in. Providing the grid coordinate of the incident and requesting EOD to dispose of the ordnance. All while the rest of my crew jumped back into their security defensive position. The TOC officer collected my information and then concluded our discussion by asking if I was coming back to the FOB?

"No. I need to continue our mission. Just because we ran into a little combat action doesn't mean we get the rest of the day off. We will suck it up and drive on." In reality, I wanted to come back and take a shot from the Civil Affairs liquor cabinet to calm my nerves down a bit, but time was of the essence and I couldn't jeopardize my opportunity to do my gold reconnaissance. The big sales job was convincing our escorts that the mission must continue for I knew they were ready to go back to safety.

After I got off the radio, I yelled over to the MP's that it was all clear for their door removal mission. They started to grab the door and position themselves for the removal, when I noticed a white Toyota pickup truck coming around the corner as it headed towards us at a high rate of speed. I yelled back over to the MP's to get their attention and we all raised our weapons and pointed them towards the speeding vehicle.

One guy appeared to be driving the white pickup truck and there were two more guys in the back. They started waving their hand in the air like they were saying, "NO!" I yelled out, "hold you fire unless you see a weapon." The truck sped past us with them still waving their hands franticly. In the back of the pickup we could see the one guy sitting on the wheel well holding on for his dear life with a gunshot wound to his belly. We could also see three other people lying down covered in blood in the bed of the pickup. We suddenly realized that the white truck was their version of an ambulance and this one was taking the casualties to the hospital. Even though I wanted to open fire on them and finish them off for what they just tried to do to us, I knew that was against the Geneva code. All I could do was let them pass. "Jesus Christ," I yelled to our group, "that will teach them to fuck with us."

As soon as the pickup passed with no incident, the MP's quickly went back to their task and successfully removed the door and placed it in a safe area without any detonation. The driver immediately jumped out of his seat and started to run down the middle of the street. In the middle of his sprint, he suddenly paused and grabbed his knees as he bent over. Then he started to puke up his lunch because the stress finally got the better half of him. I stood there for a moment and took a deep breath as I tried to collect my own thoughts.

During this surreal moment, reality began to set in as I realized that I now had my first confirmed kill. I looked at myself in the side view mirror on our HMMWV. My reflection in the mirror was still the same old Jenks, but I felt something had to be different. I knew that deep down inside I was a different person than the salesman I was back in Washington State. What this difference was would remain a mystery at this point. Many overpowering feelings came over me as I realized shooting at a person was entirely different from shooting at a target on the riffle range as I have done many times in training to prepare myself for this moment. The thousands of range targets I have shot at all went down without a second thought, but this one human target made me question if I was still a moral individual. Looking in the mirror again, I immediately realized that what was wearing on me wasn't so much as guilt but more of the heavy weight of the responsibility one feels when doing the right thing, even if it goes against your conscious. My conscious was telling me that this person who I terminated, may of had a family too and his actions may have been propelled by doing what he thought was right. My burden of responsibility wasn't to just protect my own life, but the lives of my crew just as I rely on them with the same accountability. We're no longer fighting for our country, we are fighting for each other. We were a team and we relied upon each other in order to survive. I had to take this persons life in order to safeguard Brown and Carson against any harm.

Quickly I snapped out of my contemplation because there just wasn't any time to think hard about it. I was sure that all of these deep type thoughts would come bubbling to the surface again sometime in the future. But I was going to be stinking rich by then and therefore could afford all of the private therapy and counseling that money could buy. I was going to be A-ok.

I gave the signal for everybody to load back up in order for us to move on. My security sergeant gave me the nod that he understood, but he also walked over towards me because he had something he wanted to say. "A boring day? My ass!" Then he smiled at me and went back to his vehicle.

We were able to finish off our broadcast mission and eventually make it out of Sadr City alive. We now are entering the more fashionable part of Baghdad. This part of the city is full of restaurants, modern shops, and of course where we like to purchase our cigars. We definitely made a stop there so I could stock up on some supplies, immediately popping one in my mouth to help calm my nerves a bit.

After we all took turns going into the cigar shop to buy our supplies, we decided to head on over to our favorite pizza joint called *Pizza Hot* for a late lunch. Their logo was identical to *Pizza Hut*, it was just spelled different. Definitely no copy right laws existed over here. The cheese on the pizza is also a little different. Instead of mozzarella, they use a kind of a feta or goat cheese. Since Iraq is a Muslim country, they also have no pepperoni, bacon, ham, or sausage as a topping option. We had to settle for the mystery meat, which I assumed was either lamb or goat.

I informed our security escorts that we needed to get the pizzas to go and head over to a different location to eat them. We drove over a bridge to the east bank of the river and through a middle class neighborhood looking for a place to eat our pizzas. What we are really doing was trying to find the perfect vista to secretly reconnaissance the riverbank where the gold was and the pizzas where the escort's distraction.

The neighborhood still consisted of a few businesses on some of the street corners. Though, they are mostly convenience stores and the rest of the buildings are residential. We drove parallel to the river until we found a good spot that we could use our binoculars and look across the river inconspicuously. When we stopped, I informed our security escorts that we were going to do a PSYOP planning session. I told them it was okay to chow down the pizzas as long as security was still being maintained. They nodded and went straight for their pizzas. They had their weapons in one hand and a slice of pizza in the other as they maintained a three-sixty.

I pulled out my binoculars and zoomed in on the proposed grid point on the other side of the Tigress that Milik pointed out to us on the map. The area we were scoping out appeared to be an industrial area nestled up to the river. The establishment had iron gates, an endless amount of fence, and heavily fortified concertina wire everywhere. There was only one gate entrance into the compound area where the gold was supposed to be hidden. The entrance gate had four guards at all times manning their positions with heavy assault weapons. The type that could make hamburger out of us in a matter of seconds if they decided to open fire. On the riverbank, I could see another four guards with AK-47 riffles who were making sure no one was able to pull up by boat. On the river, there were some buoys floating around in the area with some skull and cross bone symbol on them, along with a short message in Arabic. This is definitely a defense system that was strategically placed there to keep anybody or anything out because they had a dress pattern of each buoy being approximately twenty feet apart. This spacing would make it impossible for any watercraft larger than a canoe to maneuver round these buoys. I wasn't clear on what the message read or even why they placed them there so I handed the binoculars to Milik and asked him what the message on the buoys said.

"Stay 150 meters away from bank. Trespassers will be killed," he informed me.

"Well that's not much of a welcoming message now is it?" I then handed Brown the binoculars. He was still sitting up in his turret when I asked him to take a look. With Brown now studying the area with the binoculars, I took this opportunity to devote my attention to my pizza. Even though it wasn't the traditional pepperoni pizza I preferred back at home, it was still delicious because after all, it was pizza.

"Fucking eh! Did you notice the different sniper nests on the rooftops? There is also an office building inside the compound about seventy-five meters to the left that seems to have many more people. Wait a minute, hold on, this takes the cake! If you look real carefully, you can see some water mines floating just beneath the water surface under the buoys. They're a little difficult to see, but they are there. There is no fucking way we will ever be able to get into this compound. Think about it, not only would we have to blast our way in through the fortified gates, but engage into heavy combat fighting. How would we ever fight a battle while at the same time try to recover gold out of the river? If we come in by boat, I'm sure we'll just get blasted out of the water as soon as we passed a buoy. Coming from the air is fucking out of the question. They'll just shoot us down with an RPG or make mincemeat out us with one of their mounted machine guns."

"You're right. The 1st Armor division who controls this sector will respond to a battle with anything larger than a small riffle within fifteen minutes. I don't think we could even retrieve a portion of the gold in that small amount of time. That's not even including the time it would take to just find it in the water. I don't think it matters what time of day or night we do this because everything will remain the same. This place is pretty fucking secured. We need to figure out something different and pretty soon because time is ticking. "Let's roll," I yelled.

I tossed my pizza back into its box, as it now had lost it's deliciousness due to the bad news. Then we all jumped in our HMMWVS and evacuated the area in disgust of our current situation.

CHAPTER SEVENTEEN

A PLAN IS HATCHED

Later that evening after the sit-rep, we all gathered around our living room and started to try to figure out our options in order to steal the gold. Obviously we can't come by land, air, or water we concluded, because they have their right and left flank covered, and there is no way to descend from above.

"What if we come from below?" Brown said quizzically.

"What like dig our way up?" Carson asked.

Brown's statement kicked my imagination into gear. "Wait a minute Brown, I think you are on to something. I think it's worth considering to see if we can come by water…underwater that is."

Then as soon as I said that statement, I realized that was a stupid idea. I tried to recant my idea and explained "that wouldn't work because I doubt that there has ever been a submarine in the Tigress. I don't think that the river is even deep enough to navigate one through it. Besides, not only do I think the Navy wouldn't let us borrow a sub, but I think we would draw a lot of attention if we pulled up in a nuclear powered sub demanding our share of the gold."

"What if we got one of those mini subs?" Carson asked, thinking he was on to something.

"Where in the fuck are we going to get a mini sub? Did you forget that we are in the middle of the fucking desert? In addition, we are talking about millions of dollars up front for one of those Jacques Cousteau contraptions. We don't have the gold yet to make a down payment on one and there is no guarantee that we will ever get any gold. In addition, none of us has the smarts like the inventor of the first submarine William Bourne in order for us to make one on our own. Besides, they could have already thought of someone attempting to use an underwater vessel to retrieve the gold. They definitely have the surface of the water covered, so we must assume they probably have sonar devices looking for shit like that. Keep thinking."

Then all of a sudden the whole plan unraveled in my head as it came to me with one big flash, what if we went smaller, a lot smaller. Small enough so no sonar device could detect our presence underwater.

The plan that flashed in my head was this. I knew of a unit that consisted of 12C[30]'s who patrols the Tigress River. It

---

[30] 12C - Bridge crewmembers who provide conventional and powered bridge and rafting support for wet and dry gap crossing operations.

was also reported that they might have some SCUBA gear that they use when they conduct some of their underwater repairs and welding. These are the people who can place a river bridge anywhere. They have those cool flat bottom river boats that they use when they chase the portable floating bridge pieces when their counter parts drop them into a river.

Their mission eventually changed to river patrols when they discovered they had no bridges to chase. This meant the wear and tear on the boats was significantly reduced, freeing up time, material, and resources.

The plan in my head was telling me we should procure some of those freed up resources such as their SCUBA gear. If we're to get our hands on some of the SCUBA gear, then we could perform another reconnaissance of the area. This reconnaissance would be conducted where the gold actually might be. We could go upstream of the river and drop one of us off by a bank with easy access that would allow the diver in the river with all his SCUBA and reconnaissance gear. Then using the stream from the river, that person could float down to the site underwater, hopefully undetected. Then the SCUBA diver could check out what tools would be needed and more important, if there is actually any gold to be retrieved. After the reconnaissance, they could float down to a pre-designated pick up point. The more I thought about this plan and the more I ran it through my head, the more I thought that it was the perfect plan. The plan was crazy enough to work, so I decided to elaborate on it with the team and see if I was truly crazy or if I had a stroke of genius.

The only problem that materialized when I explained the plan out loud to Brown and Carson was that we would never be able to leave the front gate with only one vehicle. We would be forced to bring our security guards with us issued by 2nd CAV. There was also no way we could come up with a good enough excuse to tell our security guards why we are going SCUBA diving in the Tigress at midnight. It wouldn't be as easy as tossing a pizza in front of them to distract our intent. We were going to need some help. We only had one option at this point and that option was we had to pull in the Civil Affairs folks.

Excusing myself from our meeting while Brown and Carson tried to evaluate what I just said, I went over to Civil Affairs to try to enlist their help. When I approached the front door trying to remember this week's secret knock, I could hear Cole and his guys engaging in a major bullshit session while they simultaneously watched their satellite TV. Remembering the pattern, I knocked on the door with three quick knocks and then a pause and then another quick knock. This was this week's secret knock and apparently I had remembered it correctly.

"What do you want now Jenksy?"

"Ah hey SSG Cole, I need to talk to you for a second."

"All right, come the fuck in."

It took a few seconds before all the locks were turned and the door opened. They kept the place locked up at all times and no one was allowed inside their house unless they said so, especially after the SFC Hunter incident when he barged in to yell at me. They had a lot of booze and other contraband that was against article 1 in the US ARMY CODE, and the last thing they wanted was to be busted with it. They figured the best way to not get busted was to never let anyone come close to their stash. Luckily we all got along and they trusted our team. So as long as someone was home, it was "Mi Casa es Su Casa" with them. They never came over to our pad because we didn't have anything that they didn't already have, and better.

When I walked in through the door and entered the living room, I noticed that they were flipping back and forth between the porn channel and MTV Cribs on their forty-two inch plasma HDTV.

"Pour yourself a drink," Cole said.

I could see Sgt Butkus and SSG Vanscoy were already enjoying their after dinner toddies. They also had made some advances in their security regarding the stash. They now had a hidden bar that was constructed inside a false wall. On the outer wall was a mural of a sun setting on a beach with palm trees which helped camouflaged the secrct stash of liquor. This mural was the same exact mural that was straight out of the movie *Scarface*. Pressing on one of the palm trees, the door sprang open with all the bottles of liquor presenting themselves in a nicely fashion. They had six bottles of Johnny Walker Blue sitting there. Having that many spare bottles of the good stuff would help ease their pain when they respond to my plan, which will be proposed shortly after I find the right timing to inform them. Grabbing one of their crystal whisky glasses, filling it with ice out of their ice-making machine, I proceeded to pour myself about four fingers of the fine blended Scotch. I swirled it around in my glass as if I was a sophisticated scotch snob. I then sat down on the couch facing Cole sitting in his recliner.

"Well Jenksy, I see you found yourself to the good stuff, again."

"But of course. It's kind of funny that back at home we can't afford this shit, but here in the middle of this shit hole, we have a supply as if we were all millionaires."

On MTV cribs they were profiling a particular rapper's McMansion. The rapper was standing in his driveway showing off his pink Bentley.

This seemed to strike a note with Cole because he chimed in with his comments about the rapper. "Why in the hell does that guy get a pink Bentley because he can rhyme a couple of words? I'm making a difference in this world and all I get is an attaboy. I tell you what, this place owes me about a million fucking dollars for just being here. I never asked to be here, but here I am. I should be enjoying the lifestyle of the rich and famous like this joker. I fucking hate this shit hole." Then he proceeded to slouch a little in his recliner as his attention went back to the television.

Voodoo Gold by James H Jenks

I couldn't have teed this up any better even if I planned it and better yet, I was going to make him happy about being in this shit hole.

"I agree with you Cole, if anybody deserves a pink Bentley it should be you." He slipped down a little further in his chair as my statement had no effect on him. I needed to come up with a bolder statement to hook in Cole. "You have always been generous to me and my team. You've helped us out many of times. I would like to help you out for once."

"Why, do you have a fucking million dollars?"

"Let's say I have some information that could lead you to some cash, a lot of cash. More than that stupid rapper has."

I could see that this got his attention because he straightened up in his chair and his eyebrows widened with intent. "I'm listening," Cole replied.

"OK, gather around." I motioned to Butkus and Vanscoy for them to come over too because this would also involve their enlistment.

"If I tell you what I know, I'm gonna have to count you in. There is no turning away afterwards."

The three of them looked at each other for a second as they processed what I just said. "Spill it!" Vanscoy said, "you know we're opportunist, if you've got a plan to get some cash and you need our help, just fucking say it!"

I had never seen such a group of people before who were so excited to hear me talk. I've been on a lot of sales calls back in my old job, and most people only paid half attention to what I was saying. The CA guys are all wide eyed and now learning forward, waiting on every word I formed. They were fully committed to participate in this adventure.

"Well, to start off with, you know how in a lot of the sit-reps we sit through we hear reports of semi trucks loaded with gold being confiscated at the Turkish border? Obviously this gold is coming from Iraq locations. Well I know of a location, not too far from here, that may possibly have a couple tons of gold. I propose we take this gold before it is scheduled for one of those Turkey runs."

"Proceed," said Cole as he leaned towards me and turned off the television wanting to know every detail.

I told them about the mission we came up with in order to at least reconnaissance the site for the gold. They then wanted to know how we came across this information and I informed them about everything.

Cole was still sitting in his chair absorbing all the information. He finally had his fill and was ready to move on with the next steps. "Besides sharing the gold with us, what do you need us to do?"

Already being prepared for this question, I went on to explain their requirements. "First thing is that we need you to tell the SCO that you have some night time CA obligations to perform since he pretty much lets you do what ever the fuck you want to do. Then when you acquire permission from him on that, insist that we provide security for you instead of his guys."

Voodoo Gold by James H Jenks

"I think he will buy off on that because he knows CA and PSYOP's sometimes work together. All he cares about is enforcing the two vehicle convoy rule."

"Tomorrow, I'm going to head down to the 12C's who patrol the Tigress River and see if they have any SCUBA gear we can borrow, they might not have it, but if they don't, I bet they know who does. This comes to our first request, which will require you to offer up your first investment. Nobody is going to give up their SCUBA gear to us for free when we find it, so we need some barter material. I think I can get pretty far with two bottles of the Blue."

"Not the fucking Blue," Vanscoy cried out.

"Dude," I interjected sternly, "if we pull this off, you can buy your own damn whisky factory."

"All right, I'll make the sacrifice," said Cole because he could see the bigger picture. "You can take two, but only two!"

"Now on to our next agenda item, we need to form a team of two who will SCUBA dive and conduct the reconnaissance. On my last vacation when I was fortunate enough to visit the country Belize, I was able to get certified at the hotel's pool on the tourist island town of San Pedro. From there I was able to participate in one of their popular dives that consisted of swimming with sharks at the properly named location Shark Ray Alley. Therefore, since I have actual dive experience, I will be the one from our team who will dive the Tigress. Who do you have on your team to be my dive buddy?"

"I'm certified too so I guess it's me," Vanscoy butted in. "I don't have any stories that would top swimming with sharks, but at least I'm certified."

"Great, tomorrow at dusk, we will head out and conduct our underwater reconnaissance, provided we can get some SCUBA gear."

CHAPTER EIGHTEEN

UNDERWATER RECONNAISSANCE

The next morning we met our escorts at the staging area as usual. The CA team couldn't join us on this reconnaissance today since they had a real mission to perform. This was for the best because we shouldn't be seen together too much or people will start to get suspicious and start looking into our activities.

Today was going to be an easy day, and what I mean by easy is that we don't have to head into Sadr City and deal with another ambush like yesterday. We were headed over to the Green Zone to find the 12C unit and to see if we could utilize their SCUBA gear if they had any. This would all be accomplished under the disguise of getting Milik his new identification card at the interpreter HQ office located there. I had been putting the task of getting Milik's identification card off for a while because I loathe going to the Green Zone, but one must make sacrifices in order to advance the mission. One of my main aversions to the Green Zone is that the Army standards had caught up to the place. The Green Zone was full of "chair born" rangers walking around in their fresh starched and pressed uniforms with medals on their chests.

We never felt welcomed at the Green Zone because of the way we looked and smelled. We were only taking showers once a week and wearing the same salt stained uniforms everyday. One reason for the lack of showers and having dirty uniforms was because of the lack of facilities. We just didn't have the showers or washing machines to meet the demand at Camp Marlboro. Another reason for not showering is that after a certain point, it doesn't make a difference if you do get dirtier. When you take a shower and get clean, you can feel yourself get filthier each day afterwards. Usually after the third day, it does not make a difference if you get filthier. At this level you just plain stink and an added day's stench is no added smell.

The alternative to this situation is to shower and wash your uniform every day, as they do in the Green Zone. The soldiers at the Green Zone would always look at us as we were freaks and not up to Army standards. The smirks that we received were actually badges of honor for us. Our philosophy was that combat is an additional duty for a soldier. From the way we looked and how they were treating us in the Green Zone, it was obvious that we were the only ones performing this additional duty. This made my guys chest puff out a little more when they marched through the post and stood out amongst the masses.

The Green Zone is also full of stupid rules and standards that is imposed to protect ourselves from ourselves. For example, the Command Sergeant Major of the post issued a rule that when you park your vehicle, you must put a drip pan underneath it to catch the oil. Back in the States, that makes sense because HMMWVs do drip a little oil and we don't want to be responsible for any environmental damage. In Iraq, the oil bubbles up through the ground, so the rule makes no freaking sense.

As soon as we entered the Green Zone and parked our vehicles at an empty parking lot, I released the escorts for the day and told them to be back here at this location by 1500 hours. They were more than happy to take this opportunity and go to the Al-Rashid hotel to shop. The Army had turned the whole first floor of the hotel into a merchant's mall where you can buy everything from pirated DVD's, to hookahs, and even magic carpets.

I took Milik up to the interpreter shack and checked him in for his new identification card. "You're on your own now Milik because we got business to go take care of. When you're all done, just hang out and smoke your cigarettes with your buds and catch up on war stories. When I'm done with what I need to do, I'll be back for you."

Now the three of us were free to carry out our mission. We drove around looking for the river patrol people. Luckily they weren't too hard to find, we just drove along the road on the river bank until we found where all the Army patrol boats were gathered. This establishment we just located was definitely the place we were looking for because it looked like a boat yard as you would see somewhere in Florida.

We parked our vehicle, put a make shift drip pan underneath it and walked over to a couple of guys that were smoking and hanging out. If you ever wanted to stereotype someone and call them a redneck, these two provided plenty of opportunity to do just that. They were probably the nicest guys anyone could meet, but I just had way too many Jeff Foxworthy jokes running through my head when I looked at them. They both had ripped the sleeves of their t-shirts that was covered in grime, wore their headgear backwards, and their cigarette of choice was Marlboro Reds.

"How can we help you Sarge? Inquired the person with the Led Zeppelin tattoo on his right arm, the type where the naked angel is arched back and his wings are all spread out.

"I just wanted to check out these awesome boats. I always see them running up and down the river and I think they're kind of cool, mind if I get a tour?"

"Sure, what the hell, follow me," he replied. He appeared to be anxious to get started telling his account with the boats as we walked towards the docks, lighting another cigarette.

His name was Spec Jones and the man was into his boats. He told us that the purpose of the boats was to help the 12C's build portable water bridges. Pieces of the bridge are airdropped into the river and the boats are used to chase the modules as they floated down stream and then after they retrieved them, they placed the modules into their proper position. This information was not new to me, but I acted impressed with his narrative in order to win over his liking. It seemed to pay off because he eventually offered to take me out for a spin. Now we were getting somewhere with our plan and having some fun while we're at it.

Spec Jones handed me a life vest, took a drag off his cigarette, and instructed me to put it on before we got in the boat. "Army rules," he stated. We both got into the boat and eased out onto the Tigress as Carson and Brown stood on the dock. The other fellow was there to keep them company. We were just going to spin the boat around in the Green Zone so we didn't have to put on all the combat gear and worry about people shooting at us as we enjoyed the ride.

We were speeding down the Tigress with the wind blowing in our faces and enjoying the ride as if we were back on the lake at home in a ski boat. This feeling led me to make the comment to Jones, "it would be fucking cool if you had water skis and we could go skiing behind the boat."

"Yeah dude, that would be awesome. Unfortunately we don't have any skis, but you just gave me a new goal to shoot for because this boat is faster than grease lightning. I tell you what though, if I had this boat at home, we would be out partying on it all the time. I would definitely be picking up chicks during spring break with this thing, not to mention some bad ass bass fishing."

This was my opportunity to get him talking about what I assumed he likes most, women, cars, and booze. Since offering some women wasn't an option and having a nice car here would just be just plain wrong, I jumped to what I could offer.

"What's your drink of choice when chasing the girls and fishing," I asked? "Whiskey!" He shouted without hesitation, and to just to be sure I heard his response, he shouted it a couple more times. "Whiskey! Whiskey!"

"Whiskey I see, have you ever had Johnny Walker Blue, it's good shit?"

"No way man, I'm just a grunt. There is no way I could afford that stuff with what the Army is paying me."

"Well that's too bad. Maybe one day you'll be lucky enough to try the stuff. Tell you what, promise me that when you get back to the States, you'll buy a bottle, no matter how much it cost."

"Sure thing, I'll definitely deserve a bottle by then for being in this dump."

After the river tour, we tied up the boat and went into the maintenance shop. That is when I saw all the SCUBA tanks and the SCUBA gear. Jack pot, I thought to myself as I tried to contain my excitement.

"Are those SCUBA tanks? No fucking way!"

"Yeah" replied Jones, "they were originally assigned to me for the bridge repair personnel, but since we have no bridges to repair, I now just have additional equipment to hold onto until this war is over with."

"I love SCUBA diving, I would give anything to borrow those and just try some diving here in the Tigress."

"This river sucks. You can't see more than five feet in front of you," replied Jones with a quizzical look on his face, "and believe me because I've already tried it," he continued.

"My diving club back in Washington has this big map of the world and all the members who go on dives put a thumbtack where they have gone. I would get such a kick out of putting a tack on that map representing the Tigress. I doubt anyone has been on a dive in the Middle East."

"I don't know dude, I'm signed for that shit and if you loose it, my ass is grass."

"I can make it worth your while," I said with a smile.

"What in the fuck would you have in this God forsaken place that is hotter than a two dollar pistol that would make me let you borrow my SCUBA gear?"

"Follow me," I replied.

We walked over to the HMMWV and popped the back hatch and then I pulled out the two bottles of Johnny Walker Blue. Not the American fifth bottle size, but the larger European liter bottle size. "Oh Yeah, it's happy hour and the special is a twofer," I said wittily.

"Boy howdy, butter my butt and call me a biscuit!" Jones said with his southern drawl.

"You can have both of them if you let me borrow some SCUBA gear and a few tanks for a couple of days. I promise you'll get your shit back and who knows, we might want to borrow them again and if we do, I'll bring some more bottles for you. Besides, who's going to notice a couple of wet suits missing when nobody is using them."

"Is this Jonny Walker Blue as good as you say it is? I'm use to the stuff that you need to put a fist through the wall in order to help chase it down."

"You defiantly won't need your fist for Jonny Walker Blue or any wall for that matter, it goes down smooth like candy."

Spec Jones stood there for a minute as he tried to process all the information and then he took out another cigarette and lit it up in order to help him think. "Sure, why the fuck not. I haven't had a drink in about four months. I think it's about time to start again."

"We need two sets of SCUBA gear because it's not cool to SCUBA solo."

He agreed and we made the exchange with a condition we would have the shit back within a week. After we shook hands, we had him stand behind the vehicle and guide us as we backed out of the parking lot making sure we didn't run over anybody, per another Green Zone safety rule.

Sitting down with Cole after the sit-rep that evening, we were able to update each other with our progress. Cole was excited to see that we were able to secure the SCUBA supplies. The gear was Army issue, therefore not the best of quality, but it worked and it was what we needed. He, in return informed us that he did his part by informing the SCO and acquiring his permission for us to go out with them during a night time mission. With all the gear ready to go, we agreed that the night time mission would be tonight.

Our previous planning allowed us to already have a grid point figured out where Vanscoy and I would be dropped off, and where we would be picked up. A common theme throughout our planning session was for us to remember there was water mines floating everywhere and that we need to be careful not to bump into one and detonate it. We went through the plan over and over again until the sun finally dropped. This was our cue to put our plan in play.

We grabbed all our gear, loaded it up into the two vehicles, inventoried it more than once just to be sure, and then drove out the front gate. We were all nervous as hell because we didn't know what was in store for us. I started to have second thoughts about this mission. I was thinking to myself that the guards at the gold site had to know what they were guarding. I also started to question our ability to sneak in as planned since they did have the gold well protected from all angles. This was a big gamble for us, to think they were stupid enough to leave a gap like this in their security.

I looked over at Carson as he was driving through the city at night. Even though he was concentrating on dodging people and piles of garbage in the road, I could tell he was already spending the money in his head. He must be imagining himself on South Beach riding his Yamaha R1 crotch rocket type motorcycle with the ladies hanging on him. His look motivated me and made me feel like this adventure would be well worth the risk, as long as no one got hurt, and as long as we didn't get caught.

This was the first time we drove through Sadr City at night. The city had a different vibe to it. The place was much livelier and all the shops were open for business. I naturally assumed this was because who wanted to go shopping in 130 degree heat when all you had to do was wait until sundown and shop in a cool 90 degree weather. Lights were everywhere illuminating the city.

As we started to approach our destination and leave the city behind, the city glow faded and the moon became our only source of light. Eventually we made it to the river bank where we parked our vehicles and got out. The place was pitch dark and the only lights we could see where the lights twinkling on the other side in the secured compound.

The gear that we borrowed came with some low emitting underwater flashlights. Spec Jones informed us this piece of equipment could provide light for about six feet, and you wouldn't be able to see it on the surface of the water. Perfect for our mission.

Vanscoy and I tore off our armored vest and the rest of our gear and got down to our skibbies. We then jumped into our wetsuits and threw on our tanks. Trying to remember what to do with my buoyancy compensator and how to test out my regulator, I tried to flash back to the pool in Belize and what Ricardo the instructor/bartender said. Then it all came back to me, I was able to inflate my vest by pushing the button on the regulator and I was able to don the rest of my gear.

We started waddling into the brown murky water.

"Make sure you're at the pickup point in forty five minutes," I said to the rest of the crew.

Brown shouted back, "be cautious of the water mines." The rest of the crew gave us the nod, which meant to be careful and yes, they'll be at the pickup point. Vanscoy and I submerged under the water.

When we were about two feet under, Vanscoy tapped me on the head and gave me the OK sign, I did the same in return. We then started to let some of the air out of our vest in order to go deeper.

The water was murky brown and the visibility was poor. Spc Jones was correct, you could only see less than five feet in front of you. So our six foot light became less than a five foot light. It didn't provide much illumination, but it did help. Vanscoy and I tethered each other with some parachute rope so we wouldn't lose each other just in case it got too murky. As the current swept us down the river, we kicked our fins and were able to swim to the other side of the Tigress. I knew we had made it to the other side when I bumped into the concrete edge of the Tigress River. Then Vanscoy gave me the signal, the signal that we were to re-inflate our vest. We slowly started to rise up to the surface of the river. We stopped about four feet before surfacing to make sure that we had not been detected by anyone. Figuring it was clear, we broke the surface and where able to see where we were.

Luckily, we were still in the dark and a good distance from the secured compound where all the guards were, so nobody was even close to detecting us. I calculated that we're about hundred yards before we would cross the border and enter the complex, and if my calculations are right after studying the map the other day, I knew it would be about another sixty yards beyond the warning signs before we were close to the target.

We knew from our sources that the entrance to the chamber where the gold was supposed to be was about fifteen feet down. Not having a dive meter or any measuring devises, I had to rely on my gut instinct. I dove about two and a half body lengths and slowly hugged the wall as the current took us down stream. Once again, carefully measuring and counting how many body lengths went by, so we knew how far down the wall we had traveled. When we figured we were close to our vicinity, we started to bob up and down about every five feet looking for the entrance. As murky as it was, it was a surprise when I actually did see an entrance to something.

Then Vanscoy pointed out the entrance too, we both swam to it. At the entrance there was a metal meshed gate that was set back about five feet inside a cove. The gate had a padlock on it, preventing us from opening the doors. The lock was nothing that couldn't be cut with a bolt cutter, we just didn't have one on us.

I studied the gate to see if there was any way around it, but there wasn't. I also looked for any kind of trip wires or sensors that would alert the guards, but I couldn't find any evidence of the sort. Cole was able to squeeze his arm around the small gap on the side, but that was about it. We both shined our emitting lights into the chamber trying to focus on what we could see. The chamber was real cloudy, but I could see the fuzzy outline of the stacks of yellow shiny gold. I couldn't make out the exact shape and size of the bricks, but they looked like the ones we had confiscated from Kamal Abdallah Sultan's house. Lying around were a few loose scattered pieces of gold that were resting on the ground near the gate. Vanscoy was able to extend his reach through the gap and eventually grabbed two gold bricks. They were covered in a fine layer of sediment as with everything else in this chamber. Obviously, nobody had been down there in a long tome. We knew that no one would miss these two loose bricks if we kept them. I then pointed at my watch and gave the motion that it was time to bail.

Before heading out, Vanscoy pulled a big chalk marker from his side pouch and drew some markings on the wall so we could find the entrance easier next time on the real mission. We spent a good amount of our air in the tanks on just looking for this location. With the marking in place, we could preserve the air for the extraction of the gold. We started to swim back to the other side of the river as the current once again pulled us downstream.

I was so excited about the gold that I wasn't paying attention to my surroundings of five murky feet and because of this, I accidently bumped into one of the cables holding down one of the many floating mines in the area. The mine jerked down towards me and the little rods sticking out of the metal ball tried their best poking at me. Luckily my hard head didn't hit the cable firm enough to move it any further, so the rods missed my skull by a good quarter inch. Any closer and my big head would have detonated it.

When we were in the clear and floated far enough down the Tigress, I surfaced. Then Vanscoy surfaced immediately behind me. Having the gang waiting for us at the banks with enthusiasm was a good site to see.

CHAPTER NINETEEN

FINAL PREP

Back at our hooch we laid the two new gold bricks on the table beside the old one we had taken from Kamal Abdallah Sultan's house. They were identical. Butkus placed a bottle of Grey Goose vodka that he grabbed from the secret stash and placed it next to the gold bars and said, "let's get busy, and let's figure out how to get the rest of the gold too."

I butted in with some additional information, "the problem is we don't know how much gold there is stashed back in the cove because we couldn't see how big or how long the stack was or if there were more stacks behind it. Not that it's a problem of having stacks of gold lying around, just that we don't know what the haul will be like. Another thing we need to consider is the possibility that those visible stacks could be just a decoy and they might just be a pile of bricks or something. We will never know until the actual moment arrives when we are there stealing them."

Butkus then placed six hand carved crystal shot glasses on the table and filled them up with the premium vodka.

Then he went on to say, "that answer is easy, we take as much as there is until we fill a deuce and a half[31]. That much gold divided six ways would, well go a long way."

We decided it was time that we started working on our new list of supplies that we would need. Needing a deuce and a half truck was the first thing I mentioned, we also needed more oxygen tanks, bolt cutters, and we needed to come up with some way to transport the gold out of the cove and down to the truck waiting on the river bank. That was going to be our mission tomorrow to line up these supplies and then at night if we were lucky enough, we will pull off the heist of the century. We all grabbed a shot glass, toasted each other, and threw the drinks back.

Cole sounded as though he was out of breath as he slammed down his shot glass and his head twitched to one side as he said he could pick up a truck back at their HQ. Getting some more tanks was easy I explained to everyone, we just needed to bring some more Blue to Spc Jones at the 12C unit. This task shouldn't take us more than an hour to swing by and get the tanks. We still had more than a half tank each, we just needed some back up tanks because I knew it would take more than one trip down the river to get all the gold. The motor pool had a bunch of bolt cutters, so that was straightforward enough. The problem we have was coming up with a way to transport the gold down the river. Making numerous cycles and grabbing armfuls of gold each time didn't make sense or was very efficient. We all sat around for

---

[31] Deuce and a half - M35 - Multi-Purpose medium truck.

a while pitching different ideas, but none of them were logical or would actually work.

Then it dawned on me, I remembered back at the BIAP (Baghdad International Airport), there were a few jet airliners that had been knocked out of commission from the American's initial attack to take the airport, but they were still intact. They are sitting on the tarmac unsecured with easy access to them.

I walked over to the table and grabbed the bottle of vodka and poured a shoot into each glass. Then I motioned for everyone to pick theirs up for another toast. I explained about the aircraft to everybody and said, "what if we went on board and removed the inflatable life rafts. If I remembered correctly during all those flights I've been on before where the flight attendant pointed out the fact that they had the rafts, all you have to do was pull a string and they would inflate. If we inflated them to just the right amount, I think that it might be possible for them to float underwater stacked full of gold. Then you could just guide them down the river. We need to get at least three or four of them so we can at least experiment on one."

As I started to add up all the tasks that would need to be accomplished the next day, I calculated that we might need to put this off for at least another day or two, or at least until we could figure out if the raft floating technique would work. Besides, the day after tomorrow would be Friday night, making their security more relaxed because most of them will still be all hanging around the mosque. I picked up my glass and presented it for a toast, then we all threw back our drinks again.

Cole stood there and cusped his hands over his lips as he made sure his drink went down, and then replied with a raspy voice. "No problem, I can still get the truck and keep it for as long as we need it, it's just sitting at our HQ being unused. I'll just tell them we need it to help out with some locals transporting propane tanks to the elderly."

"Well then, let's break until tomorrow night after the sit-rep," I said.

The next day we gathered up our escorts and headed down to the BIAP. The BIAP was almost as bad as the Green Zone was as far as Army correctness. To be on the safe side, we just assumed the rules we learned over at the Green Zone also applied here. The BIAP also went all out and had set up many shopping plazas that were ran by the locals, which provided many opportunities for any military member to be separated with his money.

We informed the escorts that we had some meetings to attend and it would be unnecessary for them to be with us, so we released them to go do whatever they wanted to. I explained my only requirement for them was just to man the radio so we could call them when we were ready. The escort sergeant who was in charge of our security detail replied happily that they would be at the Post Exchange shopping and chowing down at Burger King while we did our thing. Then he put his arm on my shoulder and said, "SSG Jenks, any time you have these errand missions, please try to request us. These missions you do here at the BIAP or over at the Green Zone are definite breaks from our mundane patrols of looking for weapons in the market and dodging bullets from the bad guys." He then shook my hand and took off with his crew.

We immediately headed out to the airstrip as soon as the escorts left. Our destination was the two green and white colored commercial jetliners that sat on the tarmac. It was pretty easy to just drive up to the plane wreckage. Everybody at the BIAP has become accustomed to these planes sitting here damaged so they have now become part of the scenery on the tarmac. In addition, no one ever paid any attention to them. They just sat there unguarded. One was pretty damaged and the other was only halfway damage, that's the one we went to first and boarded it.

The plane's tail was missing, giving us easy access as it sat on its belly because the landing gears had collapsed. I couldn't tell if someone took the tail for scrap or if it was blown off during the war. It looked like it had caught on fire so I assumed the later was the cause. The fire didn't spread so the interior wasn't too bad looking. When I boarded, I looked in all the emergency areas, lifting floor panels and looking for the rafts. Luck must have been on my side today because on the first place I looked, I quickly noticed a box with a product number on it in English under the floor panel. I read further down on the box and it said, 'complies with A.D 92-14-02', then I read a little further and it said 'Life Raft Assy.' This has to be it, so I called over Carson and Brown for them to see. Since we now know where and what to look for, we were able to find all the rest of the inflatable rafts. A couple of them that we recovered were burned and a few were torn apart, but we were able to salvage five of them. They were no bigger than a footlocker size all boxed up with a chord dangling. We took those five and loaded them into our vehicle and split the scene before anybody was the wiser.

Our mission had been efficient and we had enough time to go to Burger King and get a Whopper with cheese for ourselves. Fortunately we found our escorts still there. We went on to explain to them that the plan has changed and we were now heading over to the Green Zone. They were more than happy to oblige, because to them it was another place they could spoil themselves. We finished up our crispy onion rings and washed them down with a Coke with Arabic spelling on the can, then proceeded to make the trek across town to the Green Zone.

After we arrived and dropped the escorts off at the Green Zone shopping district, we headed over to pay a visit to our boy, Spc Jones. When we pulled up, we could tell he was happy to see us. He waived for us to come on in to his work shed. We exchanged our pleasantries and he informed us that the Blue was a big hit amongst his clan. Naturally, my response was positive news for him because this time, we brought more bartering material for him to share. We were going to ask him to not only exchange the gear we had, but we also needed an extra set of oxygen tanks. We gave him two more bottles of the Blue and then we also gave him two bottles of Gray Goose vodka.

Spc Jones proclaimed that he was happier'n a preacher's son at a biker-babe rally when we presented the plunder.

I had to make up another bullshit story of why we needed them, but in the end, we were successful. I'm sure Spc Jones was thinking that he was getting the better end of this deal. This was evident because as he helped back our vehicle out, I could see his grin that was ear to ear in my side mirror.

It took a while to find our escorts because they had become tantalized with all the merchants and their commodities for sale. One merchant drew their full attention because he had pirated DVD's with all the latest movie releases, some of them still playing in the theatre back in the States. The one thing that soldiers prefer to do in their spare time is either watch a movie or play some video games. Since we were way ahead of schedule on today's mission, we let them shop for about another forty-five minutes before we informed them it was time to head back to the FOB.

Thursday evening was now upon us and after participating in the sit-rep, we proceeded to take out one of the rafts and started studying it as it lied at our feet. The instructions on the raft were all pictures and they didn't make any sense to us. I was kicking myself for sleeping through all those pre-flight safety talks. We finally decided we just need to pull the string to see what would happen. Brown gave it one good pull and within five seconds, the thing became animated as it hissed and stretched out on the floor until it became fully inflated.

"That was kind of cool," Vanscoy said, "it looks like it can hold at least ten people in this raft, if not more. That means we can fit a lot of fucking gold in there."

I did some quick math in my head and responded to everyone with, "if these rafts can hold ten people at an average of two hundred pounds a person, then this thing can float two thousand pounds. We have four of them left, so your right Vanscoy, we can get a shit load of gold in there. That is if no one beat us to the punch and there is still a shit load of gold available steal. We can probably managed two rafts per trip, so we'll wind up making a total of two trips. If we are lucky, we can haul out at least eight to ten thousand pounds of gold."

"I see a problem with you plan," Butkus said. These rafts need to be rolled up in their deflated state in order to get them across the river, underwater. You can't put the gold in the raft while it's rolled up, so you need to inflate the raft in order to stack gold in it. You will need to pull the string once you're in position under water in order to stretch the raft out to place the gold inside. The problem is once you pull that string, that thing is gonna inflate and shoot to the surface like a rocket. Apparently there is no way for us to control the air flow for inflation in these stupid things."

"That's a good point. I've been thinking about that and believe it or not, there is an easy answer for that. All we need to do is make sure the raft is tucked way back in the enclave by the gold and close the gate before we pull the string. Then when we do pull it, it will just shoot to the top of the enclave and the gate will prevent it from escaping out. Then we can

Voodoo Gold by James H Jenks

start stacking gold in it and sooner or later it will start sinking. That is when we will know we're full and time to float it out. We should bring a big sharp long knife to poke a hole in it just in case if it does go hog wild or anything."

Sgt Brown now butted in with his two cents, "OK, let's say that everything goes as planned and we extract all this gold from the secured location without being detected. Where are we going to put all of this gold once we have it? If we capture as much gold as you say there is, we're going to have a hard time hiding it. We're going to have a lot of explaining to do if anyone pops their head in our hooch and catches a glimpse of a mammoth pile of gold."

"There's an easy answer for that one too. Our product area is off limits to anybody not in PSYOP because of the sensitive material in there. Some of the literature we have locked up in there are actually secret documents. For example, the 'Muqtada al-Sadr has been arrested' flyers we have sitting on the shelves in there for the day that mission might go down. Imagine if anybody were to get hold of those before they were authorized to be released. That is why even the SCO or Sgt Major cannot enter our premise without our permission and they know that. That is also why we are here in this bombed out warehouse and the rest of 2nd CAV are set up in the nice barracks." I then picked up one of the bricks of gold and held it out as if I were presenting it and continued to explain. "This brick of gold that is six inches long, three inches wide and about a half inch thick weighs seven pounds. Now, if I have done my calculation right, eight thousand pounds of gold would only take up a space that would be twenty-one inches long by twenty-four inches wide by twenty-four inches high. So I say we just stack it here in our product area, but of course we need to hide it under a tarp or something just to be safe."

Butkus came back over after he excused himself for a minute while he retrieved another bottle for a toast. This time he grabbed the Blue! He continued to pour a full serving into each shot glass, and then distributed them to each of us for a toast. "OK, this time for real. Tomorrow we will pull off the heist of the century." We all saluted our glasses as we pinged them together and then slammed down the contents.

CHAPTER TWENTY

GOING FOR THE GOLD

Having a few drinks from last night made us a little impeded, but it didn't prevent us from getting out of bed early, because today was the day for the heist. Our excitement for the day was extremely high, but it was also met with the loll of doing nothing except sitting around and waiting in anticipation of the sun to go down. I was consumed with running the plan over in my head a million times, trying to anticipate any unforeseen situation.

The only thing that was successful in distracting me from the insanity was by playing *Grand Theft Auto Miami* on the *Xbox* while waiting for the big moment to arrive. Eventually after many hours and smashing as many cars as possible while playing the video game, the sun finally went down. With dusk upon us, we all looked at each other and with a simultaneous agreement, we knew it was time to put our plan into action. Nobody said anything to each other at this point, but instead threw on their gear, buddy checked each other, and then seized their positions in the vehicles.

Cole and his crew are to follow us to the drop zone in the deuce and a half.

Left sitting on the table in our hooch were the cigars that Jassim awarded me. They would be waiting there as a treat for us when we returned from this mission on a successful note. Hopefully Cole would precipitate with some of his Blue during the occasion.

We rolled out the front gate and I called in our departure to the TOC, "this is Voodoo Two, departing three." There weren't as many people out on the streets as there was the other night. I assumed it was because they were all at home spending time with their families as we do back in the States with our families on Sunday night. This made our travel to our destination just that much easier.

Eventually, we made it to the drop off zone without incident or being noticed. Once again, nobody had to say anything to each other as we had already done this drill before. When Vanscoy and I eventually slipped on our gear, we gave the thumbs up to everybody, grabbed our rafts, and waded into the water until we were submerged.

We had a harder time swimming across the Tigress underwater with the rolled up rafts, but the drag from them wasn't too bad. The visibility was still the same, murky and dark, but we were confident in our direction. Ultimately, we hit the wall and started floating along side of it until we hit the chalk mark that Vanscoy previously made. This was our indication to pull out the bolt cutters. We located the padlock on the gate and with one swift motion, we snapped off the lock. Then we swung open the gate and swam inside, shutting the gate behind us as planned. As we swam closer to the gold, we could see that there was a lot more than a few tons, this thing went way back and there had to be at least four or five truck loads worth. I started brushing all the sediment off the stacks to see if it was all actually gold or just a decoy. My heart started pounding fast and I had to watch my breathing as the shine from the gold started illuminating the cove from our underwater light. This scene was straight out from some Ft Knox movie, stacks upon stacks of gold! I took one look at Vanscoy through the murky water and I could see that he too was trying to contain his excitement.

The time had come for us to stop admiring our find and start getting to work. Vanscoy put his raft to the side for later use while I prepped mine for inflation. Vanscoy pulled out a K-bar knife and had it at the ready just in case if the inflation went haywire. I pulled the string and the raft instantly inflated and shot to the roof. I had a sign of relief when it worked out the way I imagined it. There was an explosion of bubbles that I didn't calculate, but luckily they dissipated before they rolled out of the enclave. The raft sat snug up against the roof and didn't budge. I pointed toward the gold and we both started slipping bars between the gaps on the rafts that was pressed against the roof. Twenty minutes later the raft was getting full. Just when it looked as if we couldn't get another bar in, the raft started to sink from the ceiling. We removed a couple of bars and then the raft floated at equal buoyancy. We pulled it forward to make room for the second raft and repeated the process. When both rafts were full, we nodded to each other that it was time to go. We then tethered the raft to our bodies and to each other and started swimming back across the river.

One of the encasement skins that the raft was rolled up in before it became inflated happen to unattached itself and without us noticing, started to slowly rise to the surface. Luckily this overlooked skin was at a slow rise to the surface and wouldn't make its appearance until after we made it through the maze of underwater mines. The underwater mines presented a new challenge for us that we didn't take into consideration. We now each possessed a weighed down raft full of gold that we had to maneuver through. We both had to take our turn swimming through the grid pattern that was created by the wires anchoring down the mines. We accomplished this by kicking our fins until we had the raft in one of the formed grids, then we let the river's current float us down to the next grid, and then kick our fins again in order to advance to the next grid. We repeated the processes over and over until we were clear of the water mines. Then we kick our fins as hard as we could to swim across the river underwater. We weren't swimming as fast as last time we crossed back, because even though the rafts were at a neutral weight, they were really dragging us down. I knew at this point we would overshoot the pick up spot, but I just didn't know by how much. All I could do was to continually kick my fins the hardest I have ever done before.

Ultimately we hit the other side and emerged in a cove. We pulled in the rafts as far as we could and tied them off to some palm trees. I knew we had overshot the pickup spot, but I didn't know if we were a hundred yards or a mile. I had no idea where in the fuck we were. I told Vanscoy to wait by the gold, stay out of sight, and I'll run up the side of the embankment towards the pickup point until I find the guys.

As I was running up the riverbank toward the crew, I appreciated the fact that at least we were clean out of sight from where we had stolen the gold. I already started doing my own mental celebration because we made a clean getaway. Then I had a sense of despair when I started to hear in the far distance the guards from the site began yelling at each other. Not too long after that, gunfire started going off. My mind stopped celebrating and shifted to problem resolution mode. I immediately knew that something was up, we needed to get the hell out of there with the gold immediately. The only solace I had was if I could here the guards, then I couldn't be too far down stream.

I traveled up the river on its banks as fast as I could run. Running in the dark while being lost, deviating from the plan, and hearing a lot of weapons being fired where I was a few minutes ago made me think I really fucked up. I was about to lose it and start panicking, when I luckily ran into the crew. Now I could get some answers and get the plan back on track. I could see Cole looking through some binoculars and shouting something at Brown. I yelled over to Cole, "what the fuck man, what the hell is going on?"

"I don't know, you tell me! All I know is we better get the hell out of here," Cole yelled back at me. "Where is the fucking gold?"

"We overshot about a half mile, Vanscoy is down range waiting on us with the gold," I said. "Let's get in the fucking truck and go get our bounty."

Cole shouted back, "we better go lights out. They may not hear us crank the engines on the trucks over all the gunfire, but they will definitely see any lights if we turn them on."

We all immediately scrambled to our vehicles and drove away towards our gold. When I jumped in our HMMWV with my guys, I yelled up to Brown who was in his turret and asked what the hell happened. Carson was too busy trying to drive away with his night vision goggles on to say anything.

"Fucking eh man," Brown shouted down from the turret. "Cole and I were waiting for you to materialize from the river. We started to hear some shouting from across the river that caught our attention so Cole grabbed some binoculars to take a look. We could see a guard shining a high-powered flashlight at the river. The guard started yelling and soon a bunch of other guards joined him at the riverbank. Then the searchlights came on and it was directed right where you were supposed to be."

"Holy Crap, this is all news to me," I said with a look of confusion.

"Here's the best part, Cole continued to watch through the binoculars without trying to panic, but we watched one of the guards grab a long pole and he fished out an object from the river. This object was the casing from the raft that

228   Voodoo Gold by James H Jenks

apparently floated to the surface. Cole and I knew we were all busted at this point."

"Holy fuck, I never realized that happened."

"Well it did and that's when the guards pointed their weapons at the river and started firing full thirty round clips at the water. Cole was freaked the fuck out. I charged my weapon and wanted to light them up from where we where. Cole was able to calm us down and explain to all of us that you two should be down far enough to where the bullets wouldn't hurt you. Cole explained that high caliber bullets like the 7.62MM round can only travel about five or six feet in the water before they disintegrate."

"Good thing he had his calm and wits about him."

"Yeah, but if they started to dive in to the river, I was then going to light them up no matter what. After about ten minutes of them continually firing into the river without your bodies ever surfacing, Cole proclaimed that you two must have been able to get out of there safely. We just had to be patient and wait for you two."

A few minutes later we pulled up in our trucks where Vanscoy was hiding in the cove. We all immediately went down to the rafts and started cross loading the gold from the rafts to the truck.

We didn't say a word to each other mostly because there was no time for talking. We wanted to load all of the gold as fast as we could and get the hell out of Dodge before the bad guys started searching the river. We started grabbing the bars by the arm loads and running up and down the trail between the truck and the river as fast as we could, but we could only grab about ten bars at a time.

A lot of action was still going on with the guards on the other side of the river. It was just a matter of time before they did venture out. More search lights kicked on and they began to scan the river and the beams started to creep up to our location.

There was a lot of fucking gold, and everybody started to drag down and run out of steam from the laborious work of transporting it out, but the adrenaline kept everybody going at full speed. As we neared the end and loaded the last piece, I said, "there is no way we are going for a second round of gold and we need to get the fuck out of here right now." Besides, we had a lot of fucking gold already. We had around four tons of gold if all my previous calculations were correct.

"What about the rafts," shouted Butkus.

"Fuck the rafts, push them into the river and let them float down. There's no evidence that will tie us to them and hopefully they'll be downstream many of miles before someone finds them."

We then all jumped into our perspective vehicles, drove with our lights out until we hit the pavement, and eventually made our way back to the FOB. Looking at Carson as we drove back, I could see he was nervous as fuck and he was all covered in sweat. I, was also nervous, but I was too worn out to think about it. Moving that amount of gold in that short amount of time can take a toll on you. We were all definitely going to need a drink when we arrive back at our pad so we can all calm our nerves, not to mention a victory cigar.

When we rolled through the front gate, we waved at the guard. He sleepily waved back at us, not noticing that we were covered in sweat in the middle of the night. He had no idea what we had just went through and no one was the wiser that we had around four tons of gold in the back of the truck.

We backed the truck in next to our restricted area where we kept our PSYOP products and we repeated the processes by unloading the truck as fast as we loaded it.

At around two hundred hours we finally hid all the stacks of gold underneath our PSYOP product. We were all beat and ready for the sack, but before we all went to our racks, I requested for Cole to pour us all a shot of the Blue, and he obliged. I tried to pass out some cigars, but everybody was too tired to smoke one and passed on them, so I went on to present a toast instead. "Here is to being stinking filthy rich." Everyone raised their glasses and cheered while we drank the content.

"The next thing we need to do is see if we can get this gold back to the States. Tomorrow I will start working on the extraction plan, in the meantime we need to get back to the real business for a while and let things cool down before we make another move."

Cole couldn't resist pouring another round for everybody, so we all clinked our glasses, consumed the contents again, and then went straight to bed.

CHAPTER TWENTY ONE

SMUGGLING THE GOLD

We are way behind on the Battalion level PSYOP initiatives because of the gold extraction mission. Today is our first day back, where we can be fully focused on our real jobs and today is the day for us to catch up. We missed a few meetings with the political leaders in Sadr City and our dissemination products are backing up.

First stop on my list was to my favorite restaurant, owned by Jassim Al-Mohammed. He always enjoyed me coming by for a visit and a smoke. Though my visit today would consist of more than just a visit and a smoke, I had an idea of how Jassim could help in getting the gold out of Iraq. I wanted to test my idea with him and see if this would be an option for us.

With Milik in the vehicle and our escorts following us, we drove through the city tossing out our product on our way to Jassim's place. Most of the time when we did this the kids would just run behind us and collect whatever we threw out. They collected them as souvenirs and kept as many as they could gather for themselves. This also meant the targeted audience who we prepared to deliver this literature to never actually received the intended message.

When we finally arrived at the restaurant, Jassim was standing out front rubbing his belly and smoking a cigarette. I could see he was as happy to see us as always. He gave his staff the gesture to bring some goat meat and bread sandwiches to our security element, and then he gestured for us to follow him back to his favorite table so we could talk. After we went through our normal pleasantries and had a few bites of his food, I decided to get straight to the point.

"Jassim, can you still make a journey to Turkey and deposit money into your account?"

Jassim flashed me a cautious look. "I suppose I could, but I would not feel comfortable traveling across Iraq right now by myself with money."

"What if we provided you an escort?"

"What do you mean?"

"Well, what if you were to ride with me in my vehicle and we'll have another vehicle fully loaded with weapons with us, and we drive up to Turkey together? When we get into Turkey, you bring us to your bank so we can deposit some money. We will of course need to open our own account, but you will be generously compensated for your efforts."

"What should I say if anyone asks why I am with you, a construction and restaurant owner sitting in a military vehicle on his way to Turkey is not normal?"

"First of all, you know from all the previous times you have crossed the Turkey boarder that it is pretty open and not guarded much. They only make the semi-trucks transporting goods go through customs. Besides, we're in a military vehicle, so I doubt anybody would stop us to ask why you're with us. But in the slim chance that somebody does ask, we'll just tell them you are one of our interpreters. Remember we are part of Special Op's so even the US military usually doesn't push the issues with us. I don't foresee any Iraqi or Turkish authorities wanting to know our business because they are accustom to us running around with weapons and all. But once again, I have an answer for them if they do. Since CA is with us, we'll just tell them we're part of the Coalition Provisional Authority. Everybody loves the CPA because they hand out all the money and no one would want to impede that."

"You have an answer for everything my friend, so can you tell me how much money are we talking about?"

"We'll get to that in a bit my good friend Jassim, but for now all I need to know is if you can do this favor for us."

"Sure, I suppose, but it will take about two days to drive there. I guess I can let my cousin know that we will be spending the night at his house. His place is where I usually stay at on my way to Turkey because he lives about sixty kilometers south of the city Zakho where I cross into Turkey."

"Sounds like we have a deal then. Before I go any further, do you swear on the Koran that this conversation will not be repeated to anybody?"

"Jenks, you are like a son to me and you have provided me with a lot of opportunity, so I will do as you ask. I swear on the Koran that this will not be shared with anybody."

"OK, then. So let me ask, instead of cash being deposited, can we deposit gold into an account in Turkey?"

"Yes, I suppose so as long as we schedule it in advance."

"We will have about four tons of gold that we'll want you to schedule a deposit for and we will give you five percent of the deposited amount. That should be enough for you to live like a king here in Iraq or even move to the USA if you desire."

"Praise Allah," Jassim responded. "Where did the gold come from?"

"We took it from Saddam."

"Even better! This is definitely a blessing. I was getting worried about my workers in the construction business. The work you have provided to us so far has helped, but it's not at the level before the war. I have a lot of families that depend on me for their livelihood and they are starting to get wrestles. This will allow me to furnish them with their needs until the business picks back up and becomes self sufficient again."

"I don't know exactly when we will go, but it will be soon and it will be at a moment's notice. So I suggest you start making your contacts and connections for us now."

After we finished our discussion and consumed all the sandwiches, we jumped back into our vehicles and finished off our days work which consisted of throwing out more literature on the ground and visiting the other intelligence points. Though, not much intelligence was gathered, because my concentration was focused on constructing my plan to transport the gold.

After we made it back to the FOB safely, I told Brown and Carson that I only had an hour before the sit-rep and I needed to get my report done. This request must have gone over Brown's head because he immediately had some questions about our ability to transport the gold to Turkey. He asked how in the hell are we going to get all the gold up to Turkey without SFC Hunter and Cpt Barker noticing our absence. He continued on and pointed out, that even if all the connections made by Jassim went smoothly, it would take us at least three days to make the journey there and back. He was adamant that there was no way we could just disappear for three to four days.

Remaining calm and collected because I always figure shit out sooner or later, I looked straight at Brown and responded in an encouraging manner and said, "I'm still working on that, hopefully a solution will present itself soon."

"We need a fucking miracle," Carson butted in as he turned on the *xbox* to finish of his level in his game.

"Now listen you two, I may not have a solution right this second, but I have learned to just think positive and Karma will always present itself. Now let me get back to my report."

As soon as I finished my sentence, Cpt Barker, SFC Hunter, and Spc McClure came barreling in with their vehicle right up to our front door. They were quick to dismount out of the vehicle and demand my attention without delay.

"Jenks! Get the fuck out here," SFC Hunter yelled as he pounded on our locked front door.

Good thing the product shack was locked up so he wouldn't wander in there. We had all the gold hidden underneath the PSYOP product so that no one would ever notice. Though with SFC Hunter, you could never be too safe. Especially when he was in these types of modes, they were very unpredictable.

I tried stepping out of our house to confront them and keep them by their vehicle, but as soon as I opened the door, all three of them came barreling in. SFC Hunter's face was red and I could practically see steam coming out of his ears. I could tell that Cpt Barker was encouraging him on to lay into me about something.

"I've had it up to here with you because your reports have been thin for the last few days. What the fuck have you been doing the last week? It's obvious that some of your missions have been performed half assed."

I butted in with my normal wittiness to try to distract him as I normally do and said, "I'm really trying to use both cheeks."

SFC Hunter gave me the death stare, "I'm about ready to put Brown in charge and have you take over Spc McClure job. When your reports are light on intelligence, it makes me look bad in front of the full bird colonel. You've got about five seconds to tell me why I shouldn't relieve you of your duty."

I stood there at a lost of words for a few seconds because I knew he was right, as far as not getting much done the last few days. The reports were light, but what can you do when you're busy stealing gold from Saddam's stash?

I needed an excuse to get myself out of this jam. Should I include them in on the heist? Though, that thought went away as fast as it came because I knew they couldn't be bribed. Should I just tell them to fuck off because I did have all the gold, but then how would I continue my extraction mission if I were to be relieved of duty? Should I butt stroke them to the head with my weapon and toss them in a back alley, but I knew I wasn't that kind of person. I was just about to go into panic mode when I had a revelation that would solve all my problems. This revelation would get me out of this bind and provide a solution for us to be able to travel to Turkey.

I leaned over to SFC Hunter and said in a secret tone, "I didn't want to report anything just yet because I haven't been able to verify, but I have been investigating into a possible location of where some weapons of mass destruction might be located. I wanted to make sure that they were there before I called you guys in so as to not make you look bad if I was wrong."

Cpt Barker jumped in and asked SFC Hunter to take a step back and let me explain myself. I knew these guys were power hungry and not experienced in the field anymore. I told them about Maqtada, the individual I meet earlier who was telling everybody he knew where the weapons were, but for a fee. I still had his contact information and I knew I could get a meeting set up.

Cpt Barker was taking the bait just as I anticipated he would. He started demanding to know everything about my intelligence gathering. "Who have you told about this information, anybody else except us?"

Coming up with another line to pull him in further, I said, "no one, you're the first. Like I previously told you, I wanted to make sure this information was accurate before I pulled anybody else in."

Cpt Barker stood there for a minute as I watched the wheels in his head start to spin. This was actually a long moment because it has been awhile since that department of his brain has worked. Finally, he responded with a cognitive thought that would continue this diversion I started. "I want you to set up a meet tomorrow with all of us so I can ask this informer of yours some questions."

"I can do that, but it will have to be the next day because I know he will be out of town tomorrow." I told them that because I needed at least a day to set up the other part to my plan with Jassim so he could get me to Turkey. I also never found out from Maqtada if his brother would accept five hundred bucks for the upfront fee that I suggested back then. I would have to convince Maqtada that this was the best offer they were going to get and they should capitalize on it now.

I continued on explaining the situation to the two, especially about needing some bribe money, and I acted eager in helping them. "The guy speaks English, but you can use my interpreter Milik just in case. There is another thing that has slowed me down in getting the intel to you. Maqtada the informant wants five hundred dollars up front and a portion of the reward when you find the weapons of mass destruction."

"I have some funds left over form our last request to pay an informant that I can access to cover his request, so that won't be a problem," Cpt Barker replied. He wasn't going to let something like five hundred dollars get in between him and fame.

"I will let you know first thing Thursday morning, if not sooner when the meet will be between you two and Maqtada. I hope you can forgive me for not having a lot of PSYOP information in the last few days, but as you can see I have been busy trying to get some hard information about weapons of mass destruction."

"If this proves to be good info, I can see the investment you have made. Also, do not let anyone know about this just yet because I think it would be a good idea for us to uncover this intelligence before the higher ups get hold of it. Because if they do, they will claim credit for themselves and rub you out."

"Good idea. Mum's the word for now."

They got back into their vehicle and left as fast as they showed up. Though this time when they left, they were actually in a good mood for once and not annoyed at me. They both actually shook my hand when they left, a first.

Brown and Carson stood there in the living room with their mouths wide open. Brown eventually was able to close his mouth and respond to the situation. "Holy fucking shit, how fucking lucky are you? I guess that was the miracle we were looking for."

"Yeah," I said back to them with my grin that was from ear to ear. "Now we just need to find that son of a bitch and let him know that these guys want to go on a goose chase with him."

CHAPTER TWENTY TWO

WEAPONS OF MASS DESTRUCTION

The next day I told Milik that his main mission of the day would be to find Maqtada. Actually, it would be the only mission of the day for him. I advised him that we would be at Jassim's restaurant around thirteen hundred hours for an update on Maqtada's whereabouts.

We, on the other hand had plenty of missions to perform today. The first mission consisted of us distributing flyers about Paul Bremer's plan to bring in a grass root election. He was the head of the Coalition Provisional Authority and this was one of his social experiments. He always wore a suit and combat boots to make the soldiers think he was one of us, but we knew he was just another bureaucrat trying to make a name for himself. Paul Bremer's election plan is to have the locals elect their village representatives, who would then compete for a council seat at a higher governmental tier. This elected council will make up the initial government for Iraq. So for the next few hours, we just drove around Sadr City tossing stacks of flyers at strategic points around the city for people to take and read. The looks on the locals faces when they read the literature was about as exciting as ours. They knew that this election would either be rigged or be puppets for the USA.

When we finally arrived at the restaurant at thirteen hundred hours, Milik was there waiting for us. Milik informed us that he had Maqtada waiting for our arrival at his house.

Before I was able to give the "move out" order, Milik approached me and asked if I would follow him over to the front of the vehicle. He wanted me out of listening distance from everybody else because he had a serious question he wanted to ask me. "I have been helping you out and keeping quiet through all of this, and I wanted to know if I will be receiving any of the gold that you have? I think from all my efforts and not telling anyone, I should get a cut."

"Milik you son of a bitch. Between the family that led us to this information and Jassim wanting his share for his efforts, I don't know if we can afford any more expenses. We all need to be fucking rich when we get back to the States."

Milik's expression quickly changed from an anticipated look to a look of despair. I don't think he caught onto my sarcasm. I could tell he was about to cry or get angry so I quickly let him in on my joke. "You fucking idiot, of course you get a cut. What did you expect dickhead? A lot of this would not have been possible without you. So fucking relax and take us to Maqtada's house."

Milik's frown turned upside down and he had a big smile on his face. "Thank you SSG Jenks! Thank you! I will always be indebted to you!"

With Milik excited to continue helping, we all jumped back in our vehicle and our escorts followed us across town to our destination. I was also now expected to be excited and pretend that I was interested in Maqtada's information when we would arrive at his residence. I have never taken any acting classes before, but it seems that ever since I've been deployed over here, I had acquired quite the skill for it. Knowing that his information was bogus, I needed to portray that we were actually interested and wanted him to take our leaders to the promised site.

When we arrived at Maqtada's house, we left the escorts outside to watch the area. When we walked up to the door, it suddenly swung open as he invited us in. He was waiting there for us with tea already prepared for all. We walked in and sat down in his living room as he served the hot tea. Even before I could take a sip of my tea that he just presented, he exclaimed, "do you have my money?"

"Slow down big boy. Here's the deal, tomorrow at this same time I want you to meet us at my office at Camp Marlboro so you can speak with my boss who will have the money. Just check in at the front gate at thirteen hundred hours and I will come and get you and bring you to our conference room. Your job is to convince these people you know the whereabouts of the weapons of mass destruction. If you do not convince them, they will not go and therefore you get no money. So I would suggest you have map points, your story straight, and anything else you might have to prove your point. If they are convinced, I'm sure they'll want you to take them to the location. Do you understand?"

"Yes," he replied.

"Now for my own curiosity, how far is this place you will take them to if you all do go?"

"It's about a day's drive from here. You already have some troops over where this place is. It's by Lake Habbaniyah, but not at the air base, it's further in the desert at a secret location."

Taking a sip from my tea glass, pausing for a second as I calculated his information, I responded with, "so I guess it would take a day of driving to get there and a day of driving to get back. Then I would assume it would only take a day or two for all of you to uncover the weapons of mass destruction."

"Yes that seems about right," replied Maqtada.

"Will we need to bring any special equipment in order to help out with the search?

"No, the funds will be sufficient. After my bother-in-law is satisfied with the payment, he will escort us to the location. Once at the location, we all can dig with the shovels that are already there and uncover the cache."

"Well OK then, unless there is anything else I need to know, we will see you tomorrow at this time at Camp Marlboro. As a reminder Maqtada, I'm sure they'll have maps for you to point out the location or at least point it out nearby, so be ready to guide them."

We all finished our tea and left Maqtada house feeling satisfied that we were going to pull this enchanted mission off. I felt a little better knowing that US troops were going to be in the vicinity, just in case something funny happened during this escapade. But then again, I knew that these two might be too stubborn to let anybody know what they were up to in order to avoid sharing information.

We jumped back in our vehicle and devoted our attention back to our original mission of handing out the flyers. In order to help accelerate this process of handing out flyers, I threw the remaining full stacks in the middle of the street and watched the oncoming traffic try to dodge the piles. Within about five minutes, every kid in Sadr City swarmed in on the flyers, stopped all traffic, and then started running away with their arms full with the prized literature. As the last kid ran off with a few shreds left over from the ravenous flyers, traffic resumed and everything went back to normal. I did this expedited process because we still needed to stop by Cpt Barker's office to inform him that the meet is set up at our location. The clock was running out and I needed to make sure I had enough time to make it to the sit-rep.

The three of us walked into Cpt Barker's office while our security guards decided to take a nap in their vehicle while they waited for us. As we walked in to the Brigade TOC, we found Cpt Barker sitting at his desk with his head bobbing back and forth as he tried to fight off the sandman. When he finally notices us as we approached his desk, he started to try to look busy. He started pretending that he was reading some emails on his laptop while he looked at some paperwork. He looked at me and acted as if he was way to busy to talk, but would give me a minute because he knew why I was there. I explained the conversation that I just had with Maqtada and informed him with the updates. He was in all smiles with this information and he even thanked me again.

The Captains chest was puffed out as he said, "thank you for setting this up. I think we're on our way to get some recognition for our hard work here. If we're lucky, maybe one day we will get to meet President Bush from all of this."

"I'm sure we will," I replied. "I'm sure we will. Ooh, and don't forget the money. He won't talk unless you have the money."

"Don't worry about that Jenks, that's not your concern."

"All right then, see you tomorrow."

The next day, thirteen hundred hours came pretty fast and the next bullshit session was about to begin. Cpt Barker was sitting at the conference room desk along with SFC Hunter. The funny thing is they were actually still being nice to me. I think I was becoming one of their favorites, but only if they knew my real intentions. I had Brown waiting at the front gate for Maqtada. When he showed up as prescribed, Brown escorted him to the interrogation room we were in and introduced Maqtada to our group.

Cpt Barker was pretty quick to take over the conversation and to make sure I knew he was in charge. SFC Hunter was right alongside of Cpt Barker being his heel like a dog.

"Hey Jenks, why don't you go and get us some coffee?" Cpt Barker demanded because he was trying to set the stage of him being the person in charge.

I smiled back knowing that as long as they took the bait I was going to be rich beyond my wildest dreams. I bit my tongue and swallowed some pride and took advantage of this unforeseen opportunity.

I went into the kitchen and took out two mugs for coffee. I looked around to make sure no one was looking. When the coast was all clear, I stuck them down my pants one at a time and scratched my butt with the rim of the mugs. I then filled them both with coffee, and was even nice enough to make sure they had cream and sugar.

I came back with the cups of coffee and served them to SFC Hunter and Cpt Barker with a smile. They already had a map pinned up on the wall and Maqtada was pointing out the location of where they were supposed to go. Knowing he wouldn't say a word to them unless he received his payment, I leaned over to Milik and asked, "have they already exchange the money?"

"Yep," he replied with a smile.

Maqtada went on to explain how his brother-in-law had seen the weapons and described how they were stacked before they were buried. He explained in detail how the chemical warheads were laid on their side in wooden crates six wide. Each one was individually wrapped in cellophane, padded in amongst each other, and then topped off with another wooden crate to start the procedure again. The stacks were four high with a black tarp as the final layer before they were covered in dirt. Each cache had four stacks. SFC Hunter was quickly writing all the information down.

"Do you think you could escort these people to the location of where the weapons are buried?" I asked.

"I could," Maqtada replied, "but I know my brother-in-law will want at least two thousand American dollars in payment before I can take you there."

"I just gave you five hundred dollars," cried Cpt Barker.

"Yes, but that was for me to pay for my expenses in order to provide this information to you. My brother-in-law has his own expense and he needs to feed his family."

"There will be plenty of food for his family when we uncover the weapons because he will get rewarded with the bounty."

Maqtada responded with, "yes, he will be mighty grateful when that happens, but they are hungry now and he has assured me that for two thousand American dollars, he will save the find for you gentlemen. He has been guarding this place ever since Saddam told him to guard it and not to leave. Saddam is no longer paying him, but he has continued to perform his duty. He will quit his post and turn it over to you if you pay him the salary he deserves for guarding the weapons."

"Insha'Allah," I said. "Cpt Barker, they have needs. That is why they are focused on such small amounts of money. They just need enough funds to get by. Besides, all he wants is his paycheck that he deserves for guarding the weapons."

"OK, OK," Cpt Barker said, as if he just lost the argument. "Are you sure your brother-in-law will take all of us there and we'll find the weapons?"

"Yes, he has been guarding the place ever since and no one has even been close to it. It's only been a few weeks since he realized that he can earn money for this information and you are the first to act upon it."

Cpt Barker processed that piece of information and he looked as if he was doing some advance math in his head and then he said, "you will take us to your brother-in-law and we will make a payment to him. I expect the two of you to guide us to the location and help us uncover the weapons."

"Insha'Allah," Maqtada replied.

"Do you know where the Army base is by the bombed out UN building?" asked Cpt Barker.

"Yes, I do," Maqtada replied.

"You will meet us there in two days before noon, and you will ride with us up to the location and help out. Just check in at the front gate and we will come and get you just as you did here. SSG Jenks, can you escort this gentleman out to the front gate and meet us back here when you're done."

"Yes Sir," I said and I even gave him a cautious proper salute.

I took Maqtada out to the front and we said our goodbyes, then I walked back to the conference room. Now was the time for me to put on my acting job again and pretend that everything they stated to me, I would be appreciative.

"Good job SSG Jenks. Looks like we're going to have to put you in for a medal."

"That would be awesome Sir!"

"We'll be gone for a couple of days and I don't think we'll need your services out in the field. I think the two of us, along with Maqtada and his brother-in-law will be sufficient in the recovery of the weapons of mass destruction, so why don't you take a few days off here while we're gone because you deserve it."

"Wow no missions and no sit-rep for a few days, this is great, now my team and I can beat that stupid game, GTA Miami."

"And SSG, when we get back with the weapons, I'll make sure you get a chance to shake the Presidents hand too."

"Cool Beans," I replied.

Then they left the room all in high spirits and headed back to their post.

I immediately rushed back to our hooch and assembled the gang. Brown, Carson, and Civil Affairs stood there wide eyed in anticipation of my information. "Game on! We leave in two days, we'll need to get to the restaurant tomorrow and let Jassim know so he can get his contacts in line and be prepared. We'll load the deuce and a half tomorrow night with all the gold and leave first thing the next morning. I know it is supposed to be relatively a safe drive to the border, but we should bring more than just a full combat load with us just to be on the safe side. This is it guys, this is actually going to happen."

CHAPTER TWENTY THREE

TURKEY BOUND

The sun was thinking about making an appearance for the new day and we had already polished off a pot of coffee. Most of us didn't get much sleep last night as the anticipation for the morning kept us awake. The truck was loaded with the gold, stacked under PSYOP product and other miscellaneous items. The gold was well hidden where no one could see it, even if they decided to give it thorough look. Civil Affairs was behind the wheel of the truck and we were in our HMMWV with Milik. We were all ready to roll. We already had prearranged with the SCO that we were all going to be over at our CA/PSYOP HQ for a few days conducting some training. This was the perfect alibi because he couldn't track it and this is also what SFC Hunter and Cpt Barker stated for their excuse to be out of the pocket for a few days.

We called in our departure as we left the front gate and headed over to the restaurant to pick up Jassim as planned. When we arrived, he was waiting out front with presents as usual. He had a bunch of flat bread and goat meat packed in a basket for our travels and he made sure we knew it. He figured these treats would be much better than the MRE's we had. Though Jassim hadn't been introduced to the cheese and crackers yet, so I could see his point of not knowing the greatness of our MRE's

We also took this stop as an opportunity to load different codes into our radios. I had saved some outdated codes from a few weeks back on a spare modular when they were issued at that time. The communication people made us load new codes in our radio once a week. I wanted to reload these old codes that were outdated so no one could hear our transmissions.

When Jassim was all situated in the HMMWV with his basket of treats, he went on to explain that it would probably take a day and a half to get to Turkey with the truck fully loaded with the gold. We didn't want to break a two and a half ton axel with four tons of gold, so we needed to take it easy. The bank transaction should only take a few hours because they have a crew on standby waiting for us. I had the foresight to have Jassim set up the gold exchange to where we could arrive unannounced. They were also under the impression that it was Jassim coming in for the transaction. They knew nothing about the military making a visit. The bank crew would be called in for the exchange after Jassim's arrival. This was safer so they couldn't anticipate our arrival and ambush us. When talking about this much gold, anything is possible. After our money is secured in our new bank accounts, we could make our journey back in about a day's time.

The plan was to travel to this village where Jassim knew a couple of people, including his cousin. They had already agreed to let us park the vehicles in their garage so we could remain inconspicuous. They too were not informed about the gold, they were under the impression that we were just helping Jassim travel to Turkey for business. After we all had a good night's sleep, we would travel across the border the next day into Turkey to convert the gold into cash which would be deposited into a bank account run by a western bank. By the time we finished out our business there, it would probably be getting close to dark and not safe to travel back into Iraq. We would then be forced to spend the night there in a five star hotel and party our asses off.

Even though our destination in Turkey's upper class tourist district would be a relative safe place for us, I figured we need to be cautious and be on the safe side. Continuing to provide security for the vehicle would be the smart thing to do. That meant we would have to take turns while half of us enjoyed the spoils and the other half lounged in the vehicles. So technically we could only party our asses off half way.

The next day, all we would have to do is drive back and pretend like nothing ever happened. After we were all deployed back to the States from our tour of duty, all we would have to do is travel back over to Turkey as tourist and collect the cash. With Turkey being part of the Euro Zone now, we could drive to Greece and take a ferry to Italy without any customs or boarder crossings. From Italy, we could drive right into Switzerland and deposit our money there for safe keeping.

As we traveled down the road, we passed the time by talking about what we would do with our share of the money. This time instead of fantasizing about what we might do, we actually put some thought into it since we now actually possessed the gold.

Carson wanted us to know how he was going to buy about five different motorcycles. He listed the Yamaha R1 as his top choice, then quickly changed his mind to a Moto Guzzi like the one they used in the *Matrix* movie. Then he changed his mind once again and declared, "with all this gold we have, I'm going to buy a motorcycle company and produce the fastest production bike available. Think about it, Carson Motor Works and my signature bike will be the C1. Oh yeah!" Then Carson's list changed back to what he always proclaims, which is fast cars, big screen TV's, and rolling through Hollywood with 22 inch rims on his Cadillac Escalade.

Brown jumped in, "oh shit, you gonna waste your money on popcorn and bubblegum. That's the problem with being young and stupid like you are. All you know about is sex, drug, and rock & roll. It won't matter if you have a million dollars or fifty million dollars, you will eventually blow it all and be broke within a couple of years." Brown continued and said, "I still like the idea of having a Hall named after me on campus, but I'm going to invest the rest of my money into the housing market. I'm going to own homes all over the States, maybe even throughout the world. Donald Trump might start working for me when I'm done. Real estate is always a sure investment, you can never lose."

Then they both looked at me and asked, "what are you going to do with your share Jenks?"

Having already thought about this question previously, I was able to respond quickly. "Well first thing I'm going to do is create a charity foundation so my name can live on, like what Brown is doing with his Hall.

Next, I will then pay off everyone's bills in my immediate family, and then finally do some traveling around the world. Then after all of that you would think that I would just take it easy and enjoy the day because I'll be super wealthy. Especially since I've been busting my ass all my life just so I can keep afloat.

The problem with that is I know myself too well. If I sit idle, I will either become some strange eccentric individual whom people will run away from or a full blown boozer. The temptation to party like a rock star, then get caught up in that party scene will be too immense for me, if I'm inactive. Eventually I would just lose everything, just as Carson would do.

In order to keep busy, but still be able to enjoy some type of adult beverage on regulated bases, I have come up with an idea to incorporate the two. I think I might buy some land over there in Yakima and then start a winery with a bed and breakfast. They are starting to turn out some first class wines over in the Columbia Valley, it's geared up to be the next Napa Valley. I could get about a thousand acres overlooking a wine valley and build a couple of nice little rentals. Of course, I'll have my own little chateau overlooking everything. I'll definitely grow some first class wines and ship my product all over the world. So, I guess I'll need to have a huge ass underground cellar to go along with my Chateau.

While I'm at it, I will definitely have the world's largest walk in humidor full of all the finest cigars. This humidor will be bigger than my house that I have now. So that's about it. Me keeping busy in Yakima in order not go off the deep end, drinking wine, and smoking cigars."

The drive was un-eventful and we were getting close to our destination for our overnight stay. We're just a couple of hours out and it looked as if we'd get there shortly before sunset. This was apparently going to be one of my easiest missions I had ever done. Jassim even assured us that everything has been lined up and we had nothing to worry about while he retrieved another goat sandwich and tried offering it to me.

A few miles before we arrived at our final destination towards the village, we approached an old shepherd tending his flock of goats on the road. This road was the only way into the village. As we drew closer, I noticed the old shepherd started waiving as if we were his best friends. He also surprisingly pulled out a military issued radio and gave us the thumbs up. This definitely caught my attention, so I told Carson to pull over and asked Milik to translate for me. Jassim sat there stuffing his face with goat sandwiches.

The old shepherd was more than happy to enlighten me on why he had a military issued radio. He leaned on his cane as if he were taking a break as he started his tale.

This old shepherd went on to explain that he was tired of being a shepherd and was tired of other people coming to his village and taking advantage of his friends and family. So when this old shepherd was handed a flyer by the US Army a few weeks back, saying if you have seen any of these people on this particular flyer, let us know and we will give you a lot of money. These faces on the flyer were the new enemy that started to filter into Iraq. They are members of the Al-Qaeda organization. The old shepherd figured this could be an opportunity to not only retire from herding sheep because the reward money was sufficient to do so, but also stop people from pillaging his village. Especially, since he did recognize the faces on the flyer. The reason he recognized the faces was because they were the ones who would come to his village and take advantage of his friends and family. They would always speed by him on this dusty road in their convoy and they would never pay any attention to him, probably because he is just an old shepherd tending to his sheep.

The 3rd CAV who handed out the flyers were also smart enough to know that intelligence needs to be received and acted upon as soon as possible. That is why they also provided him with a transmission radio that would have direct access to their HQ. They also made some pre-arrangements with the old shepherd. The next time he saw a group of people who matched the description of the flyer, who were driving by and not paying any attention to him, he would call it in to the HQ unit with the 3rd CAV.

We thanked the old shepherd for the information and we drove away and then he quickly vanished as our cloud of dust that we kicked up from the road concealed his whereabouts. The information about Al-Qaeda visiting this village didn't settle very well with me though. We would need to stay on extra alert tonight.

CHAPTER TWENTY FOUR

AL-QAEDA IN THE VILLAGE

We arrived at Jassim's cousin house and we made it there right at sunset. The village which he lived in was nestled at the foothills of some treacherous mountains in northern Iraq. Jassim jumped out of the HMMWV and went inside the house to find his cousin, Tahir Al Nuhman's, and to find out where he wanted us to park our vehicles.

Tahir came out and motioned us to follow him to a large building that looked like a garage that was about fifty yards away. When he approached the building, he opened the barn doors to let us in. Once we were all inside the building, he closed the doors so the rest of the village would not know we were here.

The village was small, it had about ninety houses with a few stores, a school, and a mosque. All in all, it was about a half square mile. From the inside of the building that we were hiding in, we could see Tahir's house and some of the other houses, plus the mosque.

Tahir explained to us that he didn't think anybody saw us arrive. He continued to explain that he thought it would be best if we stayed put for the night and left early in the morning. A few weeks ago they had some Al-Qaeda come into town and establish itself as their security. Tahir continued with, "when Al-Qaeda decides they will provide security for you, you have no choice but to accept it." Tahir continued with his rationalization and mentioned, "that every once in a while they do come back and when they do, we have to take care of them by providing food and shelter. They would never want to sleep in a garage because they know they can take our house, so hopefully you will be safe there."

"Ah shit Jassim, how come you never told us about this being an Al-Qaeda strong hold?" I demanded to know.

"My apologies, this is the first I have heard of this too. I know these people here are peaceful and will mean no harm on you," said Jassim as if he were pleading for his innocents.

Tahir butted back in and said, "even if they do show up tonight, they travel in small groups of four or five, so you would have no problems handling the situation if they do in fact find you."

Cole jumped in to explain to our host about our desire to be concealed. "Yes, it is true we can handle a small engagement, but we want to be unnoticed not just by the people in your village, but also by the US Army. That is not possible if there is a fire fight."

Knowing we really didn't have any other options I said, "fucking eh, well it's too dangerous to travel at night so I guess we are kind of stuck here for now. Let's hope for the best. Let's figure out the watch list and I suggest we go with noise and light discipline immediately."

"I think that it's a good idea Jenks," responded Cole.

Tahir opened the door to let himself out, but before he left he turned to us and said, "Insha'Allah," then he left and walked back towards his house.

"Can we trust this guy?" Brown demanded to know from Jassim.

"Yes my friends. His intentions are well. It's just unfortunate that this situation is upon us."

I stood there for a minute and contemplated our situation and then said, "well shit then, I guess no cigars for now, so pass me a cold MRE." This was not an ideal situation to be in, but instead of panicking, I decided to accept the situation and prepare for the worst. If a couple of Al-Quada members on the slim chance come snooping around tonight, I had confidence that we all could figure out a solution and continue our mission. Everything we have done so far has led us to this place at this moment under these circumstances. These particular new circumstances were not going to cancel out our payday.

We were well into the night and the darkness had settled everywhere. Carson was now keeping watch over us while we slept. He was sitting in a corner of the barn that had a strategic view of the outside surrounding area. He was sitting there in the dark and trying to be quite as a mouse, watching for any movement outside. Carson was trying to stay awake by running many scenarios in his head with trying to determine which spring break party he would participate in first. Those thoughts soon vanished when some motion outside caught his attention. He couldn't believe his eyes in what he was witnessing. He sat there for a few minutes to be sure this was for real and continued to watch. Finally, Carson concluded that he had enough, so he came over and shook me in order to draw me out of my sleep.

"I think a couple of those Al-Qaeda assholes are mongering around the village. The mosque has opened its doors and it is quite busy in there. A few guys keep going in and out of the mosque," he whispered to me.

I immediately went over to where Jassim was sleeping and woke him up.

"Fucking eh Jassim, I thought I asked you if we could trust your cousin."

Still half asleep and rubbing his eyes he said, "we can."

"Then why in the fuck are there bad guys out there? Seems like quite a coincidence."

"I swear to you, my cousin is truthful and I am sure he doesn't want them here as much as you do."

"Well, we'll see. We'll see."

I sat there on the ground for a second and rubbed my face as I contemplated our next move, which logically was to grab my weapon and take it off of safe. I then motioned for everybody else who was now awake to lock and load their weapons and take guard on all four corners of the garage. I whispered to everyone that all we can do is hope Jassim's cousin is on our side. Hopefully we can wait it out here until they leave. If they don't come looking in the garage like Tahir said, then we can wait it out. One big question remained for me, does the old shepherd tend to his flock of sheep on the road at midnight? Chances are I wouldn't be that lucky for he would most likely be fast asleep with his sheep.

Hours went by with all of us on full alert, waiting for them to get what they needed and leave. I had Milik sit with Cole and I had Jassim sit next to me the whole time as he interpreted what he could hear for me. Jassim was able to piece some information together to explain that they were here for some kind of hand off. He couldn't figure out what it was that was so important, but he was pretty sure that a lieutenant in the Al-Qaeda was due to arrive at any time and pick up a package that was being safe guarded in the mosque.

I was starting to get short with Jassim because the trust factor with his cousin was fading. "A package in the mosque? You're cousin is getting shadier by the minute, but I'm sure he has an excuse for not letting us know that piece of information too."

A few more hours went by as we all waited in our perspective corners and there was still no sign that they were going to leave any time soon. Milik was able to pick up on a few more pieces of the puzzle too as to why they were there. Milik said they had a sword to help cut the head off the infidel.

"What in the fuck do you mean by that?"

Brown had heard enough at this point. "Jenks, you need to load the valid codes so we can call this in. Gold or no gold, we have a duty to protect any of our brothers from getting their heads cut off by these assholes."

"I know, I know, you're right. But we can wait it out a bit more to see what happens. Maybe we can get a glimpse of what it is when they transfer the goods. For all we know it could just be a couple of regular swords, right? Anyway, if it is something substantial, we can call it in and give the directions and grid reference. We can boogey out of here at the same time. That way, everybody wins."

"I suppose. Just make sure that we are not responsible for any good guys getting killed because we were greedy for the gold."

"I agree, I guarantee you that no American blood will tarnish this gold."

The sun was coming up, it was now daybreak and the bad guys were still busy by the mosque. A few more of them had materialized, their numbers where multiplying. There were now twelve of them that we knew of. Some of them were taking naps while the others performed their weapons maintenance and drank tea. More hours went by and the lieutenant had not yet made his presence.

I was running the calculations in my head and figured this was going to put us behind on our payday schedule if they don't evacuate the area soon. I asked myself what would be the worst thing to happen? Fighting these bastards and taking all them out or explaining to SFC Hunter where we have all been these last few days. The later didn't sound too exciting especially knowing he would come up short on his mission with no weapons of mass destruction. If I had the payday secured in my Turkish bank account, I would then be able to handle anything he dished out to me. It became apparent to me that in order to get to the payday, I would have to choose between two options. I would have to either wait these bad guys out or take them all out. Not wanting any blood on my hands at this point, I voted for the first.

A few of the soldiers were getting agitated and started arguing with each other. I asked Milik what was going on. He said he couldn't tell what they're arguing about, but they were at odds with each other. The one soldier who seemed to be in charge, motioned to three other Al-Qaeda soldiers to follow him. Then they all marched to Tahir's front door step. They stood there for a minute discussing something and then, all of a sudden they kicked in the front door and went inside.

CHAPTER TWENTY FIVE

PANIC IN THE MOSQUE

"Holy fuck! They just kicked in the front door to Tahir's house. This is not good, not good at all." This was exactly what I didn't want to happen.

Jassim started to get hysterical and demanded that we do something. He was starting to pace around frantically. I was worried that he might panic and do something stupid.

With a desperate plea, Jassim grabbed my arm and exclaimed, "if I have to, I will go in there myself and rescue my cousin."

"Now hold on Jassim. Let's think this through. There are six of us and twelve of them that we know of, and probably more on the way. If we do anything, we need to make a plan first."

I motioned for the guys to gather around. Then I explained that if this gets any worse, we would have to jump in and take care of the situation. I knew we had the element of surprise, and I had hoped that element would be good enough. If I had my choice though, there would be no surprises for anybody. Though, in order to present a surprise if needed, we needed to have our "gifts" readily available. I assigned two Al-Qaeda guards as targets per person. That way if I gave the signal, everyone will know which two to take out. I assigned myself the guy who seemed to be in charge and one of the other guards who went into the house. I assigned Carson the other two guards that would be coming out. The rest were up for debate on who would take who.

A few more minutes went by, but it seemed like a couple of hours. We could hear a scuffle going on inside the house and a lot of yelling was going on. Then all of a sudden we watched Tahir being pushed through the front door along with his wife. The kids that were inside were crying and didn't know what to do.

The supposed leader was pushing around Tahir and his wife as he continued yelling at them. When they were escorted to their front yard which was more of a dirt patch, they were shoved to their knees and forced to put their hands behind their head. The kids started running towards the mother, but were quickly intercepted by a couple of guards and where shoved to the ground. They continued to lay there crying on their bellies.

"Do something, please Jenks," Jassim begged. "They are going to be executed."

The leader then took out his handgun, cocked it, and started to waive it around franticly.

"Fuck!" I said.

I motioned for everyone to focus on their targets and wait for the command to fire. I placed the center mass of the leader in my sights with the aiming post from my weapon on his chest. I had the other target in my peripheral vision so I could quickly switch to him before he could return fire.

After he was tired of waiving his pistol around, he placed it on the back of Tahir's head. I took a deep breath hoping that this was all just a ploy. When I realized that the situation was only going to get worst, I pulled the trigger on my weapon three times quickly and simultaneously yelled, "FIRE!"

The leaders chest exploded and blood splattered all over Tahir who just stayed in his knelt position and didn't move an inch as the corpse fell backwards. His wife looked at him in a confused state.

I placed my second target in my sights and pulled off another three quick rounds. As I watched him fall to the ground, I could see Carson had taken out his targets because they too were also on their way down with bloody wounds to their chest.

Looking down the barrel of my weapon, I could see a little plum of smoke rising out from the flash suppresser. I wanted to concentrate on the smoke to distract myself from what just happened, but I couldn't. I had to quickly scan the sector for a few seconds to see if there was any movement from the two I just shot or if somebody else that I did not account for was coming out of the woodwork. As I scanned the sector, I realized that killing these two individuals did not have the same effect on me as it did the first time I terminated a life. I was going to chalk it up as me getting in the habit of taking someone's life, but then I realized that wasn't the case at all. I concluded that the reason I wasn't bothered with their bloodshed was because they were just plain assholes and they needed to be eliminated.

Not seeing any movement, I turned my attention to the Civil Affairs guys and Sgt Brown. Trying to get a grasp of the situation I yelled out, "are all targets down?"

Brown was the first to respond back. "Fuck Yah, both of my targets are toast."

Carson and Cole each chimed in with their report and said, "targets down."

Tahir and his wife were still kneeling with their hands behind their head, still thinking they were about to be executed. They were in shock and they had not processed the current events yet. The children were just as confused. They wanted to run over to their parents, but didn't know if they had permission to do so. They chose to stay put on their bellies in the dirt and continue to cry. I was starting to think that we were all in the clear when I heard Butkus and Vanscoy yell out at the top of their lungs, "negative!"

"What in the fuck do you mean by negative?"

"Negative means not all targets are down" explained Vanscoy.

"The two guards who were still in the mosque when all the firing started are still in there. They weren't ready for their seventy-two virgins so they slammed the door shut for protection. We have two hostiles in the mosque."

"Let's blow that fucking mosque to kingdom come," yelled Carson.

"No! You must not," interjected Jassim as he jumped to his feet.

"Yeah he is right," I replied. "If we even touch that mosque, more bad than good will come of it. Jassim, I think now is a good time to go and tend to your relatives, they appear to be a little shook up. You can also tell them that I said you're welcome. Also Jassim, I guess Tahir was telling the truth the whole time?"

We shifted out focus back on what to do with these two guys in the mosque. I knew as soon as we leave, they will torture Tahir in order to get information out of him like where we are going. Then after they kill him and his whole family, they'll radio their people where we are going and they will have an ambush waiting for us down the road.

"Milik, how about we go and talk these guys out. Carson and Butkus, you stay here and help everybody else provide a three-sixty parameter, let's go!"

As we started to head over to the mosque, I grabbed a couple of cigars out of my personal bag from the HMMWV that I had been saving. I was in desperate need of a drink, but the cigar was the next best thing and the only thing I had available. I took the cigar that was neatly packed in the aluminum tube and placed it in upper pocket on my blouse for safe keeping. Then I took the other one and lit it up. After a couple of puffs from my cigar, Milik and I walked up to the front door of the mosque and knocked on it. Milik was ready to translate everything I said and vice versa for them.

"Hey, we are the Americans out here. How many of you bad guys are in there?"

They yelled back and Milik translated their words with "you will soon feel the sword of Allah."

"That's not what I asked, can you stay on the subject here? I want to make a proposition to you. I'll give you some money so you can go home and take care of your families. So, how about you all come on out, get paid, and go home. I promise you we will not enter or do anything to this mosque."

"You are too late. It is you Americans who need to surrender. We have great number of our people only about fifteen minutes out from here. If you lay down your weapons and kneel towards Allah, then we will take pity on you and let you live as our hostage."

"I don't think we can do that, like I said we are Americans and we never surrender."

"Then you shall die today!"

Milik was getting a little uncomfortable with these translations because he was worried that I might start thinking that it was he who was making these statements. So I told Milik that he was doing a good job.

I had him continue translating for me, "well why don't you come out here and say that to my face, maybe it is you who will die today."

A long pause pursued before the subject in the mosque responded. "Even if I die today in battle, I will die as a martyr and I will go to heaven and be welcomed by Allah. If you die today, you will just go to hell."

"And I suppose you will get your seventy-two virgins. I want to let you in on a little secret. There is a reason why they are virgins. I have this female cousin who is so butt ugly, that no man will ever touch her and guess what, she is a virgin. I take pity on you if you have to deal with her and times that by seventy-two."

Then Carson whistled and pointed to the west. We could see in the far distance dust being kicked up from a convoy of trucks. We couldn't count how many there were, but we could tell it was more than a few and they were not the US Cavalry.

The entrance to this village had only one way in, which meant there was also only one way out. The way in was being traveled by a group of people who are going to be pissed off that I just killed their friends. This same group is also blocking the way out. The mountains cut off any other avenue for escape. This left us no choice but to take a stance and fight because I don't think they were going to understand my point of view.

I refocused on the two guys in the mosque, "this is my last offer. If you do not surrender now and tell your boys to

Voodoo Gold by James H Jenks

leave, I will then personally come in there and put a bullet in your head when this is all done and over with."

"Insha'Allah!" they replied back.

"Fuck these guys, we'll deal with them later. What we need to do is form a plan, like right now!"

We went back into the barn, took a knee and formed a circle.

"OK," I said. "Besides crossing our fingers that the old shepherd is tending his flock today, here's a plan that I derived. I'm sure they know we're here in the village, but they do not know how many of us there are or where exactly we are in the village.

First, everybody take a radio so we can keep in constant communication. Second, let's set up a convoy ambush at the front of the town where the road enters the village. We'll use the one way in and one way out to our advantage.

Cole, you and I have the M-203's. Our plan is I will take out the last vehicle in the convoy when they enter the kill zone and you take out the first vehicle so we can pin the rest in. Then we will start taking them out one by one. As soon as the last vehicle crosses the entry point, I will fire on it and this will be the signal for us to start rock and rolling. Cole, after you take out the first vehicle, start working your way in and I'll meet you in the middle.

I'll be on that building roof over there on the east side of the main road. You should take that one on the west side from that window. Brown and Vanscoy, you have the SAW's so Brown, I want you in that building over there, as I pointed to the center building on the east row. Vanscoy, you should be in that one over there, as I pointed to the center building on the west row. As soon as that first 203 frag goes off, I want you two to light them up with your SAW's.

Once again, Brown you go from front to back and Vanscoy you go from Back to front. Carson and Butkus, you two need to take position to the rooftop of those two tall buildings so you can provide sniper fire, as I pointed to the buildings to the south end. After the initial assault, I'm sure a lot of them will scatter into the surrounding buildings and hide and regroup. We need to keep the pressure on them until they're all gone. You two need to pick off the stragglers one by one.

So, Carson and Butkus, you will also be our eyes and you need to guide us over the radio with what you see. That way the one you don't get, we can go after them for the cleanup.

Those four buildings on the outside of the village to our left will be our fall back point. This garage will be our rally and last stance point.

Milik, you better just go in with Jassim and just hope we succeed, just play stupid if they run into you. We better get moving because from the looks of it, they will be here in about five minutes."

We all ran to our prospective points and took our positions. When I was well situated, I did a call check to each of my men to make sure we were all in communication.

Voodoo Gold by James H Jenks

"Listen up guys, they're about a few minutes out."

"Cole you read?"

"Yes."

"Carson you read?"

"Yes."

"Brown you read?"

"Yes."

"Vanscoy you read?"

"Yes."

"Butkus you read?"

"Roger."

CHAPTER TWEENTY SIX

SHOWDOWN

The convoy was about a half mile out, I could see that they had a total of fifteen vehicles. They were all white Toyota pickup trucks that were not armor plated. As they approached the entrance of the village, they cautiously slowed down and a lot of the dust they were kicking up from the dirt road caught up to them and became part of the convoy too.

"Cole, hold, hold, hold," I whispered over the radio.

When the last vehicle was in my sight and was approaching the kill line, I adjusted my side sights on my M-203 and calibrated it to two hundred meters, which is what I approximated the last vehicle in the convoy would be at when it was time to fire. I had the aiming pin centered on the target and I was tracking as it became closer. I had all ten of my M-203 frag round out and lined up in single file next to my firing position. I knew I had to get as many rounds off as possible before they could figure out where the rounds were coming from. I had the ammo out of their protective casings and ready to be fired, I knew I could get one off every five seconds or so.

"OK Cole when you hear my first frag go off, it will be time to light them up."

I sat patiently in my fighting position as drops of sweat dripped down over my eyebrow and into my eyes as it tried to blur my vision. Patiently waiting as the last vehicle crossed the kill line, I took a deep breath, focused on the target and then pulled the trigger. The M-203 kicked back as if I were shooting a twelve-gauge shotgun. It felt like someone was punching me in the shoulder. The round traveled down range, and hit the vehicle on target. I watched the round enter the white truck through the windshield and I could hear the clunking of the round as it bounced around inside the cab before it exploded.

When it detonated, the windshield busted into a million pieces and I could see the two passengers inside become shredded to pieces.

The truck's momentum slowed down as it rolled to a standstill. Then three people jump out from the back of the truck and started running into the side alleys. That is when I heard the SAW with its three to five rounds burst and witnessed two of the targets that were trying to escape go down with fatal wounds. The third one got away, so I jumped on the radio and told Carson that he needs to keep an eye out and take him down.

As all this was happening, I grabbed another round and chambered it into the tube for the next shot. I could hear

Cole's round go off, followed up with the thumping of the other SAW.

The next round that I fired off missed the target by a couple of feet because I was now rushing myself. I had to remind myself to keep calm and slow down, because in these type of situations, slow is actually fast. I could see the round detonate as it ripped a hole into the front passenger side tire, but it did not stop the vehicle.

Cole got another round off and his second vehicle exploded.

Before I could shoot my third round, the remaining vehicles scatter into different directions and then disappear into the village.

"Fuck, this is not what I planned." Just like that, my great plan turned to shit and we would now need to resort to the Alamo.

Over the radio I told everyone to go to the garage building where we would create a defense perimeter.

Next, I ran down the steps of the building I was in and dashed out onto the street. As I ran down the street, I hugged close to the buildings looking for every point of cover that I could jump to in case they started shooting at me.

When I came to an intersection that I needed to cross, an insurgent jumped out from nowhere who came running at me from a different direction, and he had his AK-47 pointed directly at me.

I hit the dirt rolling to the left while dodging his bullets. He persistently fired off more rounds at me as he continued to run towards me. I rolled onto my belly and fired back with a three round burst, which made his bullets pause for a second as he tried to take cover. I took advantage of this pause so I could jump up and take cover behind the nearest brick wall too. After I caught my breath, I looked around the wall with my weapon drawn and saw three more of his buddies running towards me.

I quickly pulled my trigger in a rapid motion as fast as I could, spraying rounds towards them. Two of them went down quickly, but the third took cover behind an abandon vehicle. I jumped back behind the wall for cover. I tried to peer around the corner again but every time I did, I could hear him fire his weapon and debris from the wall would spatter on my face. It felt like pins and needles were being thrown at my face as the flakes hit it.

I took one of my M-203 round that I was able to salvage, placed it into the chamber, and then fired the round at the old car. I took cover behind the wall, barely glancing over the edge, and waited for the explosion. I could see the dirt in the road ripple from the shock wave after the round discharged. I could not witness if the fragments from my round was able to neutralize the target. I continued to peer over the wall and watched for any type of movement. After a minute of nothing moving or experiencing any more debris stinging my face, I decided the coast was clear and I took off running again towards our fallback point.

As I came around another corner, I noticed Brown and Carson were in front of me. They had taken a defensive kneeling position by a brick wall.

When they eventually acknowledged my presence, they waved for me to come over and join them. I ran to the other side of the street as fast as I could as I stayed hunkered down. I knelt down next to them when I arrived and then Brown immediately told me that there were about five guys around the far corner.

"Well the only way back to the garage is to go through them, so let's get going. Cover me while I move!"

I popped around the corner and saw an insurgent about thirty feet away. I was able to raise my weapon and get a round off before he was able to shoot at me.

His expression was of surprise and then quickly changed to disappointment as my round went directly into his chest, spraying blood everywhere.

I kept running as fast as I could and eventually I made it to the next corner where I took up a prone fighting position.

I applied suppressive fire to the other four insurgents so they couldn't fire back as I motioned back to Brown and Carson to advance up to where I was.

As soon as they were able to advance to my position, we saw two trucks with built in machine guns mounted onto their roll bars. They started to advance towards us. The four other insurgents considered us to be a done deal. They were going to let the trucks finish us off while they proceeded to search for other targets throughout the village.

In the corner of my eye, I saw a building with the front door open that we could run in and take cover. I pointed it out to Brown and Carson and we made a mad dash to get inside it as fast as possible. We were able to stay at least one step in front of the bullets that the trucks was now firing at us.

When we were all able to make it inside the building safely, we quickly set up a hasty defensive position and got a few shots off, but they seemed to have no effect on their advancement. My radio squawked. It was Cole.

"Jenks, we're back at the garage and it's starting to get a little messy. Where the hell are you?"

I instructed him to take position in the garage and to keep on the defense. We'd be there as soon as possible.

Then the two trucks pulled in front of the building that we were occupying. They are about seventy-five meters out. A few insurgents dismounted the trucks. One of them started yelling at us in English with a heavy Arabic accent. He informed us of our situation and that there was no way for us to escape. As he went on with his speech, I could see some of the other trucks pull up and position themselves around the building.

The insurgent who was speaking in English continued to inform us that if we surrenderd, he would allow us a quick death with an execution bullet to the back of the head, but if we didn't cooperate, then he would behead us on video for our loved ones to see.

I looked over at Brown and Carson and I could see in their eyes that this was going to be our Alamo and not back at the garage. We were going to fight to the end.

"We'll let's see how many we can take down," I said to the two of them. They nodded their heads back in agreement and displayed their war face. I thought for a second that this might be the time to make a speech on how I was glad to serve with them and it would be an honor to die in battle with them. Though I had a feeling they already knew that and besides, now was the time to concentrate on taking out targets because we would need a miracle to get out alive with this predicament.

We took up our fighting positions and took aim at our targets. I looked through my aiming post and lined up a headshot on one of the drivers. I wanted to acquire a shot on the guy who had been talking, but he was smart enough to take cover.

A second after I pulled the trigger I watched the driver's head explode.

Then a rain of bullets returned our direction and there was nothing we could do but duck and hide behind the brick wall.

As we hunkered down, we knew it would only be a matter of a minute or two before the bricks crumpled from all the bullets impacting them.

"Well this is it I guess, let's go out fighting." Once again, they were in agreement. "On the count of three, let's rush them with all guns a blazing, true grit style."

I began the count down. "One...Two..." Just before I was ready to say three, we heard a familiar explosion that seemed to be out of place and even more unusual was the bullets stopped raining. I peeked out the mutilated window and witnessed a Kiowa Helicopter firing its small missiles at the trucks. This made the remaining insurgents scatter and retreat into the village.

"Holly Mother of God!" I yelled to Brown and Carson with excitement. "See I told you someone up there likes me," as I pointed straight up and posed a colossal grin.

My radio started squawking with the helicopters pilot's voices. At first I thought this was weird, but then I recognized we must be frequency hopping together with the same codes because I was picking up their transmission. The old codes that we were using now must have been recycled to them. Then I realized if I can hear them, they can hear us. The question was, were they listening to our transmission and are now reacting to our conversations? If this was the situation, then I'm sure they know about our gold and our names. If they know about the gold and our names, then the gig is definitely up. Hopefully this was not the case and they were here responding to the old shepherd request.

As I listened to my radio I heard, "K-One, this is K-Two, we need to track these vehicles down and destroy them."

"Roger that K-Two, I'm calling it in. Red One this is K-One, we have the targeted enemy hostiles at location, there also appears to be a squad of US Soldiers currently engaged on the ground. At least they look like US Soldiers."

"K-One this is Red One, we have no knowledge of any US forces in this area, proceed with caution. We are thirty minutes out, over."

Well that answered my question, that old shepherd must have called it in when they passed him on the road. This was a huge relief for we were back in business. Though, a new problem just presented itself. Besides them now picking up my radio transmissions, I only have thirty minutes to get the hell out of here.

The helicopters made another pass, firing off their missiles and taking out a few more of the trucks. All we could do was sit back and watch the show as if we had front seats to a fourth of July extravaganza.

Then I heard Cole on the radio.

"What the fuck is going on over there and why am I picking up helicopter pilot communications?"

"We're on the offense now, we'll be there in a second. And if you haven't already figured it out yet, no names over the radio for the time being."

Then I heard a voice come in over the radio that was giving commands a few minutes ago. "This is Red One, please identify yourself."

I paused for a second and then responded on the radio to his request. "This is Lieutenant McClane, I'm on a special mission from Delta force and I'll fill you in on the situation when you arrive. Until then, I need to concentrate on this current battle." This was probably the lamest excuse anybody could come up with, but it was all I had at the moment. I just hoped he would buy off on it.

"This is Red One, understood. See you in thirty mikes"

Carson and Brown looked at me as if I was an idiot. Brown said, "really, Lieutenant McClane? Are you supposed to be John McClane as in *Die Hard* and we are fighting Hans Gruber and his men? I'm surprised you didn't say yippee-ki-yay, motherfucker!"

Not providing any more encouragement for them to mock my storyline, I sternly instructed them to go to the garage and get everybody ready for us to move out with the gold because it's starting to look like this situation in getting wrapped up. "Besides, you heard the man, in thirty minutes, the whole God Damn US Army will be here. In the meantime, I'm going to track down the asshole that made those stupid remarks about us, and I'm going to personally take him out."

I could see various fireworks shows go off in different parts of the city as the Kiowa's kept the heat on. Then I noticed two more combatant trucks that come out of the woodworks and raced by with a crew of insurgents armed with RPG's in the bed.

Then the two trucks scattered to different corners of the street and when they stopped in their strategic spot, the insurgents jumped out from the back and set up a firing position for their RPG's.

The helicopters came swooshing down as they made another pass, they fired their missiles, but were only able to take out one of the trucks.

The surviving insurgents waited patiently and did not allow the blast from their comrades truck distract themselves. They took careful aim with their RPG's that was resting on their shoulders, pulled the trigger, and fired the rounds towards the helicopter.

Two RPG rounds sizzled through the air. The first one was off target and missed the helicopter that it was aiming for, but the other one was on target to hit its objective. I clinched my weapon in disgust as I prepared for the round to detonate. Then excitement went through my veins as I realized the round bounced off the helicopter because it was a dud.

Before I could even enjoy that moment of victory, a third RPG round came from a non disclosed location and hit the cowl on the same helicopter. It's engine started to bellow out massive amounts of black smoke.

"K-One this is K-Two, my panel lights are going off like a Christmas tree here, they must have spliced a line. I'm heading back to base before I go down," the pilot said over the radio.

"Roger that K-Two, I'll make one more pass and try to neutralize this place before the SCO shows up, I'll catch up in a couple of minutes."

The healthy helicopter made another pass before banking around a turn at the corner of town. As the helicopter aligned itself to fire off more missiles, I watched as an insurgent jump into a truck that was already in position. Even before I could react and neutralize this situation with my riffle, he already had pulled out an RPG and fired it towards the helicopter. The helicopter also was able to fire its missiles at the truck.

The arsenal from the helicopter screamed towards the truck as the RPG simultaneously raced towards the helicopter, passing each other mid-distance. The truck exploded in a huge ball of fire as the missiles struck it with precision. Then the RPG round hit the tail boom section of the helicopter and exploded. This made the helicopter spin out of control, rocking back and forth like a cradle, before diving towards the ground.

Smoke was coming out on the engine and it was spewing everywhere. The helicopter tried to gain control of itself but was unsuccessful. Then the tail rotor hit the side of a building, which made the rotor disintegrate and a million pieces of brick went flying everywhere. The helicopter tilted to one side as gravity took over and made it strike the ground with a thunderous effect. The momentum the helicopter carried from flying around in the air made it skid down the street towards the building I was hiding in. The belly was exposed as it slid on its side with the blades hitting the ground and scaring the dirt with deep trenches until the blades finally fell apart. Debris was flying in every direction. Immediately jumping backwards into the far corner of the room, I curled up and braced myself for the impact. When the explosion of bricks didn't happen when I anticipated they would, I looked up and saw the helicopter had finally come to a rest. It persisted to rock back and forth a couple of times until it finally lay there in total silence. Dust and dirt was everywhere.

I ran over to the damaged helicopter and discovered the two pilots who were lying in the cockpit with their eyes wide open. They were bruised up and bloody, but at least they were alive. Taking the butt end of my weapon, I busted away the remaining broken glass so I could clear a path to drag them out. When I entered the cockpit, I could see that they both had busted up legs. At least they had to be busted up because I never saw legs that were in a zigzag fashion as theirs were and not be busted up. I told them both to relax and I would take care of them. They seemed a little surprised and excited to see me, but then their expressions quickly went back to the agony look as they waited for my help.

Starting with the right seat pilot, who was now the pilot on top, I unlocked his safety harnesses, threw him over my shoulder and laid him down on the ground. Next, I grabbed him from the underarms and dragged him into the building behind me that I was using for shelter. After I leaned him up against the wall and took out his canteen, I went back for the other pilot and repeated the process. The final process was securing their weapons and placing them next to them so they could defend themselves.

"You guys OK?"

Both of them where now fully conscious of the situation and tried to regain their composure as soldiers. They knew that I was trying to give them field medical aid, so they got straight to the point and pointed out the fact that their legs were broken. Other than that, they were only bruised up a bit and felt fine.

As I was applying a field pressure dressing over a wound on one of the legs where the bone was sticking out so I could stop the bleeding, one of them mustered up enough strength and said, "Fucking eh man, there were only two more targets for us to destroy before the SCO shows up and then this shit happens!"

"So there are only two targets left?" They both gave me a dumbfounded look when I asked this question. I tried to explain my purpose. "I just need to know what I'm in store for when I go back out."

"Yeah there are only two left, but they're fucked when 3rd CAV shows up. There is no need to go out there and try any brave shit, just hang here with us and rescue will be here shortly."

Staying put wasn't an option for me, but I didn't tell them that. They would never understand, nor did I want to explain that I needed to get back to my guys so we could exit this village with a truckload of gold.

As I was finishing up applying aid to the second pilot, he looked directly at me and asked, "by the way, who the fuck are you?"

I looked down on my right chest to just make sure that I did unvelcroed my name tag. This is a common practice that soldiers in Special Ops do in order to conceal their names. To my relief I did remove my name tag and my unit patches, so my natural response to his question was, "didn't you hear? I'm John McClane. Sorry guys I would love to stay and chat, but I gotta run now. When this is all over, you two come out to the coast, we'll get together, have a few laughs..."

I knew they would be safe inside the building with their weapons, besides I was going to take care of the remaining threat myself and not 3rd CAV. Not because I wanted to be a hero, but because I had to eliminate the last two targets in order to exit this village safely before the SCO arrives.

I quickly picked up the radio and reported that there were still two enemy trucks out there to the rest of my crew.

I peered out the front door looking in both directions to ensure the coast was clear, but I noticed one of the trucks was resting down the street by the intersection. Luckily it did not see me. Then all of a sudden, its tires spun out and threw dirt everywhere as it started to take off up the road as a wild animal would do with chasing its prey. A minute later I then heard Sgt Brown's SAW open fire.

This enemy truck was able to race through the maze of alleys in the village and somehow was able to zero in on

Brown with a Russian made DUSHKA[32] mounted on a fixed tripod in the back of the truck. He opened fire on Brown's position and was determined to get its first kill.

"Help anybody, I'm pinned down," Brown squawked over the radio.

"Holy Shit, are you OK?" I yelled back into the radio.

"Fucking eh man, you need to come and get these bastards, like right now."

"Hold tight and I'll be there in a few, don't try to be a hero just yet."

I was out of frags, so the easy option of firing a M-203 round at them wasn't available. I would have to do it the old-fashion way and use bullets. I ran out of the building once I knew I was in the clear. I maneuvered myself through a couple of alleys toward the sound of the gun fire, and took up a position about hundred meters out from the truck firing at Brown.

I placed my aiming post directly on the insurgent who was manning the DUSHKA. I took a deep breath and steadied my nerves because I knew I would only get one shot at this. I squeezed my trigger very gently so it wouldn't jerk to the right. A fraction of a second after I felt the recoil from

---

[32] DUSHKA - also written DShK - Degtyarov-Shpagin Krupnokaliberny - Russian / Soviet 12.7 mm Heavy Machine Gun.

my weapon, I witnessed the neck of the bad guy in the back of the truck explode and then the body went lifeless.

There was no time to celebrate this victory because the other insurgents in the truck didn't like the fact that they just lost their gunner to me. Their response was immediately spinning the truck around towards my direction. It kicked up dirt from the tires and started racing towards me as another insurgent kicked the dead body of the previous gunner to the side and he manned the DUSHKA.

I spotted an alley down the road on the right about hundred and fifty meters away, and in that ally there was also a building that had an accessible entrance just a few meters further. This building with the access could provide cover and from there I could figure out what to do next, but for now I needed to run like hell. I just didn't know if I could run fast enough to make it to the building before they could shoot me or run me over.

I started sprinting as fast as I have ever run before. As I ran, I looked over my shoulder and I could see the truck had its sights locked on me as it was racing towards me at as fast as it has ever chased anybody before. The Insurgent in the back was trying to keep his balance as he tried to get a foothold and aim his weapon. Calculating the remaining distance to the building and the rate the truck was gaining on me, I knew that this might be a real close call.

I thought of turning around and opening fire on the truck. But I knew I couldn't get an accurate shot off to neutralize it in a hasty situation like this. Even if I did get off an accurate shot to the driver, the end result would be me dying in a hail of bullets as the rest of them in the truck returned fire.

As I sprinted down the road a little further, I realized that the escape access wasn't close enough. Is this how it all ends? Am I going out running like a coward and not even take a stance? I couldn't go out running away from a fight, so I started to reevaluate the option of at least getting one shot off and dying in a hail of bullets. As I passed a small gap between two buildings on my right and still contemplating my choice, I was surprised at what I just saw out of the corner of my eye. The small gap wasn't a surprise as they were plentiful throughout this village. The surprise was a person hiding inside this small gap who was completely cloaked in a black outfit. This person seemed to be out of place standing there in the gap between the two buildings, but my instincts told me not to worry about it. My instincts told me that this out of place person was there for a reason and I should switch back to my original choice of running like hell. As I gained some distance from the gap and hoping my instincts weren't wrong, I looked back one last time to confirm my notion. When I looked back, I noticed this person jumping out into the middle of the road for some reason. This person then proceeded to throw down what look like an anti vehicle mine toward the front of the truck as hard and far as he could. Then this person vanished back into the gap never to be seen again.

The truck tried to weave to the right as it slid on its brakes, but it couldn't maneuver around the object or stop in time. The truck expectedly ran over the intended object.

With my nose now facing forward as I was still running as fast as I could possibly move, I could feel the bright flash behind me as it tried to lunge over my shoulder. This bright flash seemed to stop time in its tracks and everything went in total silence. With everything seeming to be in an enhanced slow motion state, I could see the dust particles in the air get sucked backwards towards the flash as if everything was about to implode. With this I felt as if my pounding heart was being ripped out of my back along with every last breath of air that was in my lungs. Next a huge ball of flame consumed the truck, reversing the effects to an explosion. The sound came screaming back with a vengeance as the thunderous explosion resonated in my ears. My heart was thrown back in its proper place, pumping faster than ever and my lungs vibrated as they felt the air being forced back in. The blast from the explosion tossed the truck about ten feet in the air. While the truck resembled an exploding rocket, I looked down at my feet. I noticed they were barley touching the ground as I tried to run. I was more or less flying at this point, with my feet touching the ground about every twenty feet. The truck finally reversed its trajectory and struck the ground with its full momentum right next to me as my feet skimmed over the ground. The truck was now doing cartwheels next to me as it continued to chase me.

The full force of the explosion had finally caught up to me as its thrust threw me frontwards flat on my stomach.

Voodoo Gold by James H Jenks

When I hit the ground, it knocked the breath out of me as I did a power slide on my belly through the dirt, getting a mouthful of dust and rocks.

The flame ball that used to be a truck decided it wanted to take one last shot at me. I rolled over and looked up as the flaming truck bounced over me. I could see every detail of the truck such as bolt patterns on the undercarriage and I could feel the intense heat from the flames as it tried to land on top of me. I quickly did a combat roll to the left and avoided the truck as it slammed right next to me on the right, missing me by a mere few inches. It continued down the road as it tumbled over and over for about fifty meters before it eventually came to a crashing stop.

I was just lying there for a few seconds, trying to figure out what the fuck just happened as I was spitting mud out of my mouth. I looked back over to where the gap between the two buildings was supposed to be and saw that the person who had saved my life was long gone.

Then in the distance, I heard dueling SAW's firing for about thirty seconds and then silence again.

There was a high squelch in my ears and in the far distance I could hear someone saying, "McClane, we got them, we got the other truck." This seemed to be weird, because why would anyone call me McClane?

CHAPTER TWEENTY SEVEN

THE AFTER MATH

I picked myself up and then sat back down in the middle of the road and tried to refocus on everything that had just happened. I patted around the chest part of my blouse because I knew that I should have a cigar that was ready in a tube. I eventually found it, unbuttoned my pocket, and then wrestled the cigar out. The cigar was a little difficult to retrieve because the tube was all bent out of shape and damaged.

The cigar had definitely seen better days, but it was still smokeable. I pulled my lighter out of another pocket, bit the end off the cigar, and then lit it. I then took a few draws of my tasty but damaged Cuban cigar.

"McClane, do you copy, we got the last truck," Vanscoy shouted over the radio again. He said it a few more time as I continued to look at the blue sky watching the birds fly around, until it finally registered that I should answer them. I came out of my trance from the shock and I remembered everything.

"Hey good job," I replied. "I took this one out too. I'll be there in one second, let's get ready to roll. Also keep an eye out for snipers in case one of those sons of bitches that escaped might try to take one of us out. This is John McClane, out."

When we all met up, everyone was quiet. We couldn't believe we actually made it through this ordeal. Brown broke the silence to everyone by stating, "SSG Jenks, let me state some infantry 101 here. After a successful mission like this, we need to do a sweep through the kill zone and make sure there aren't any stragglers."

I responded back to his logical request, "normally I would agree with you, but the 3rd CAV will be here in a few minutes and we need to hit the road. Besides, when the 3rd CAV does get here, they'll accomplish that task for us."

As we all started to head over to the garage to jump in our trucks, Jassim and Tahir suddenly came out of the house with their hands pointing up in the air shouting, "Insha'Allah." Then they ran over to our location and threw their arms around us.

"Thank you, thank you," shouted Tahir. "We can now live in peace in our village and not worry about the Al-Qaeda anymore."

"I would love to stay and celebrate with the rest of the town, but as it is now, we will be lucky to make it to our bank and meet our contact before close of business today. In addition, we need to make it out of this village and onto the main road before 3ʳᵈ CAV comes into sight, so you're welcome Tahir. Jassim, we gotta split."

"Wait Mr. Jenks, what about the men in the mosque?"

I captured a glimpse of Tahir's curious expression when he asked me the question. I felt obligated to give him a response. Besides, after all we have been through I should be able to spare at least one more minute for him.

Looking directly at Tahir I said, "I don't know, let me go see."

I walked over to mosque with both Jassim and Tahir in tow. I tried to open the door but it was still locked. I then decided to pound the door with my first to alert whoever was still inside that we wanted a response from them. As sarcastically as I could be, I said, "hello Mr. Bad guy? Looks like the wrath you warned me against didn't pan out for you. You want to come out and surrender now?"

No answer.

Feeling that I at least placated Tahir's request, I said, "looks like he's your problem now. Sooner or later they will come out and you can deal with them at that point. Don't worry about them retaliating because 3ʳᵈ CAV will be here shortly to deal with them. We would really like to stay and discuss this issue, but we have got to get going so we can make our deadline."

As we were making our second attempt to head back to the garage for our vehicles, Tahir shouted from the top of his lungs, "look! Someone else is on their way here!"

Voodoo Gold by James H Jenks

I grabbed the binoculars that were nearby and took a quick look. "Fuck! It's the US Army, they finally made it on time for once. Now what else can go wrong?"

We were so close to getting out of here, and what made matters even worse was that now I was going to have to extinguish my bent up victory cigar.

The people from the village started emerging from their hiding spots because it was now safe to come out. They started to get curious as to who we were and started to form a crowd in the streets. This crowd would make it difficult for us to travel through with our vehicles and make our exit. Then an idea came to me that would use this situation to my advantage and help us exit the village without the 3rd CAV noticing. This brilliant solution placed a smile on my face, so naturally I took another big drag off of my cigar to celebrate, reviving its life.

"Carson, Butkus! Grab a bunch of gold bricks and toss them over there by the mosque, off the side of the road." As Carson and Butkus went to go grab a handful of gold, I grabbed Tahir by the shoulder to get his attention. Tahir's attention immediately shifted from the two men in the mosque and on to me. I proceeded to explain my idea and demands to Tahir. "You need to make an announcement to your people that we will donate a bunch of gold in a pile by your mosque if they can help us out."

Looking straight at Tahir so I knew he was focused on what I was saying, I continued with explaining my plan. "We are going to park up by the last alley before we jump on the road that heads out of town. I need a bunch of your locals to stand in front of our trucks to help conceal them as the US Army drives by our hidden location and straight into your town. As soon as the last truck enters your village and ensuring they all pass us, everybody in this town needs to come out to greet the Americans. You will then need to seal them off with a crowd of people so they can't get back to us. You need to act like you are throwing a big parade for them and welcome them with open arms. Break out the hookahs and pour the tea, have a good time and celebrate with them. When they are caught up in the joyful moment, we'll slip out the back. You need to make sure they are surrounded with a large mob of your people so that if they notice us, they won't be able to follow at all."

"Yes Mr. Jenks, I understand."

"And one more thing Tahir. You can count on these guys asking you a thousand questions about what happened here. In order to protect Jassim and not have the Army looking for him, you need to convince them that we were not here. If they figure out it was us who was here, they'll be able to connect the dots to Jassim."

"What do I say to convince them of this Mr. Jenks, especially since your bullet casing are placed everywhere?"

You can just tell them some independent security contractors came through here. These trigger happy guards use the same NATO ammo as we do. They should buy off on that explanation. Just make sure you and your village all stick to the same story."

Carson and Butkus came running back and threw the pile of gold down where I instructed them to. Tahir's eyes lit up when he saw the amount of gold being placed over by the edge of the mosque. He immediately made the announcement to the locals. The women began retrieving the gold from the pile and concealing it under their garments. The men started to clear the road for our vehicles and they began to waive as if they were giving us directions. About five of them patted on our hood and motioned for us to follow them. They ran in front of us as we drove our vehicles down the road until we reached the alley by the entrance to the village.

We backed up and parked in the alley, waiting for our signal to leave. A bunch of locals stood in front of us, concealing any evidence that we were there. Sure enough, when the US Army finally arrived, they drove right passed us. The only thing that stopped and found us was their dust cloud they kicked up on their way in. This dust cloud was actually a good thing because when we left and kicked up our dust, they would just assume it was from them and not realize it was ours.

We could see the villagers playing their parts with enthusiasm as we left. Everyone in town participated in stopping the convoy by surrounding the vehicles and wanting to shake every soldier's hand, they were all chanting "USA! USA! USA!"

We slipped out as planned and the 3rd CAV was never able to piece together the chain of events that happened in the village. Tahir was also an additional insurance card because he made sure the villagers would all tell a different story other than what actually happened. I just hope nobody would try to explain to the 3rd CAV SCO that there was a policeman hero here who walked through glass with his bare feet and saved the Nakatomi hostages.

We eventually made it to the bank in Turkey with only a half hour to spare. To celebrate our arrival, I reached in my personal bag to grab a smoke because I knew it was going to be a long night to finalize our transaction. When I reached into my bag, I had a paralyzing realization hit me like a ton of bricks. "Shit, I'm out of cigars!"

THE END

EPILOGUE

JENKS: The Jenks Winery sits on two hundred acres of rolling hills in the Yakima Valley. James is often found sitting on the deck of his estate sipping wine with his wife Sue, while gazing at the beautiful snow capped Mt. Adams, when he is not in his vineyard tending the grapes. He is never seen without his signature Cuban cigar.

CARSON: Lives in a mansion on Latigo Canyon in the Hollywood Hills. He owns one of every type of street motorcycle, but his two favorite rides are his Yamaha R1 and his Moto Guzzi. He is often seen cruising Sunset Boulevard on one of his various motorcycles or in his black Cadillac Escalade with twenty-two inch rims.

BROWN: Is a successful real estate mogul. He owns several luxury homes through out the States. Even though he is a millionaire many times throughout, he is still frugal with his money and refuses to spend it on anything that would not make more money for himself.

COLE: Started his own private security company that provides protection for diplomats in Baghdad. He is currently back in Baghdad under this pretension while he secretly tries to find a way to get the rest of the gold that was left behind.

BUTKUS and VANSCOY: Started a brokerage firm called B&V Enterprise. They are heavily invested in the Diageo company (who own Johnny Walker Blue). It is also rumored that they purchased some land in Scotland and are trying to launch a new high quality brand of blended scotch where they control the process from field to glass.

MILIK: Took advantage of the American dream from his proceeds and now runs an ESL franchise based in Manhattan.

CPT BARKER and SFC HUNTER: Around the same time that Jenks deposited the gold in the Turkish bank, Cpt Barker and SFC Hunter had arrived at Maqtada's brother's house expecting to be taken to the weapons of mass destruction as promised. After Maqtada's brother took their money, they escorted them to the extraction site. They spent the next two days digging holes everywhere. On the third morning, Maqtada and his brother were nowhere to be found. Not being able to explain their whereabouts or account for more than two thousand dollars that was missing from the Coalition Provisional Authority funds, they were busted down two ranks each.

Voodoo Gold by James H Jenks